SWANS in SPACE 2

STORY & ART by
Lun Lun Yamamoto

HOW TO READ MANGA!

Hi there! My name is **Instructor**, and this is the latest volume of **Swans in Space!** It is a comic book originally created in the country of **Japan**, where comics are called **manga**.

A manga book is read from **right-to-left**, which is **backwards** from the normal books you know. This means that you will find the first page where you expect to find the last page! It also means that each page begins in the top right corner.

START HERE!

If you have never read a manga book before, here is a helpful guide to get you started!

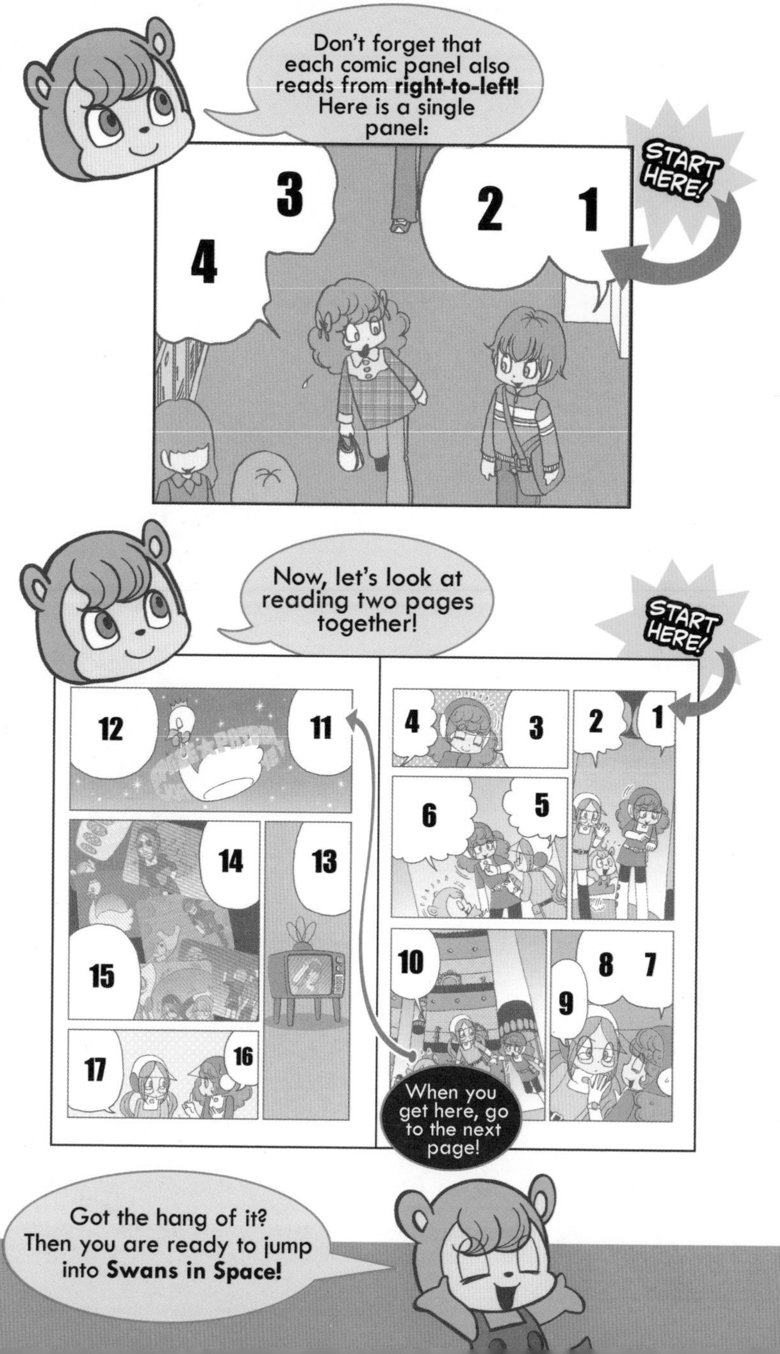
Don't forget that each comic panel also reads from **right-to-left!** Here is a single panel:
START HERE!
Now, let's look at reading two pages together!
START HERE!
When you get here, go to the next page!
Got the hang of it? Then you are ready to jump into **Swans in Space!**

SWANS IN SPACE

CHARACTER INTRODUCTIONS

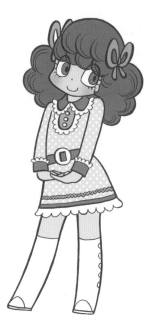

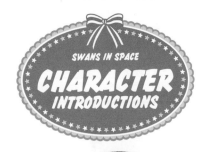

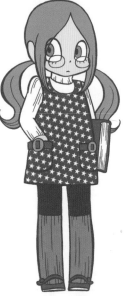

CORONA HOSHINO

A sixth grade student at the Cosmos Institute, Corona is an honor roll student who has high grades and does well at sports. Corona is the acting student council representative for her class, and her classmates often call her "Class President." A perfectionist to a fault, Corona's world is turned upside-down by Lan.

LAN TSUKISHIMA

One of Corona's classmates. A hardcore "Space Patrol" fan, Lan lives at her own pace. Lan does not particularly stand out in her class, as she can usually be found off on her own, reading a book. A rather lazy girl, Lan enjoys snacking on junk food.

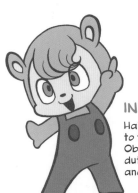

INSTRUCTOR

Hailing from the planet Omora, he acts as instructor to the trainees of the Space Patrol's Earth division. Obsessed with games, he often slacks off where his duties are concerned, but it is said that he is a kind and reliable father to his son.

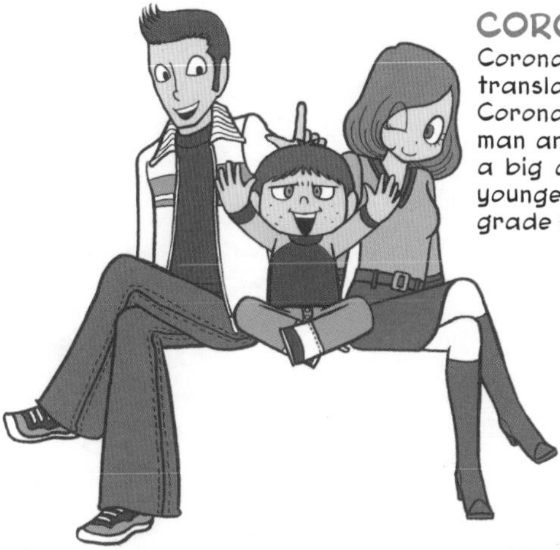

CORONA'S FAMILY

Corona's easy-going mother is a translator and works from home. Corona's father works as a stunt man and hopes to some day become a big action star. Subaru, Corona's younger brother, is an energetic first grade student.

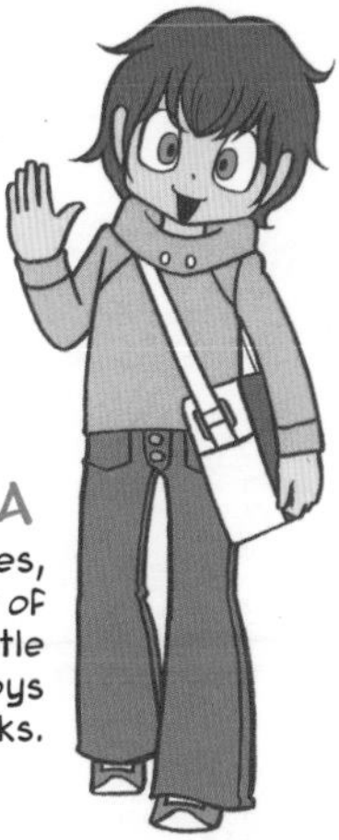

HINATA

One of Corona's classmates, Hinata is the vice president of their class. A kind and gentle young man, Hinata enjoys reading books.

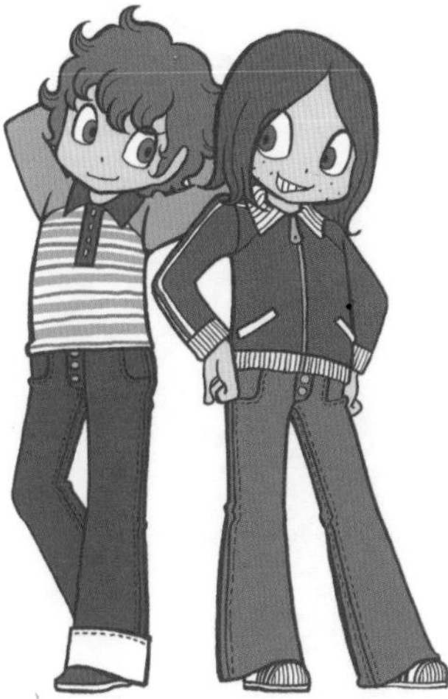

TORU YUYA

The troublemakers of Corona's class. They are always up to no good.

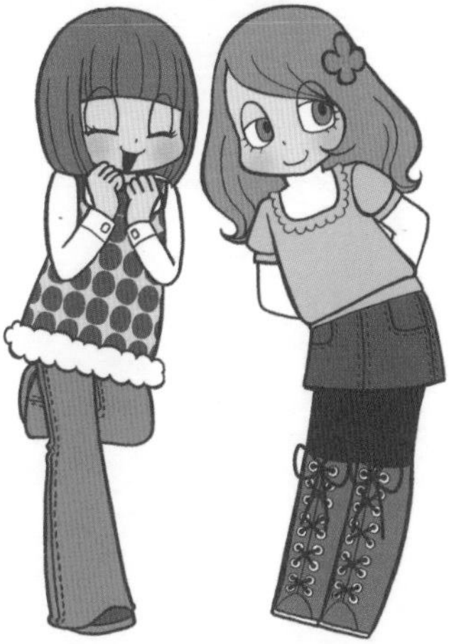

NIJIKO KASUMI

Corona's friends. Interests include fashion.

SWANS IN SPACE

CHAPTER 5
LAN IS...

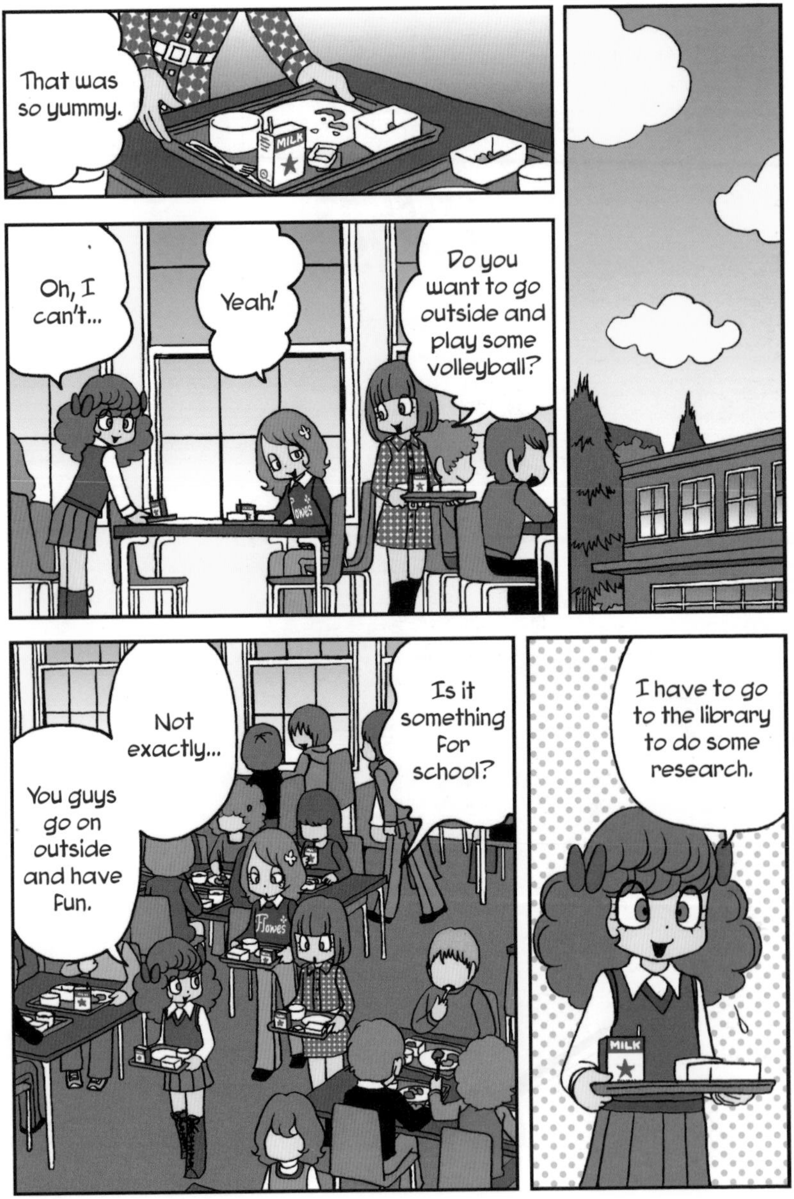
That was so yummy.
Do you want to go outside and play some volleyball?
Yeah!
Oh, I can't...
I have to go to the library to do some research.
Is it something for school?
Not exactly...
You guys go on outside and have fun.

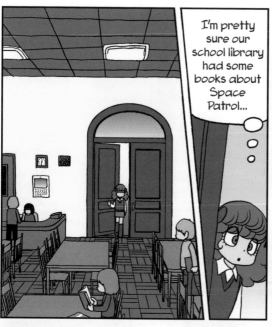

I'll probably be summoned for a mission soon...
I'm pretty sure our school library had some books about Space Patrol...
Wow...
Oh, there's one.

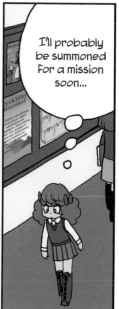

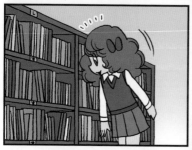

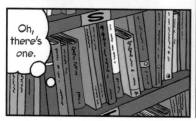

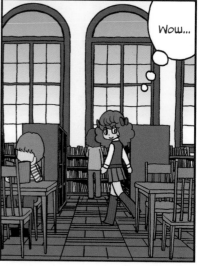

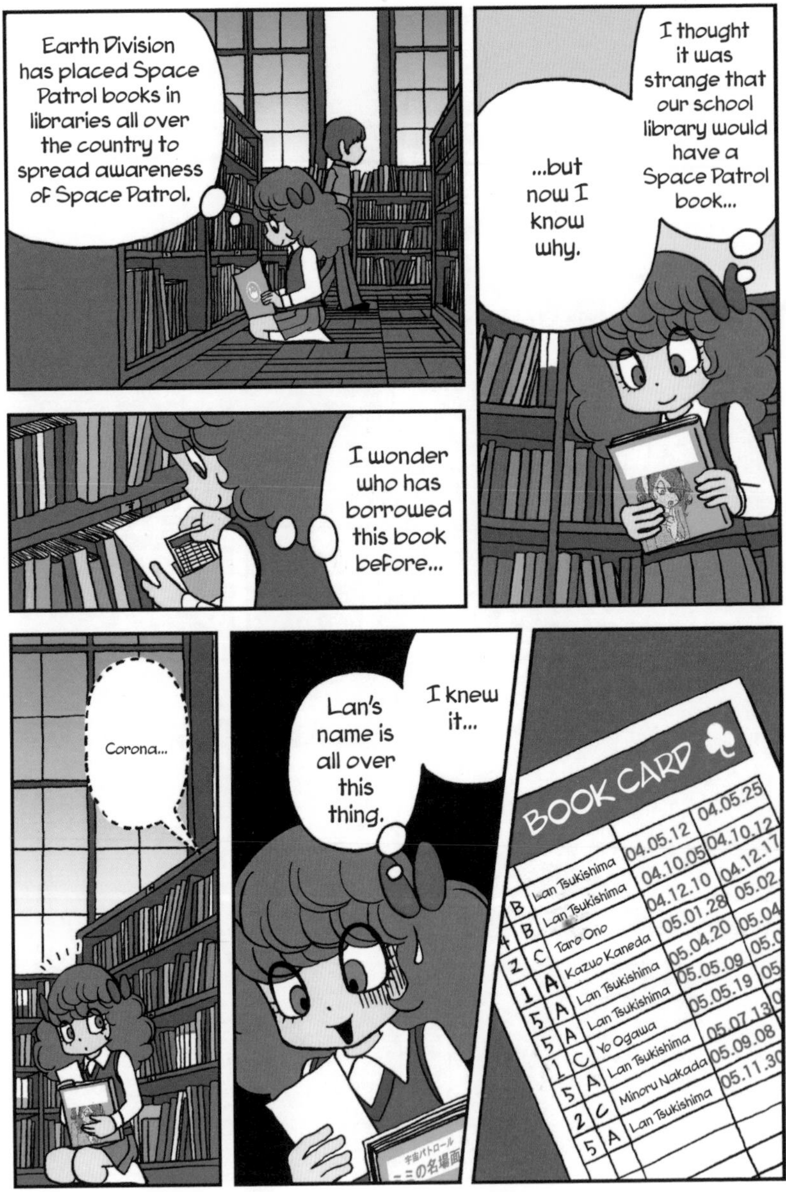
I thought it was strange that our school library would have a Space Patrol book...
...but now I know why.
Earth Division has placed Space Patrol books in libraries all over the country to spread awareness of Space Patrol.
I wonder who has borrowed this book before...
BOOK CARD
Lan Tsukishima
Lan Tsukishima
Taro Ono
Kazuo Kaneda
Lan Tsukishima
Lan Tsukishima
Yo Ogawa
Lan Tsukishima
Minoru Nakada
Lan Tsukishima
04.05.12 04.05.25
04.10.05 04.10.12
04.12.10 04.12.17
05.01.28
05.04.20
05.05.09
05.05.19
05.07.13
05.09.08
05.11.30
I knew it...
Lan's name is all over this thing.
宇宙パトロール
Corona...

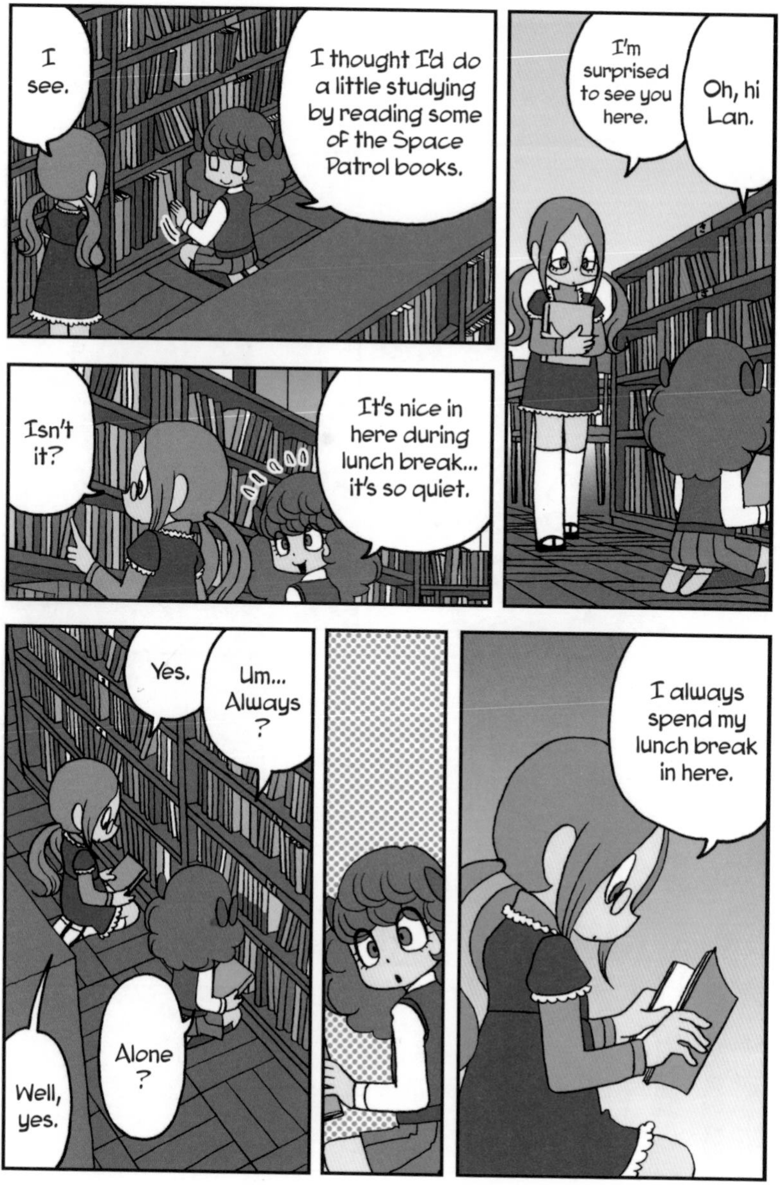
Oh, hi Lan.
I'm surprised to see you here.
I thought I'd do a little studying by reading some of the Space Patrol books.
I see.
It's nice in here during lunch break... it's so quiet.
Isn't it?
I always spend my lunch break in here.
Um... Always?
Yes.
Alone?
Well, yes.

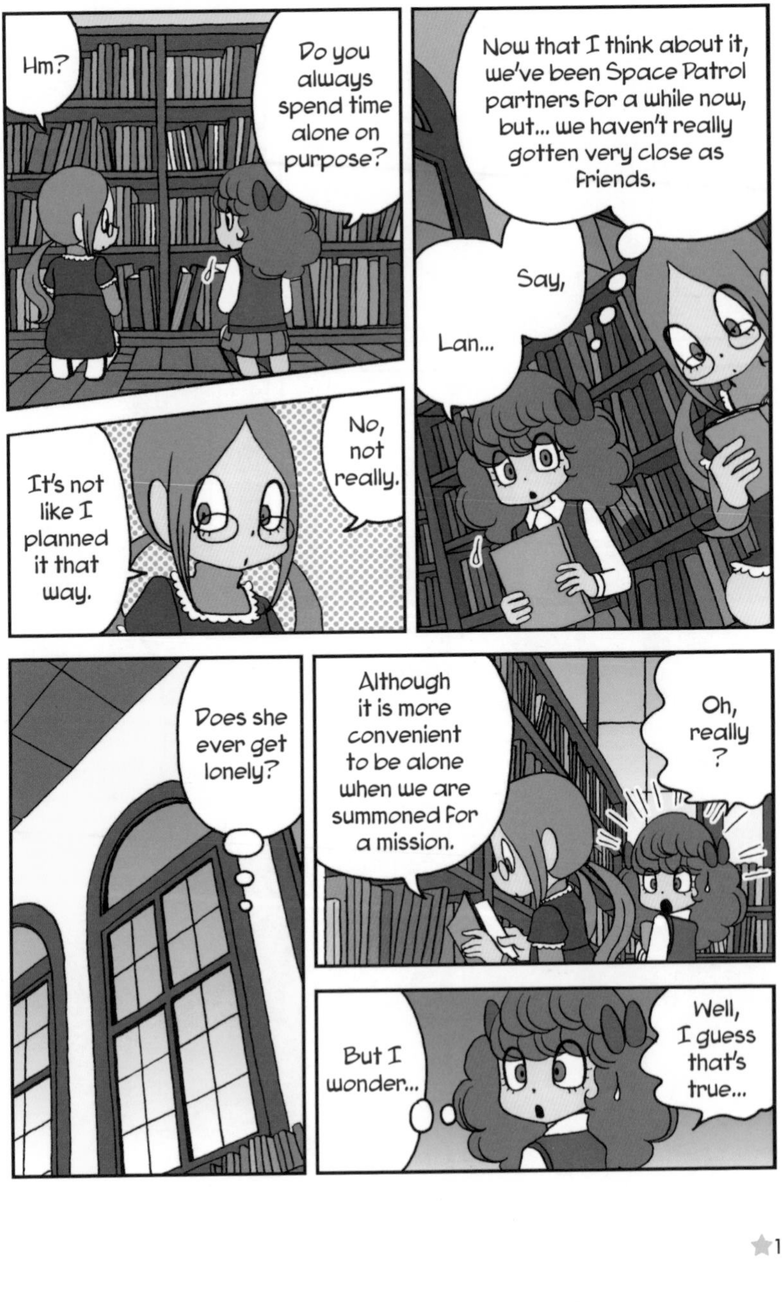
Now that I think about it, we've been Space Patrol partners for a while now, but... we haven't really gotten very close as friends.
Say,
Lan...
Do you always spend time alone on purpose?
Hm?
No, not really.
It's not like I planned it that way.
Although it is more convenient to be alone when we are summoned for a mission.
Oh, really?
Well, I guess that's true...
But I wonder...
Does she ever get lonely?

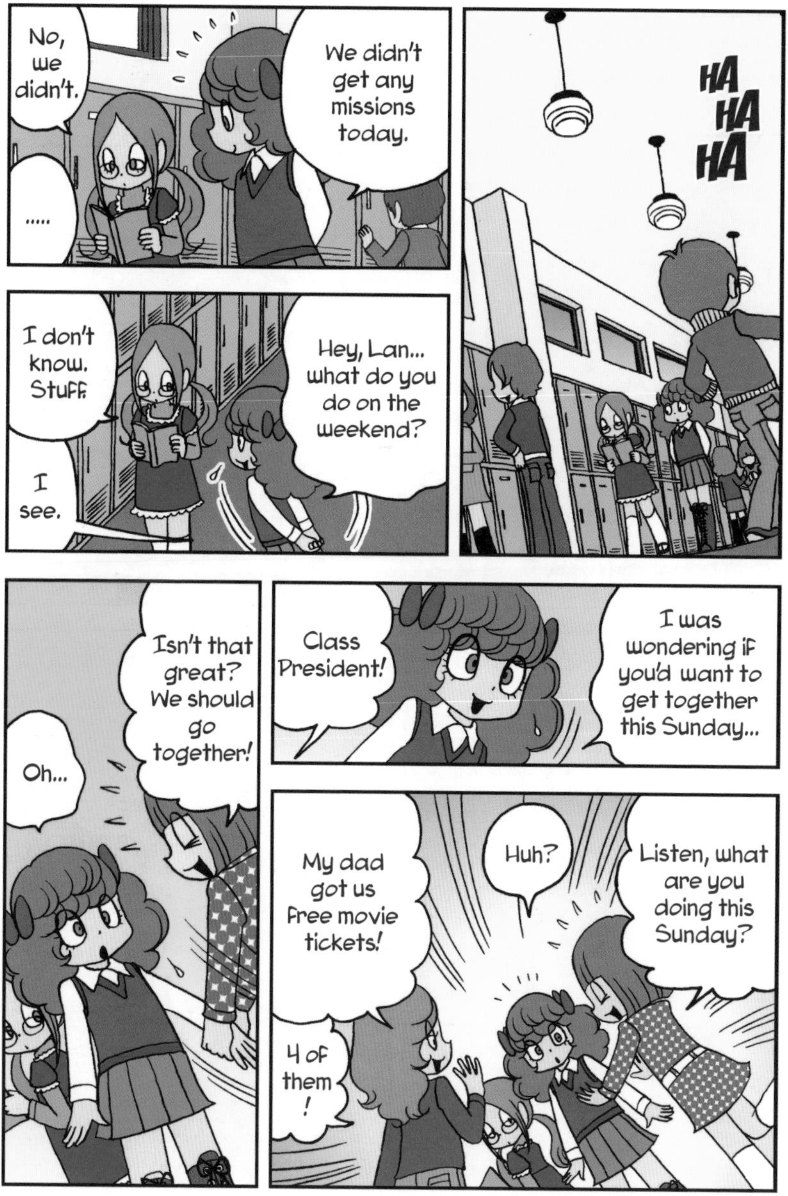
HA HA HA
We didn't get any missions today.
No, we didn't.
.....
Hey, Lan... what do you do on the weekend?
I don't know. Stuff.
I see.
I was wondering if you'd want to get together this Sunday...
Class President!
Listen, what are you doing this Sunday?
Huh?
My dad got us free movie tickets!
4 of them!
Isn't that great? We should go together!
Oh...

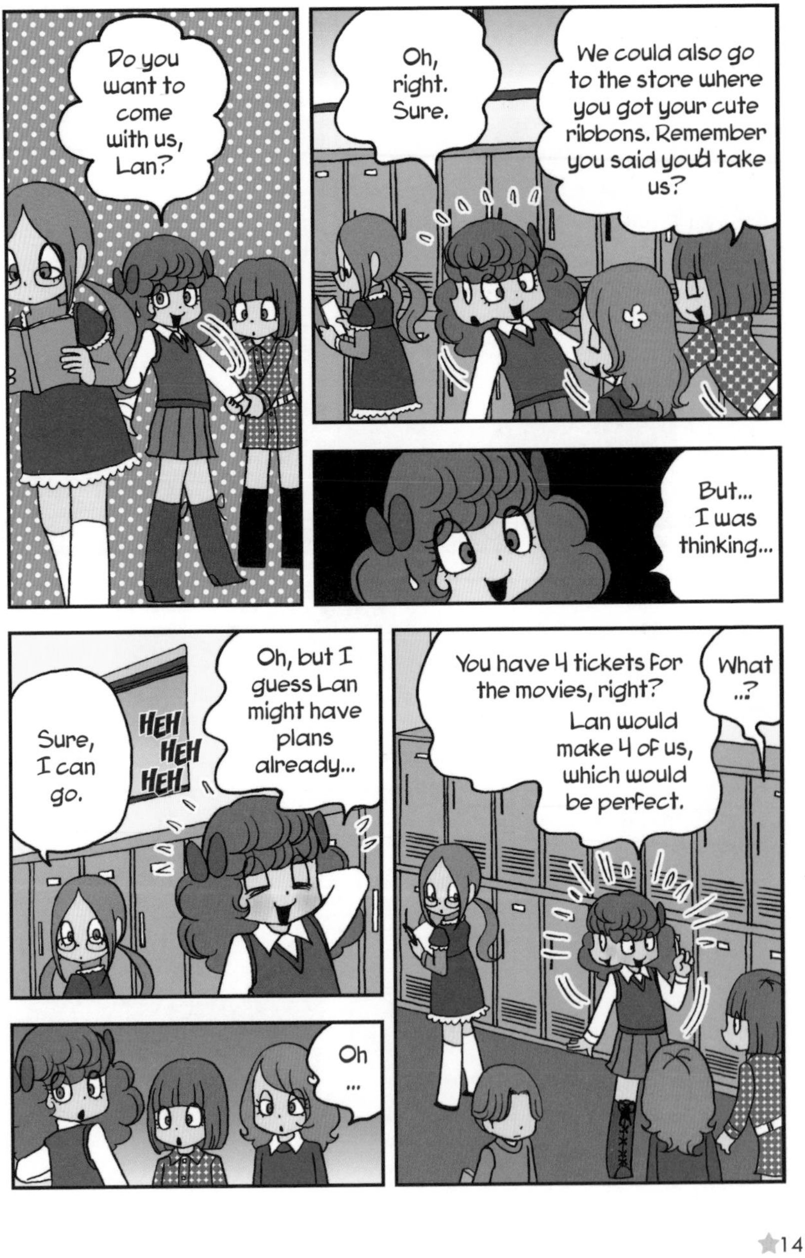
We could also go to the store where you got your cute ribbons. Remember you said you'd take us?
Oh, right. Sure.
But... I was thinking...
Do you want to come with us, Lan?
What ..?
You have 4 tickets for the movies, right?
Lan would make 4 of us, which would be perfect.
Oh, but I guess Lan might have plans already...
HEH HEH HEH
Sure, I can go.
Oh ...

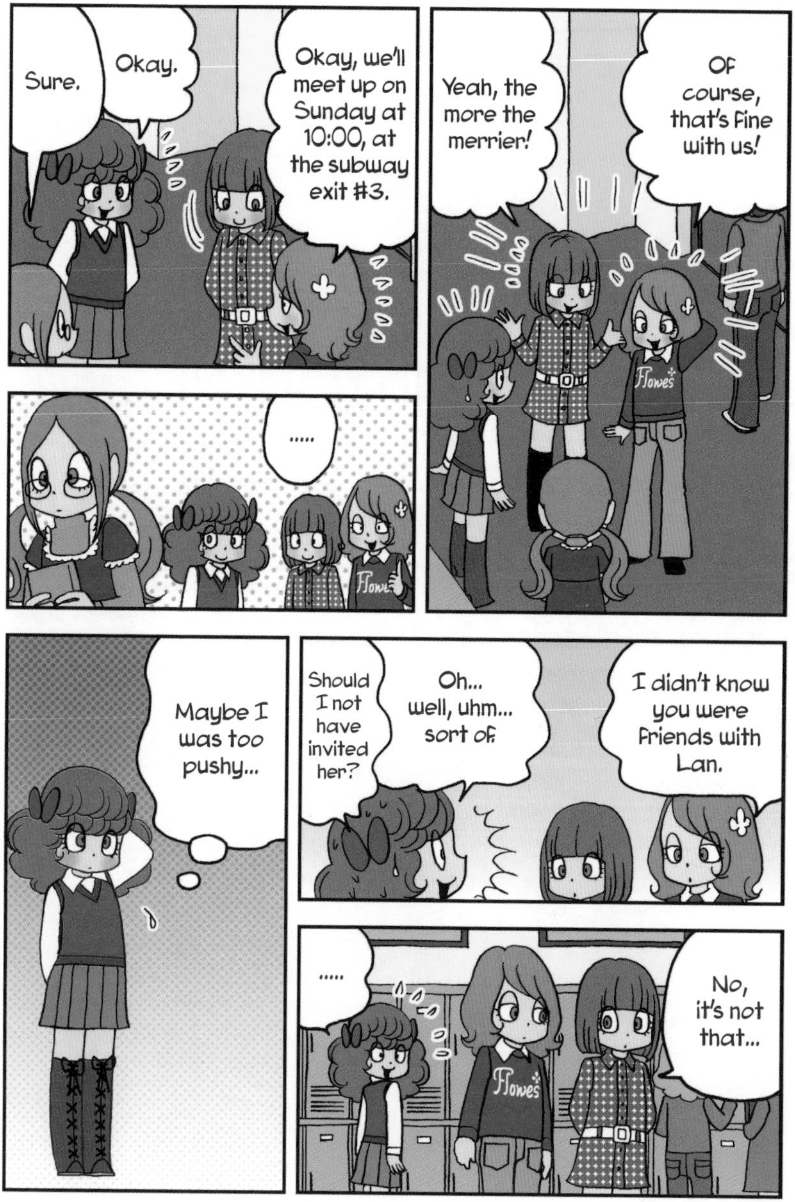

Of course, that's fine with us!
Yeah, the more the merrier!
Okay, we'll meet up on Sunday at 10:00, at the subway exit #3.
Okay.
Sure.
.....
I didn't know you were friends with Lan.
Oh... well, uhm... sort of.
Should I not have invited her?
No, it's not that...
.....
Maybe I was too pushy...

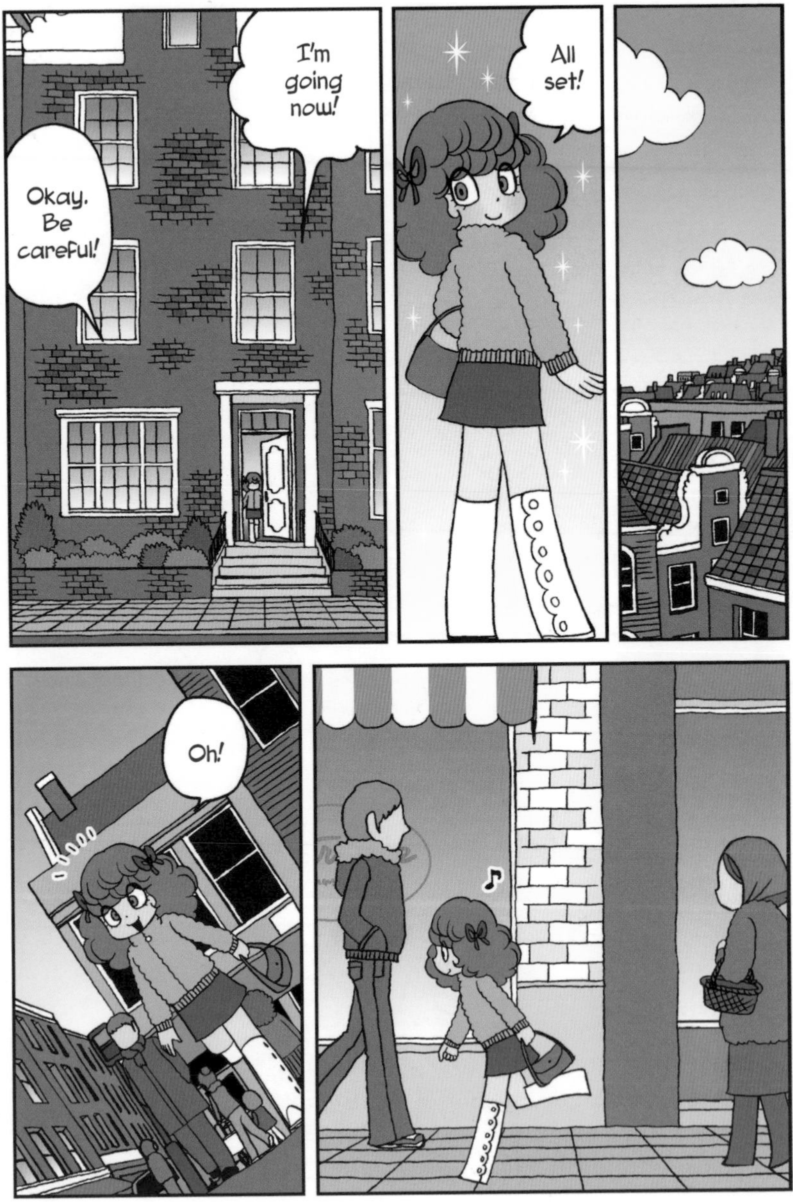
All set!
I'm going now!
Okay. Be careful!
Oh!

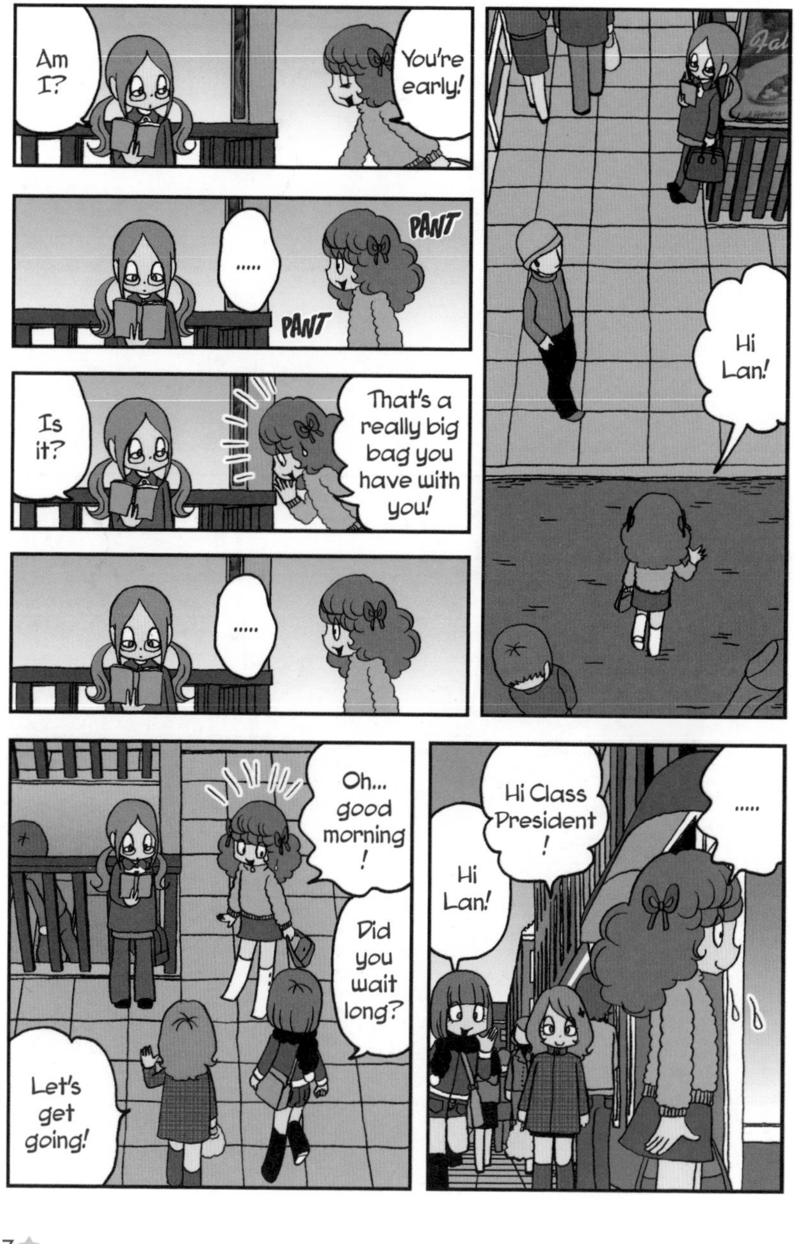
Hi Lan!
You're early!
Am I?
PANT
.....
PANT
That's a really big bag you have with you!
Is it?
.....
.....
Hi Class President!
Hi Lan!
Oh... good morning!
Did you wait long?
Let's get going!

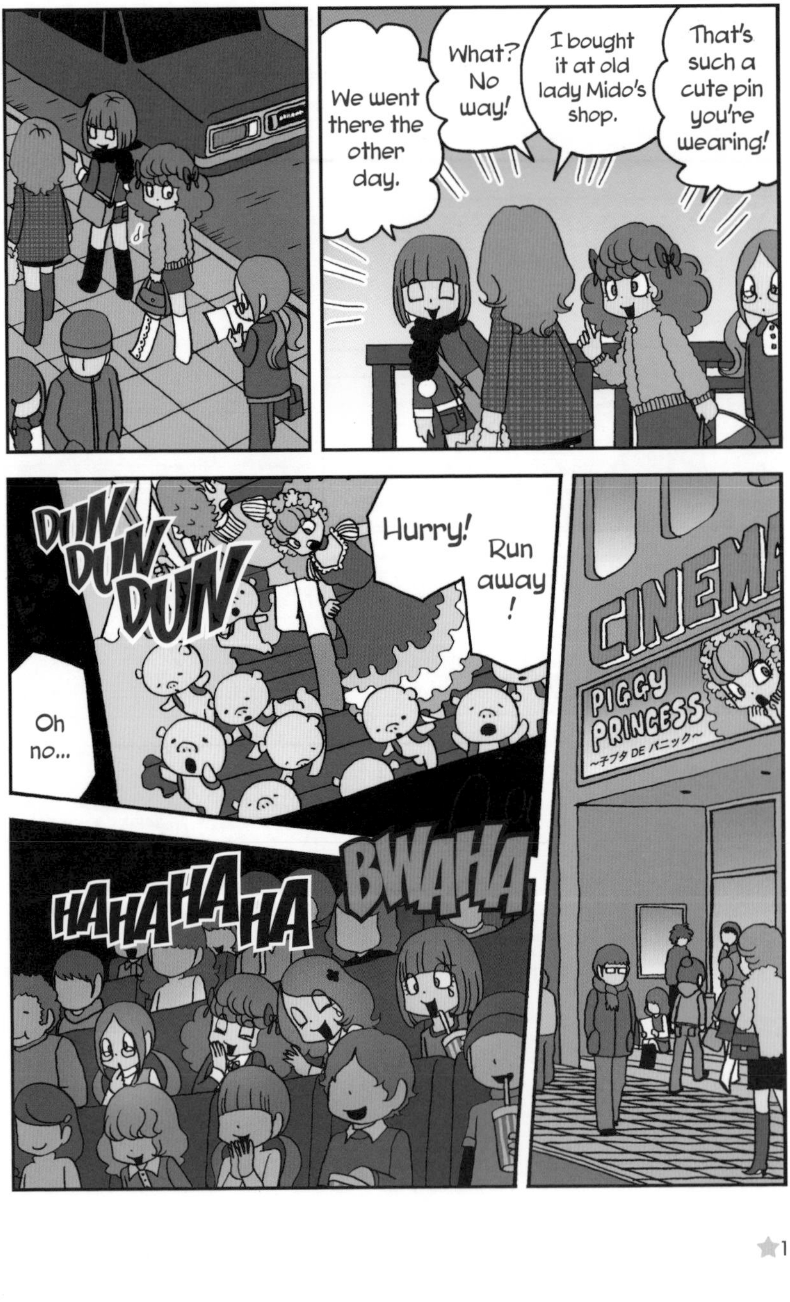
That's such a cute pin you're wearing!
I bought it at old lady Mido's shop.
What? No way!
We went there the other day.
CINEMA
PIGGY PRINCESS
~子ブタ DE パニック~
Hurry!
Run away!
DUN DUN DUN
Oh no...
BWAHA
HAHAHAHAHA

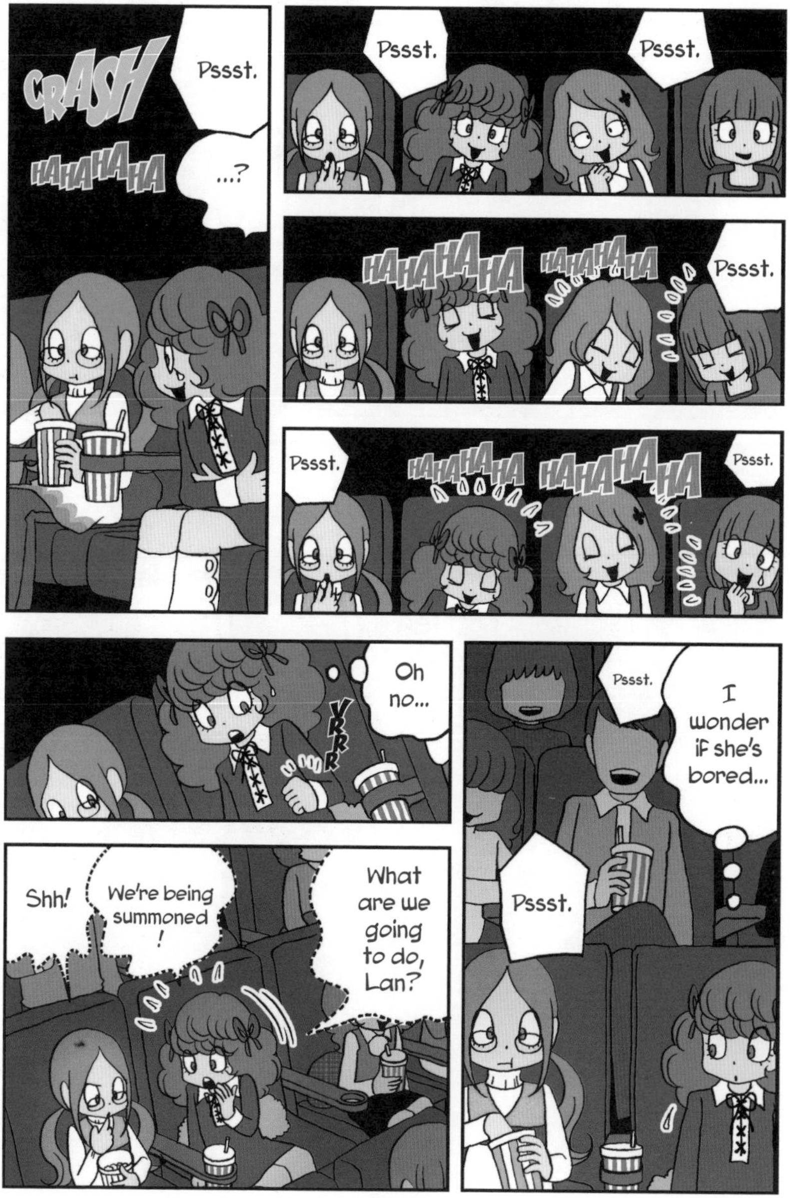
Pssst.
Pssst.
Pssst.
HAHAHAHA
HAHAHAHA
Pssst.
HAHAHAHA
HAHAHAHA
Pssst.
Pssst.
CRASH
...?
HAHAHAHA
I wonder if she's bored...
Pssst.
Pssst.
Oh no...
VRRR
What are we going to do, Lan?
We're being summoned!
Shh!

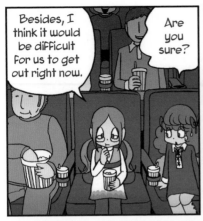

Let's not go this time.
We're in the middle of a movie.
Are you sure?
Besides, I think it would be difficult for us to get out right now.
I... I guess you're right.
I'm surprised.
I didn't think she was enjoying the movie.
SMOS INEMA
YADA
PIGGY PRINCESS
PIGLET PANIC
I laughed so hard!
Me too! That was so funny!
Bacchus
YADA

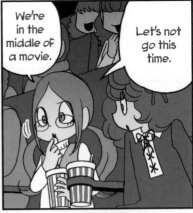

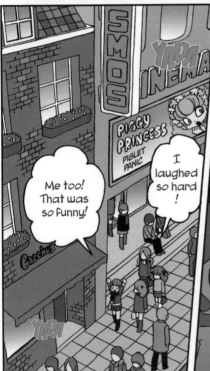

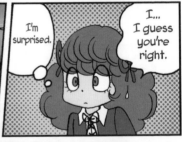

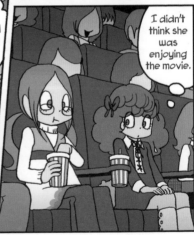

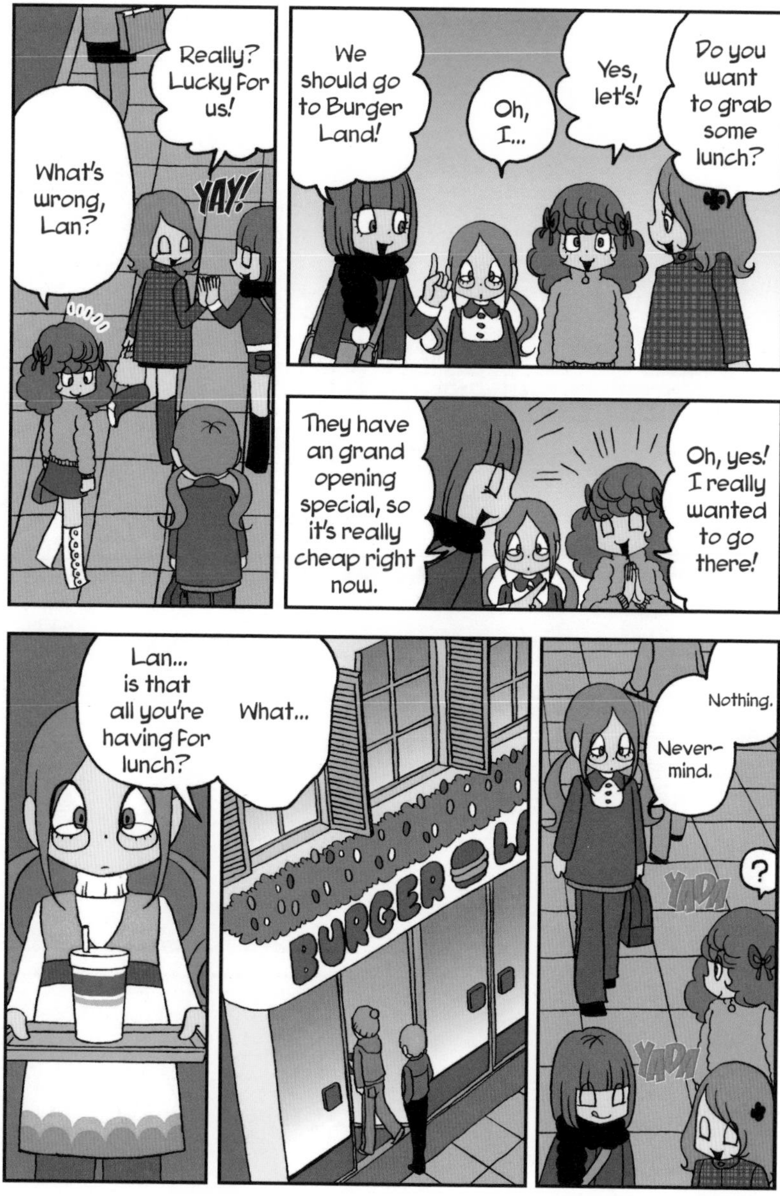
Do you want to grab some lunch?
Yes, let's!
Oh, I...
We should go to Burger Land!
Oh, yes! I really wanted to go there!
They have an grand opening special, so it's really cheap right now.
Really? Lucky for us!
YAY!
What's wrong, Lan?
Nothing.
Never-mind.
?
YADA
YADA
What...
BURGER L
Lan... is that all you're having for lunch?

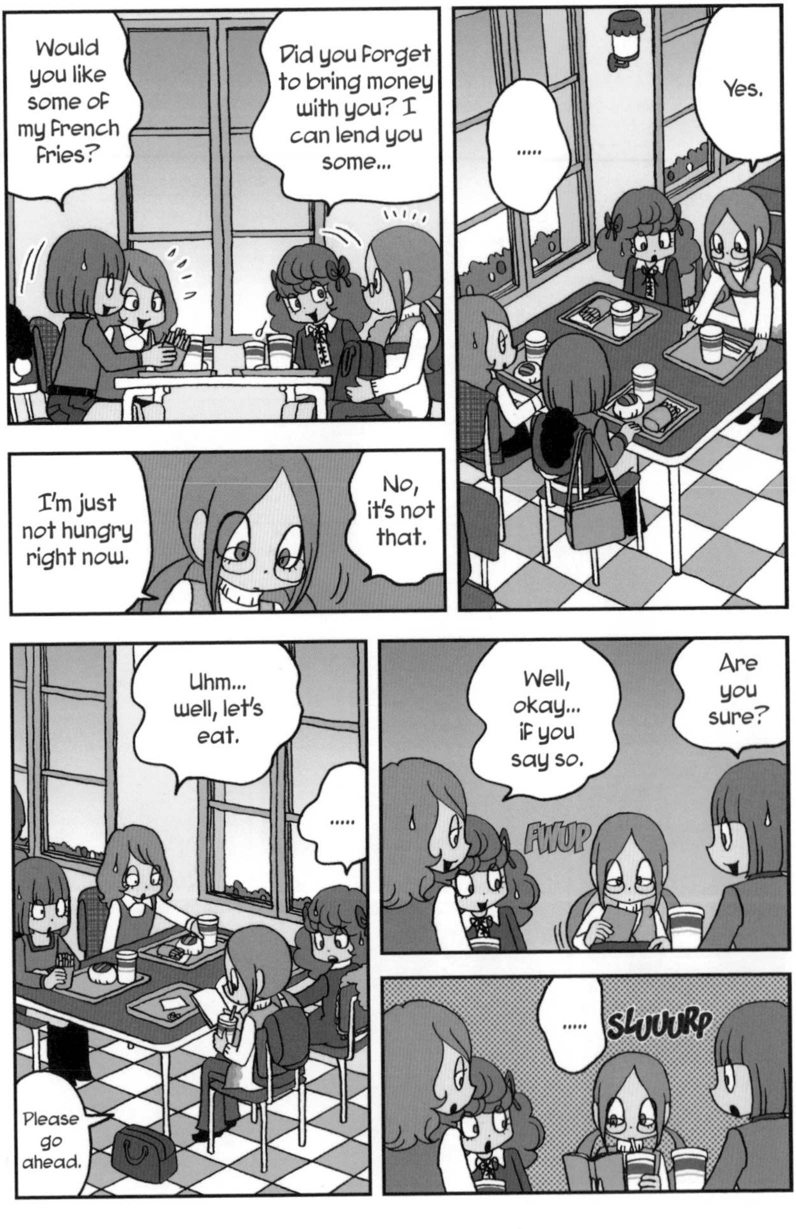
Yes.
.....
Did you forget to bring money with you? I can lend you some...
Would you like some of my French fries?
No, it's not that.
I'm just not hungry right now.
Are you sure?
Well, okay... if you say so.
FWUP
SLUUURP
.....
Uhm... well, let's eat.
.....
Please go ahead.

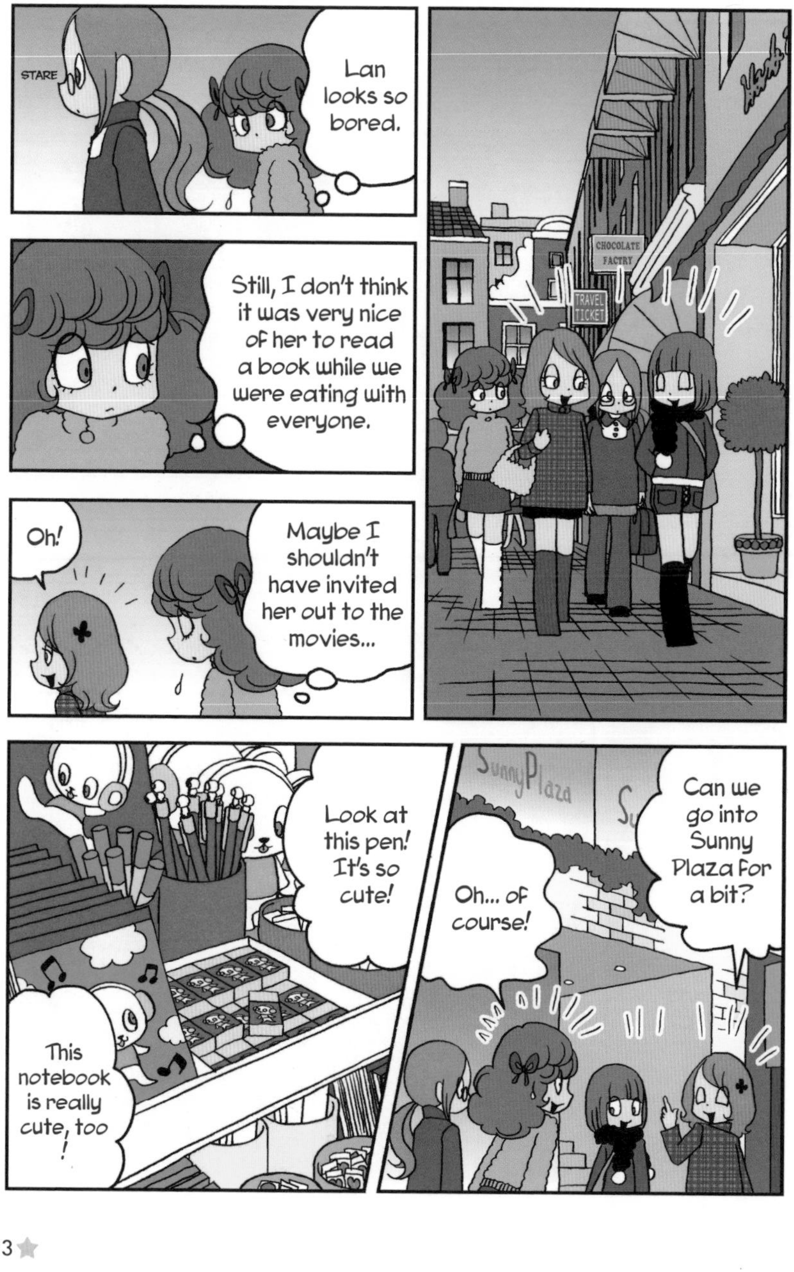
CHOCOLATE FACTRY
TRAVEL TICKET
STARE
Lan looks so bored.
Still, I don't think it was very nice of her to read a book while we were eating with everyone.
Maybe I shouldn't have invited her out to the movies...
Oh!
Sunny Plaza
Can we go into Sunny Plaza for a bit?
Oh... of course!
Look at this pen! It's so cute!
This notebook is really cute, too!

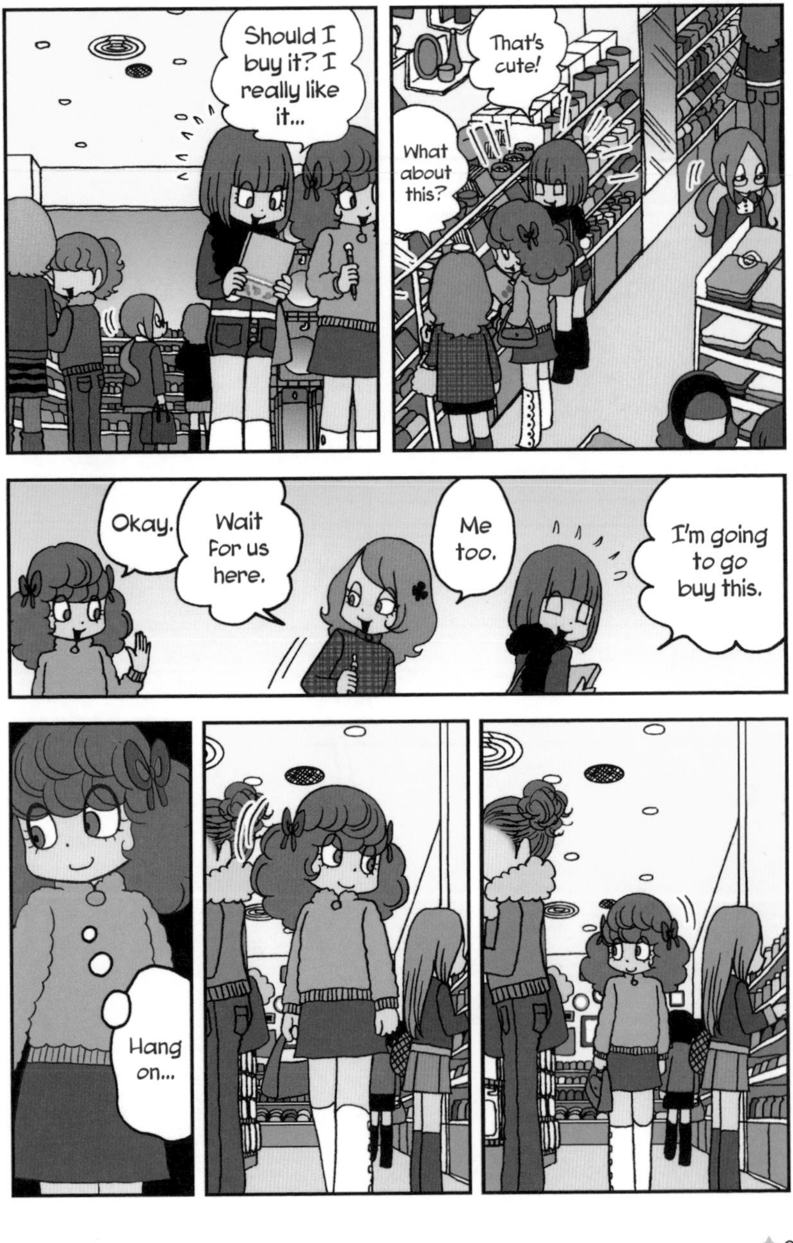
That's cute!
What about this?
Should I buy it? I really like it...
I'm going to go buy this.
Me too.
Wait for us here.
Okay.
Hang on...

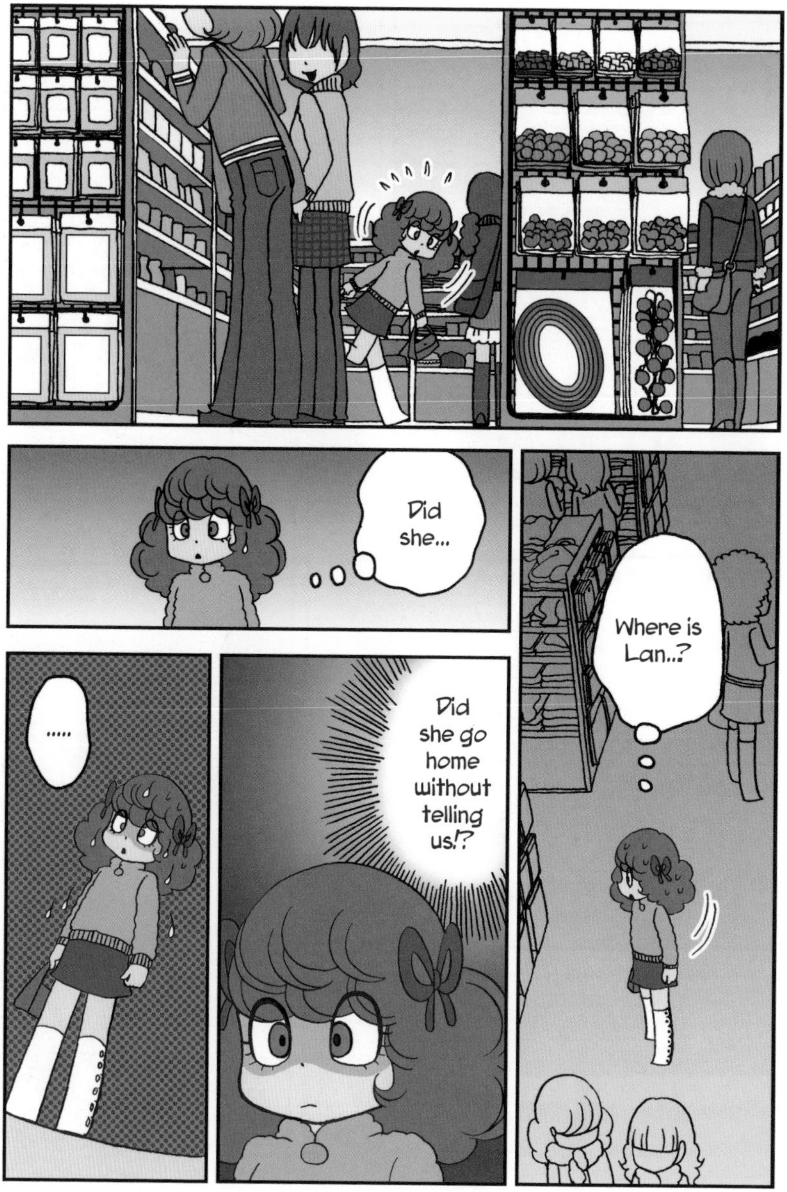
Where is Lan..?
Did she...
Did she go home without telling us!?
......

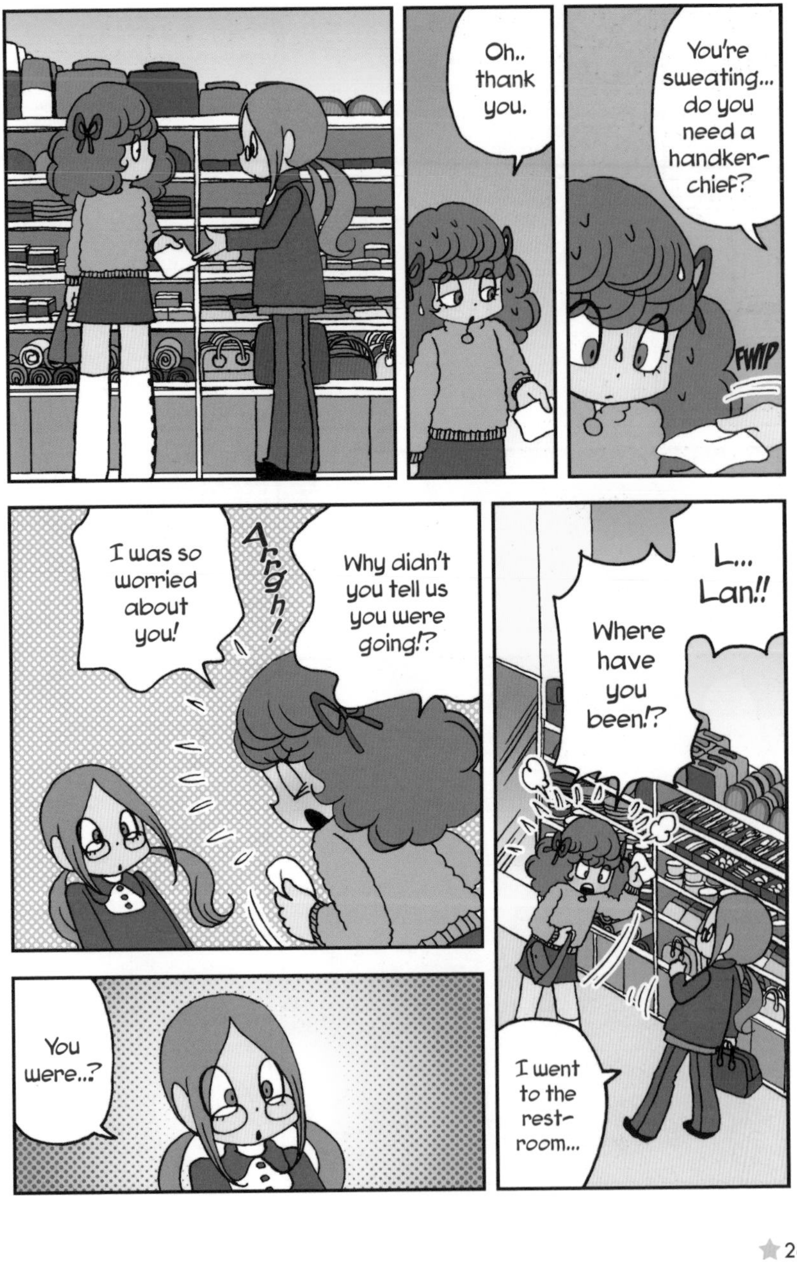
You're sweating... do you need a handker-chief?
FWIP
Oh.. thank you.
L... Lan!!
Where have you been!?
I went to the rest-room...
Why didn't you tell us you were going!?
Arrgh!
I was so worried about you!
You were..?

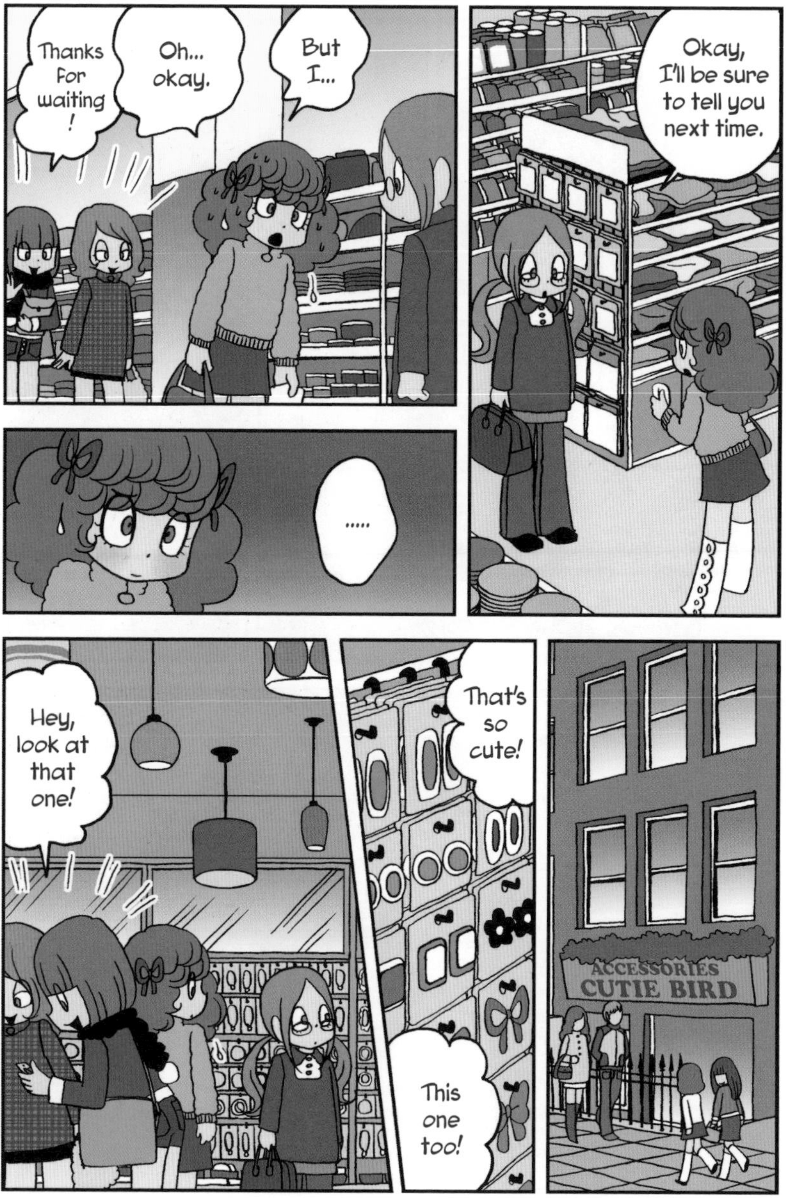
Okay, I'll be sure to tell you next time.
But I...
Oh... okay.
Thanks for waiting!
.....
ACCESSORIES
CUTIE BIRD
That's so cute!
This one too!
Hey, look at that one!

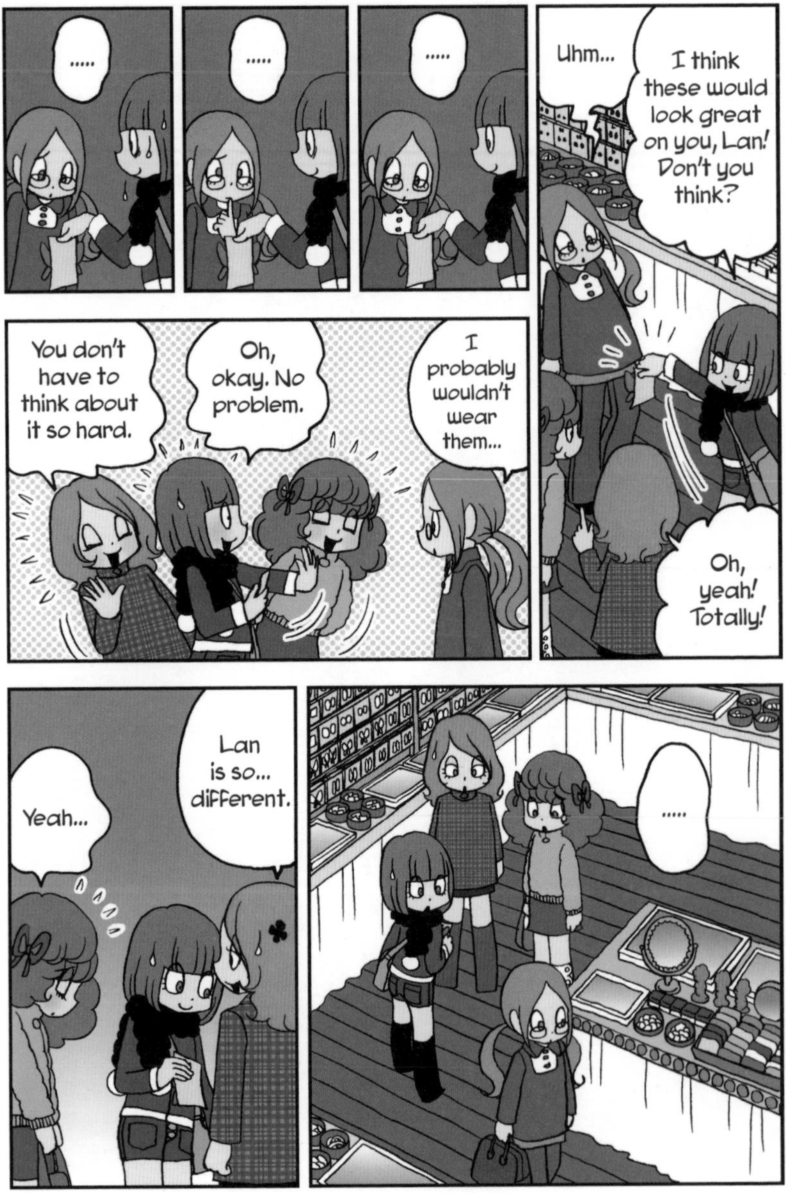
I think these would look great on you, Lan! Don't you think?
Uhm...
Oh, yeah! Totally!
.....
.....
.....
I probably wouldn't wear them...
Oh, okay. No problem.
You don't have to think about it so hard.
.....
Lan is so... different.
Yeah...

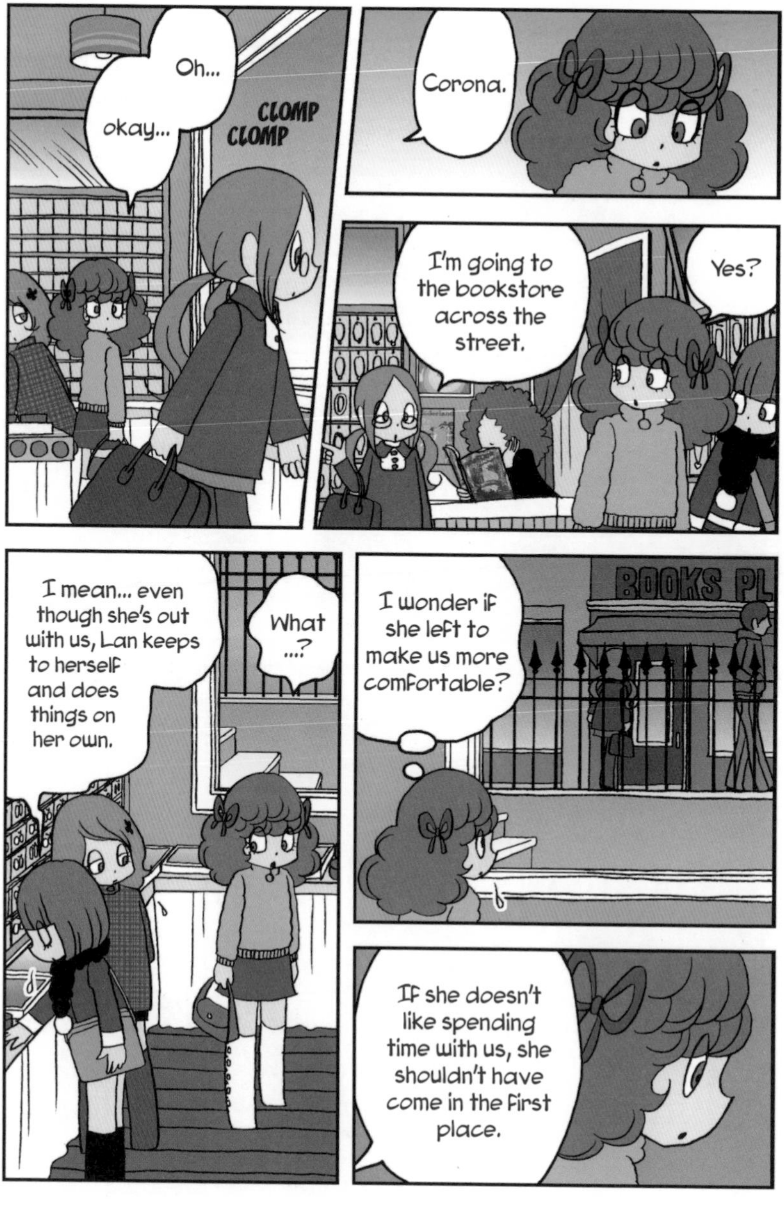
Corona.
Yes?
I'm going to the bookstore across the street.
Oh... okay...
CLOMP CLOMP
I wonder if she left to make us more comfortable?
BOOKS PL
If she doesn't like spending time with us, she shouldn't have come in the first place.
What ...?
I mean... even though she's out with us, Lan keeps to herself and does things on her own.

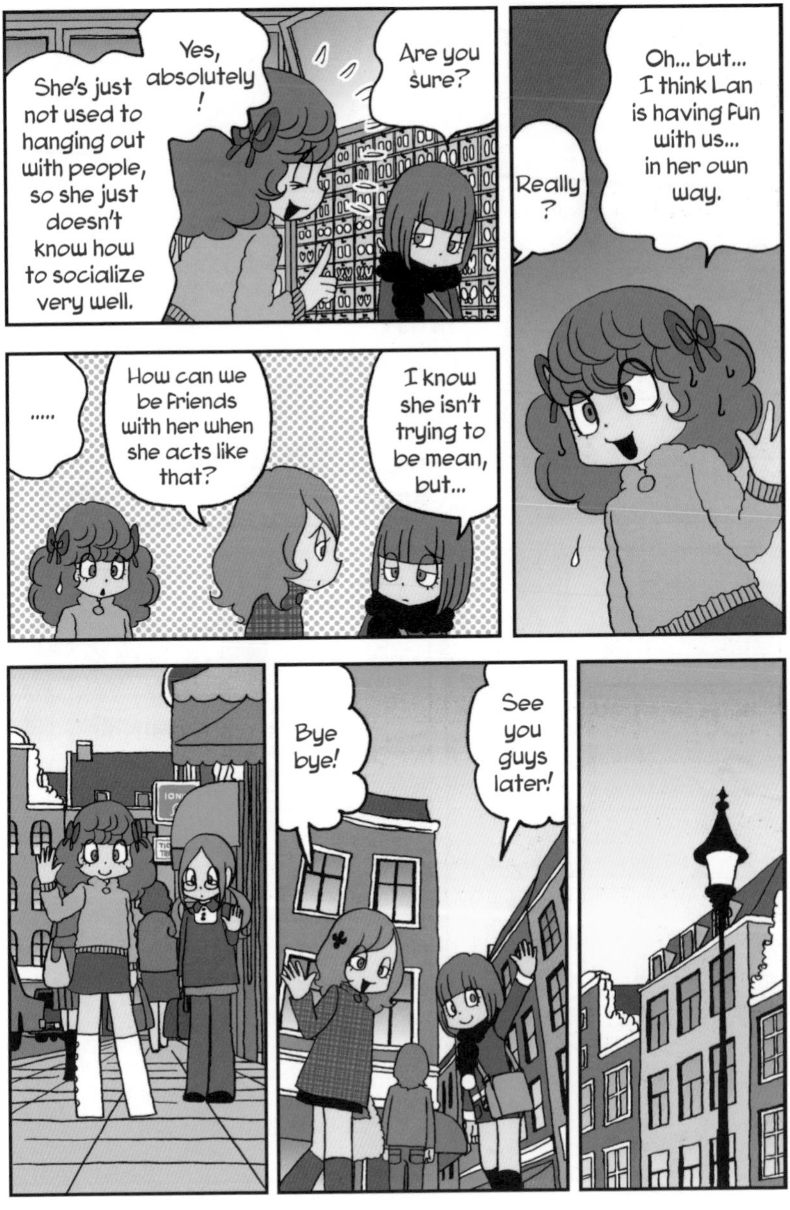
Are you sure?
Yes, absolutely!
She's just not used to hanging out with people, so she just doesn't know how to socialize very well.
I know she isn't trying to be mean, but...
How can we be friends with her when she acts like that?
.....
Oh... but... I think Lan is having fun with us... in her own way.
Really?
See you guys later!
Bye bye!

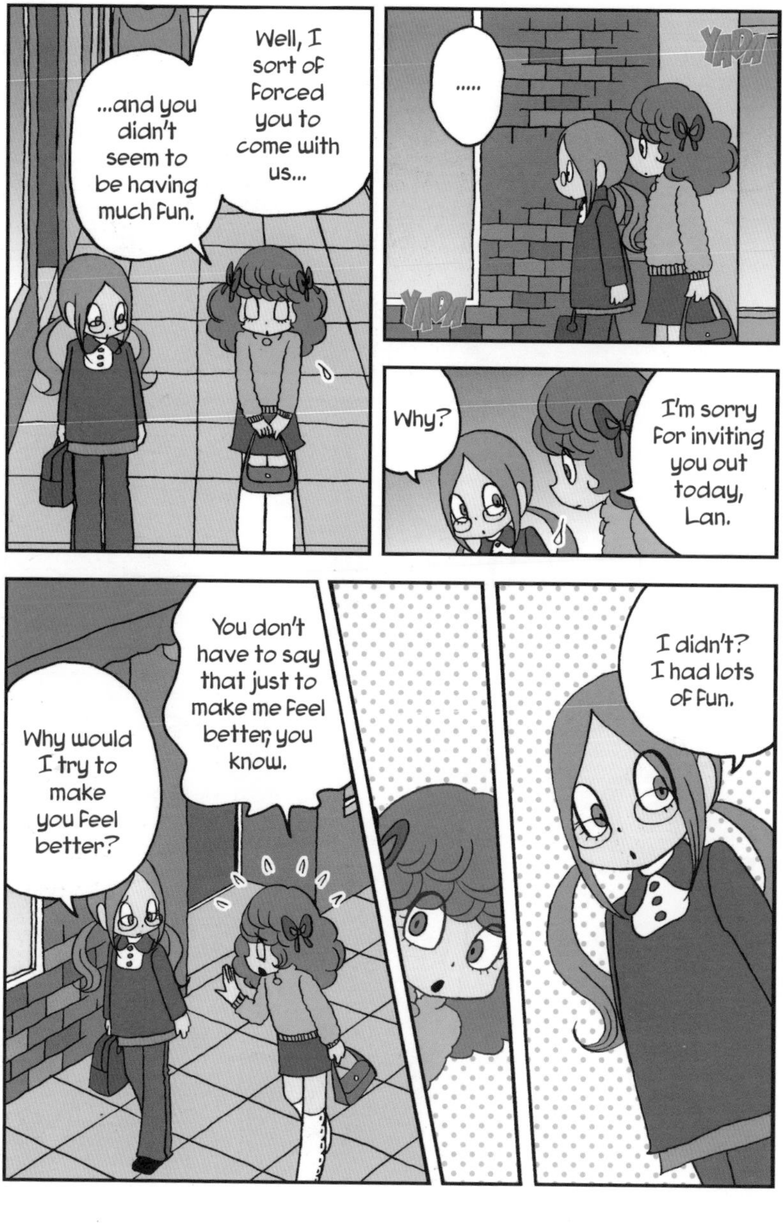
YADA
YADA
.....
I'm sorry for inviting you out today, Lan.
Why?
Well, I sort of forced you to come with us...
...and you didn't seem to be having much fun.
I didn't? I had lots of fun.
You don't have to say that just to make me feel better, you know.
Why would I try to make you feel better?

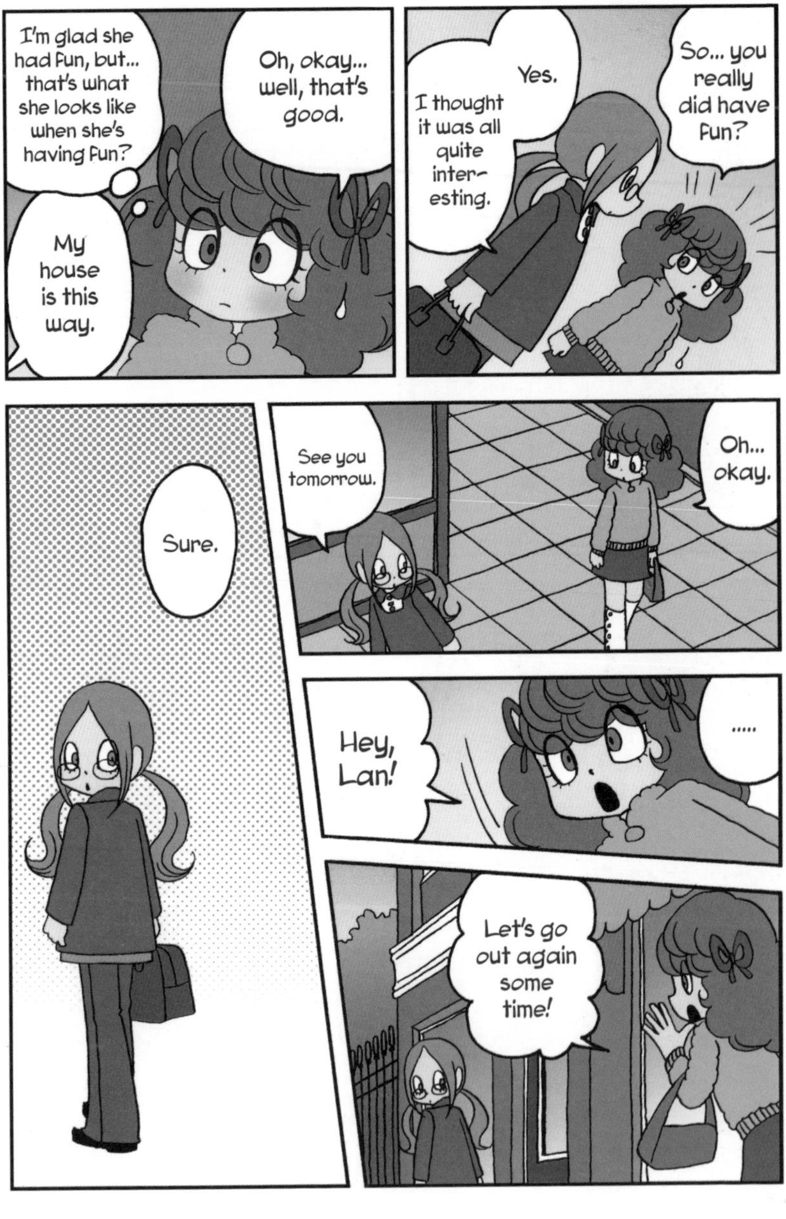
So... you really did have fun?
Yes.
I thought it was all quite interesting.
Oh, okay... well, that's good.
I'm glad she had fun, but... that's what she looks like when she's having fun?
My house is this way.
Oh... okay.
See you tomorrow.
.....
Hey, Lan!
Let's go out again some time!
Sure.

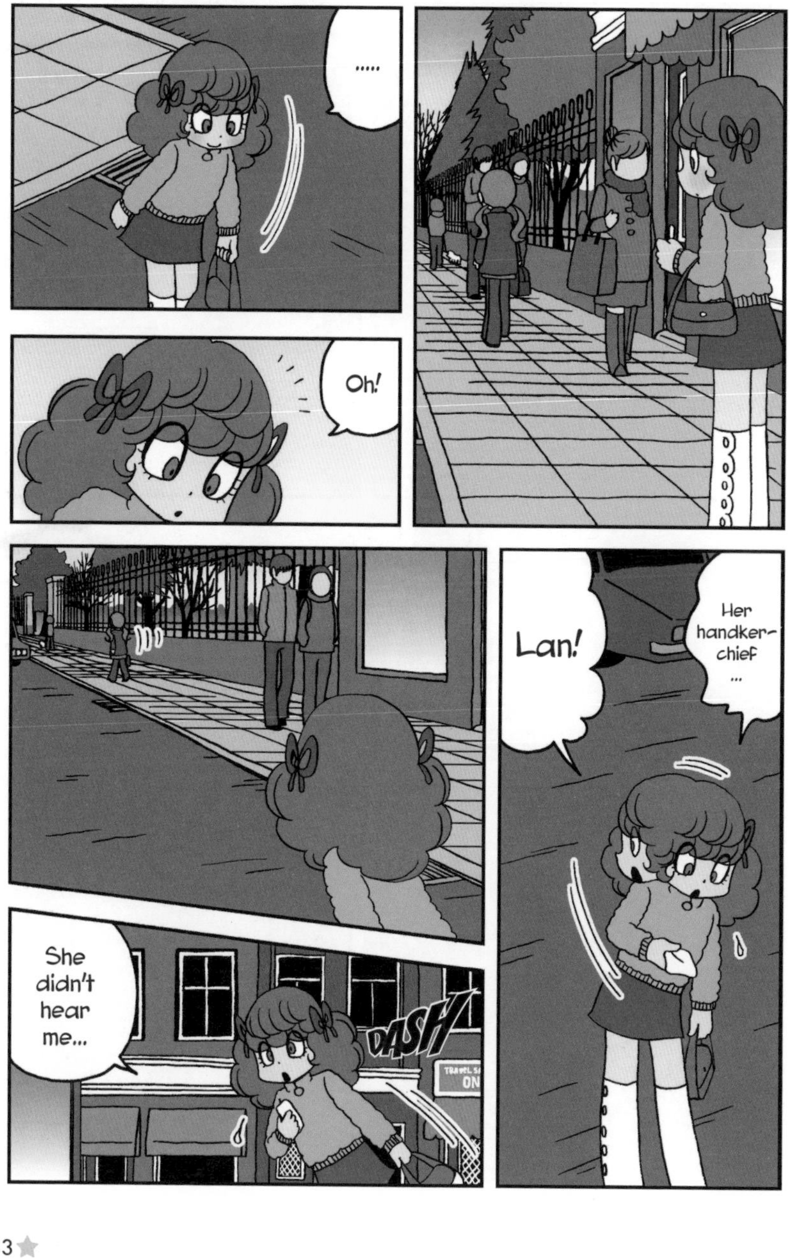
.....
Oh!
Her handker-chief ...
Lan!
She didn't hear me...
DASH

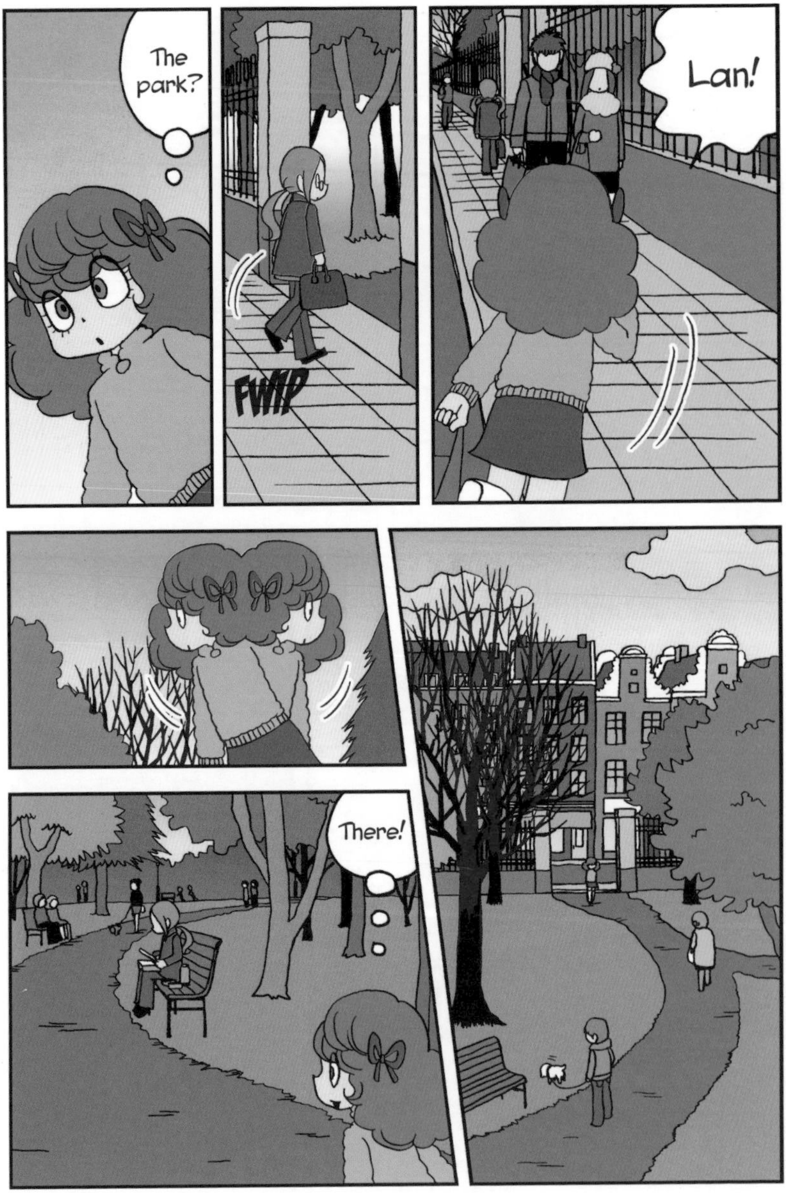

Lan!
FWIP
The park?
There!

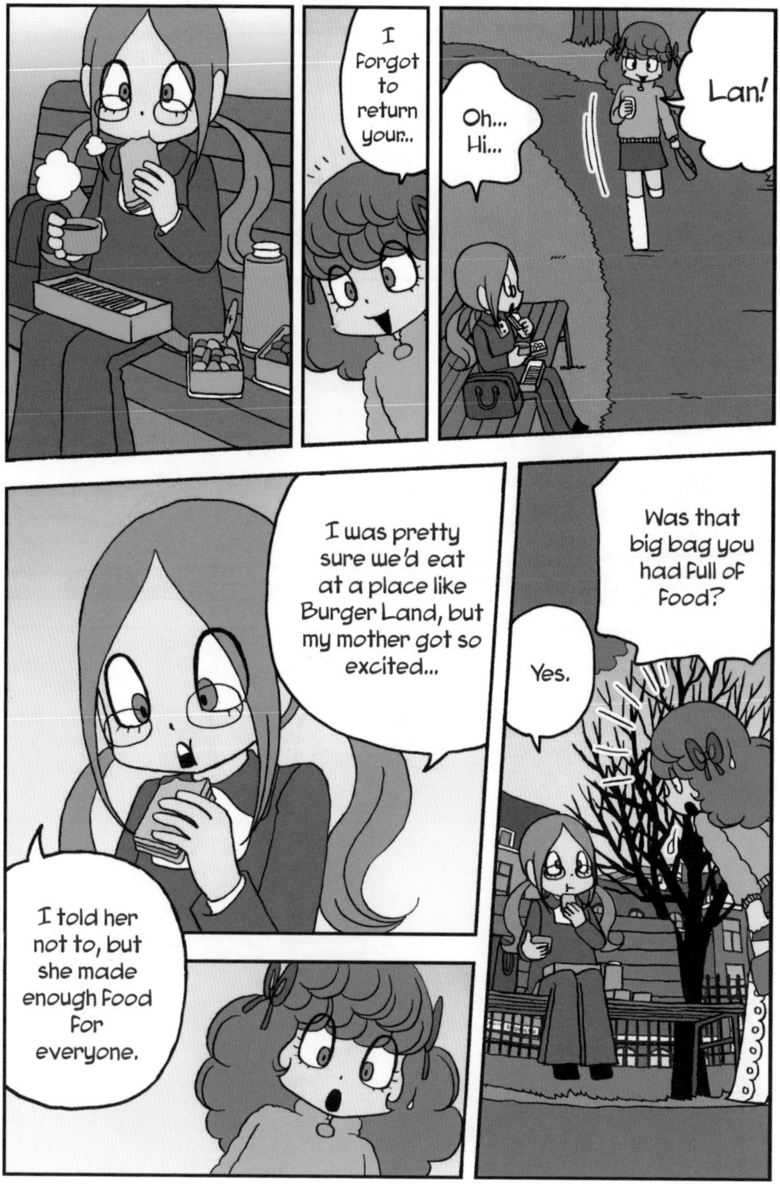
Lan!
Oh... Hi...
I forgot to return your..
Was that big bag you had full of food?
Yes.
I was pretty sure we'd eat at a place like Burger Land, but my mother got so excited...
I told her not to, but she made enough food for everyone.

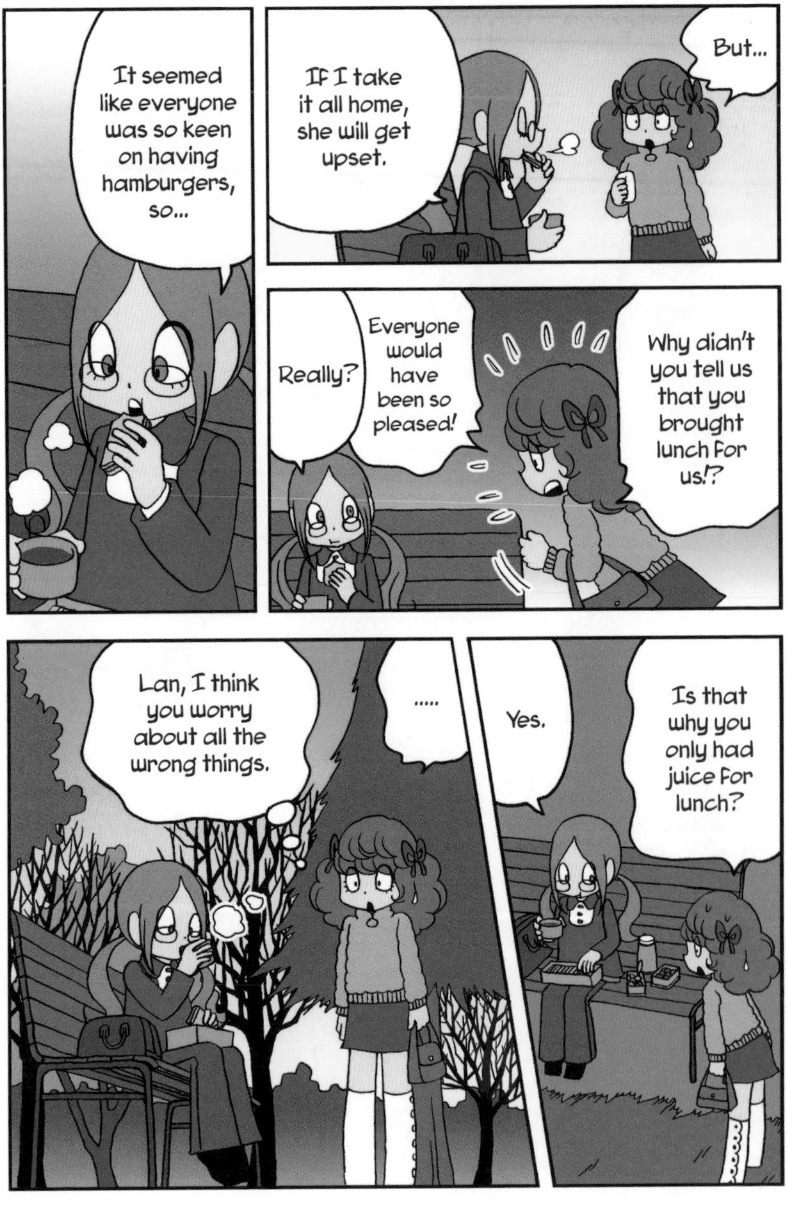
But...
If I take it all home, she will get upset.
Why didn't you tell us that you brought lunch for us!?
Everyone would have been so pleased!
Really?
It seemed like everyone was so keen on having hamburgers, so...
Is that why you only had juice for lunch?
Yes.
.....
Lan, I think you worry about all the wrong things.

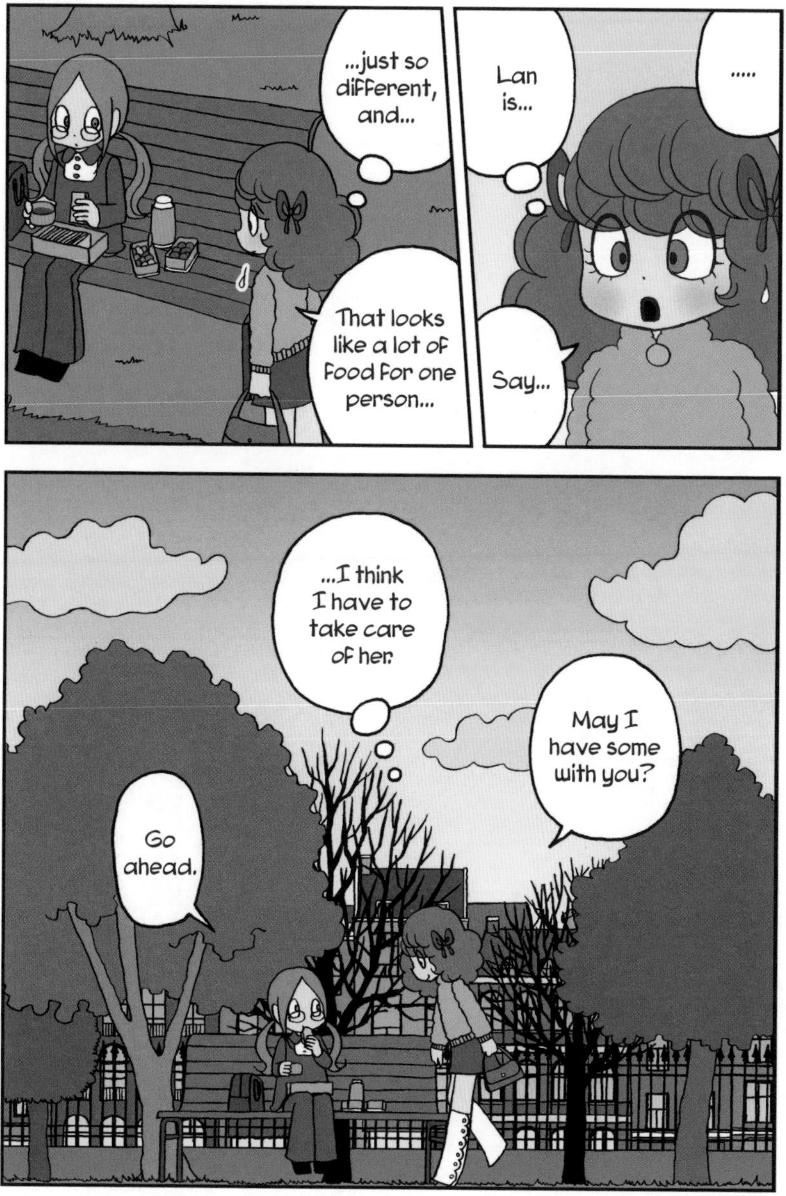
.....
Lan is...
Say...
...just so different, and...
That looks like a lot of food for one person...
...I think I have to take care of her.
May I have some with you?
Go ahead.

CHAPTER 6
THE TWO SUPER STARS

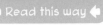

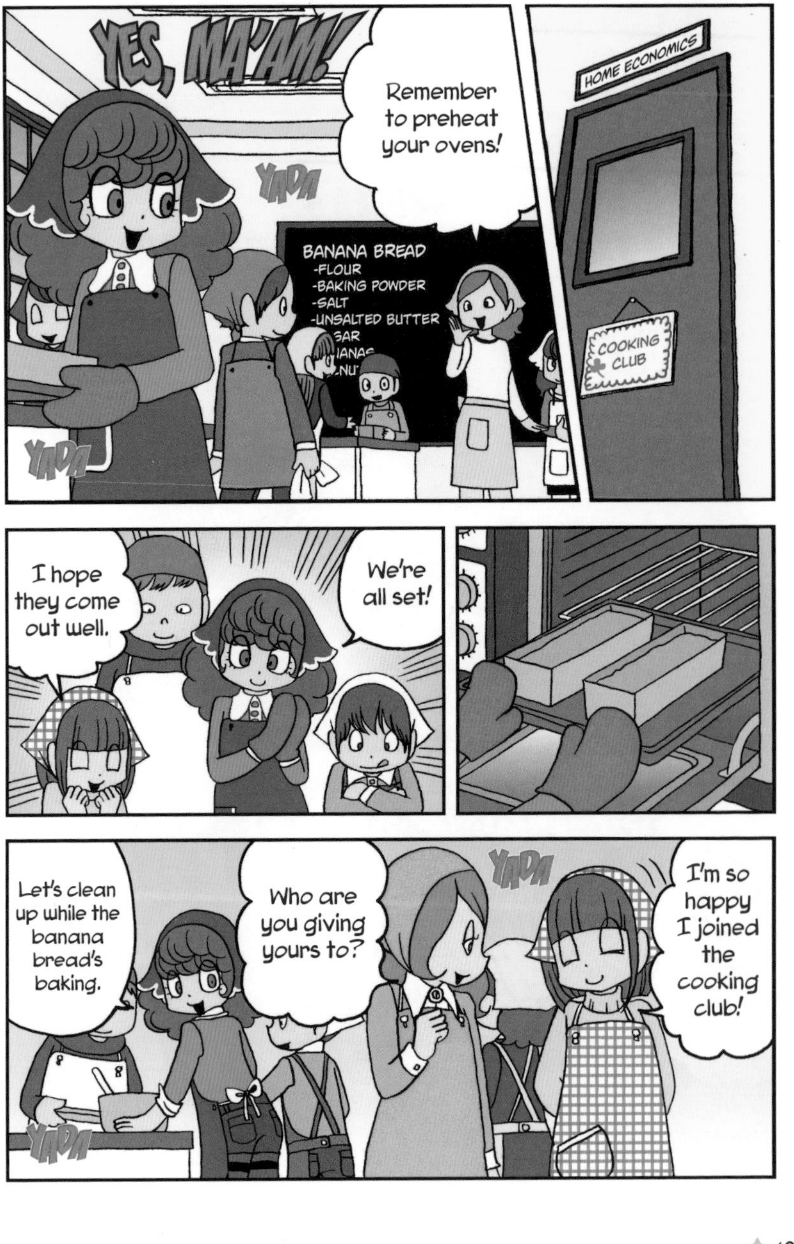
HOME ECONOMICS
COOKING CLUB
Remember to preheat your ovens!
YES, MA'AM!
YADA
BANANA BREAD
-FLOUR
-BAKING POWDER
-SALT
-UNSALTED BUTTER
YADA
We're all set!
I hope they come out well.
I'm so happy I joined the cooking club!
YADA
Who are you giving yours to?
Let's clean up while the banana bread's baking.
YADA

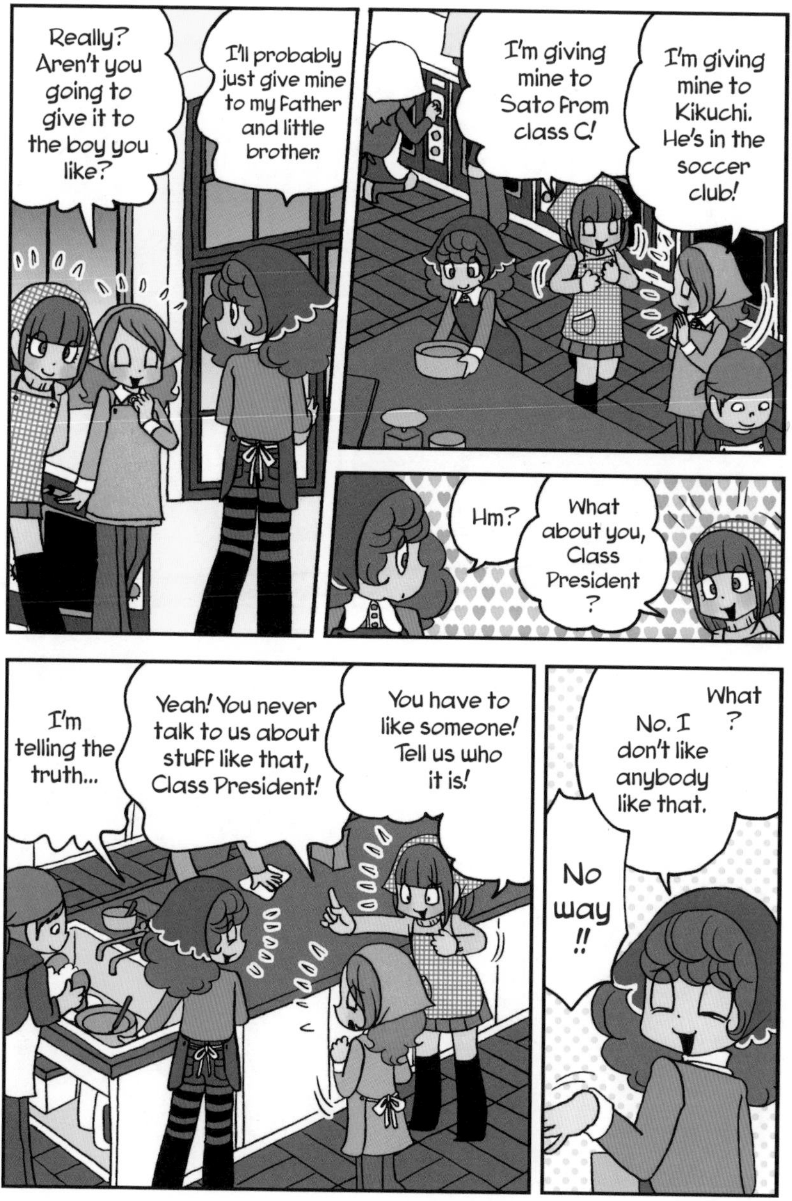

I'm giving mine to Kikuchi. He's in the soccer club!
I'm giving mine to Sato from class C!
I'll probably just give mine to my father and little brother.
Really? Aren't you going to give it to the boy you like?
What about you, Class President?
Hm?
What?
No. I don't like anybody like that.
No way!!
You have to like someone! Tell us who it is!
Yeah! You never talk to us about stuff like that, Class President!
I'm telling the truth...

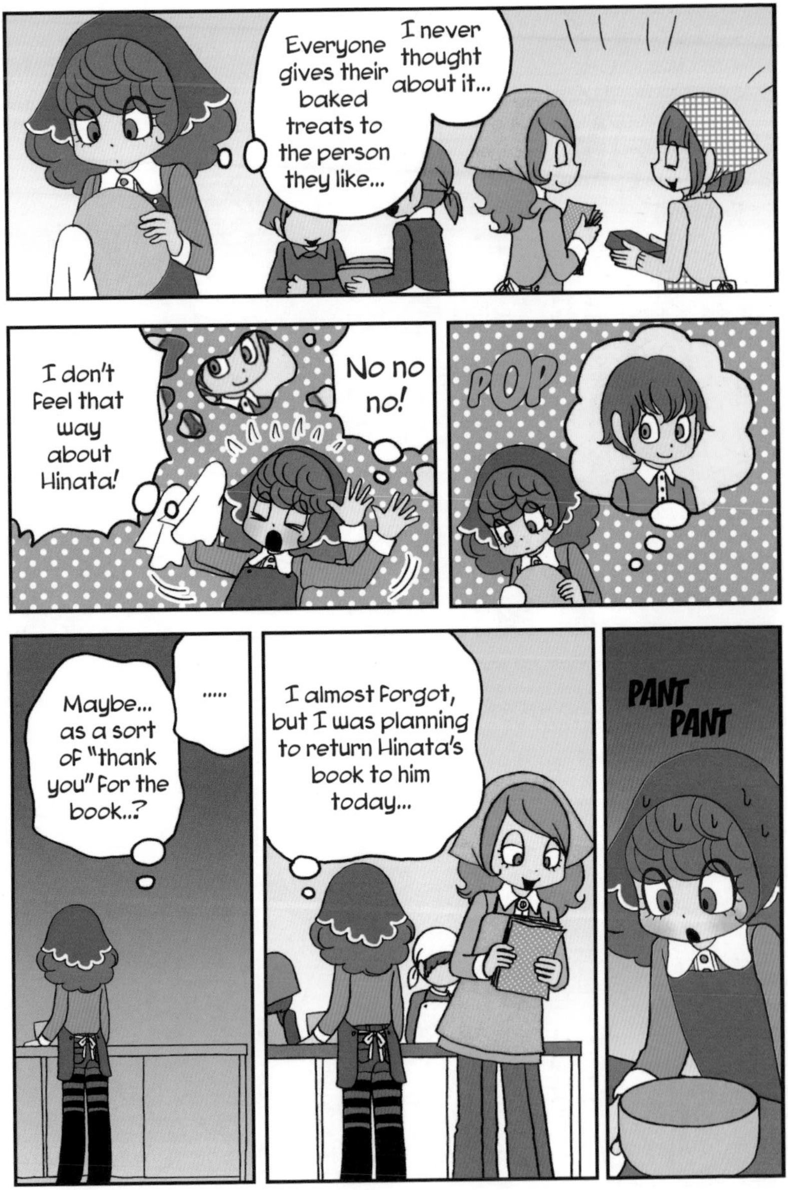
I never thought about it...
Everyone gives their baked treats to the person they like...
POP
No no no!
I don't feel that way about Hinata!
PANT PANT
I almost forgot, but I was planning to return Hinata's book to him today...
.....
Maybe... as a sort of "thank you" for the book...?

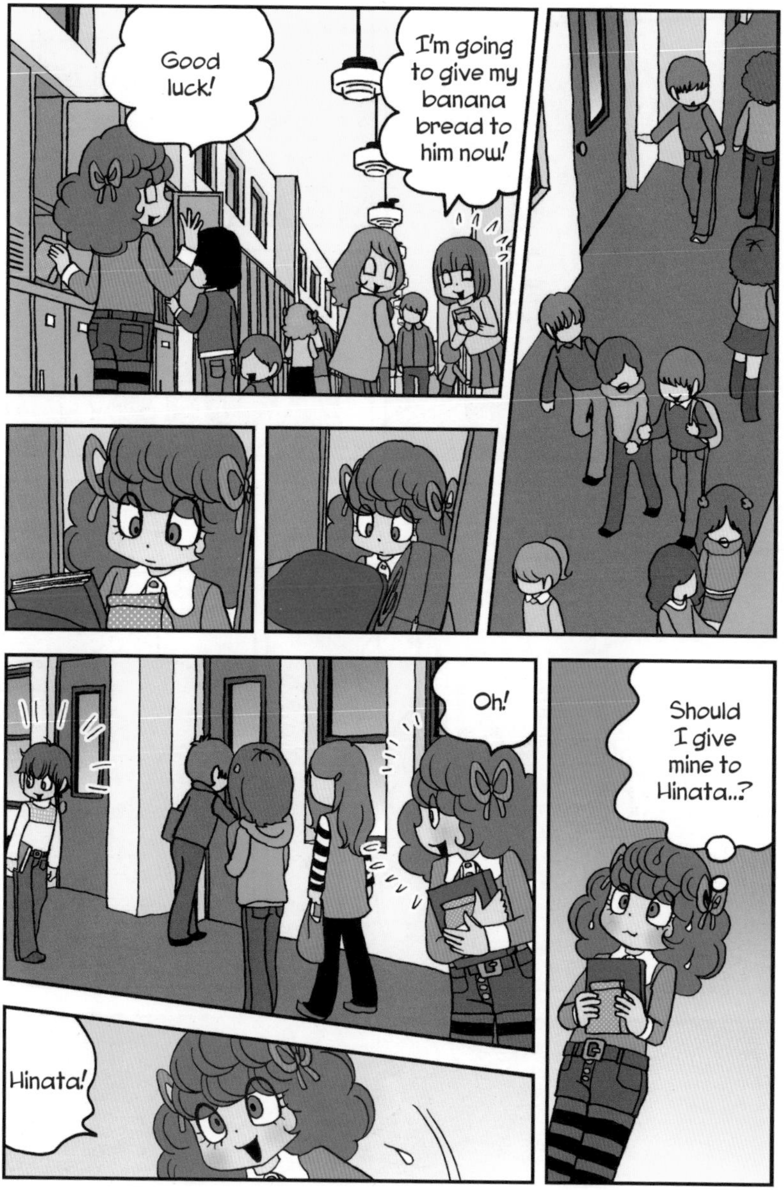
I'm going to give my banana bread to him now!
Good luck!
Should I give mine to Hinata..?
Oh!
Hinata!

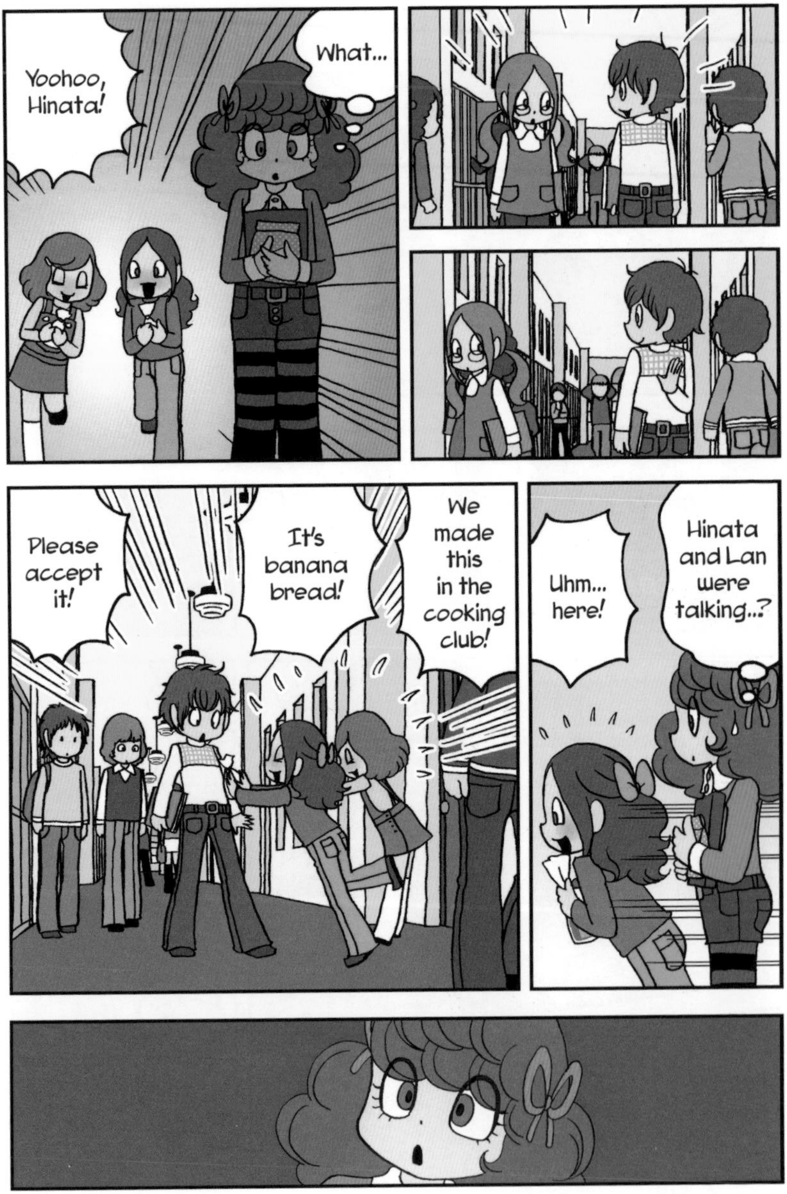
What...
Yoohoo, Hinata!
Hinata and Lan were talking..?
Uhm... here!
We made this in the cooking club!
It's banana bread!
Please accept it!

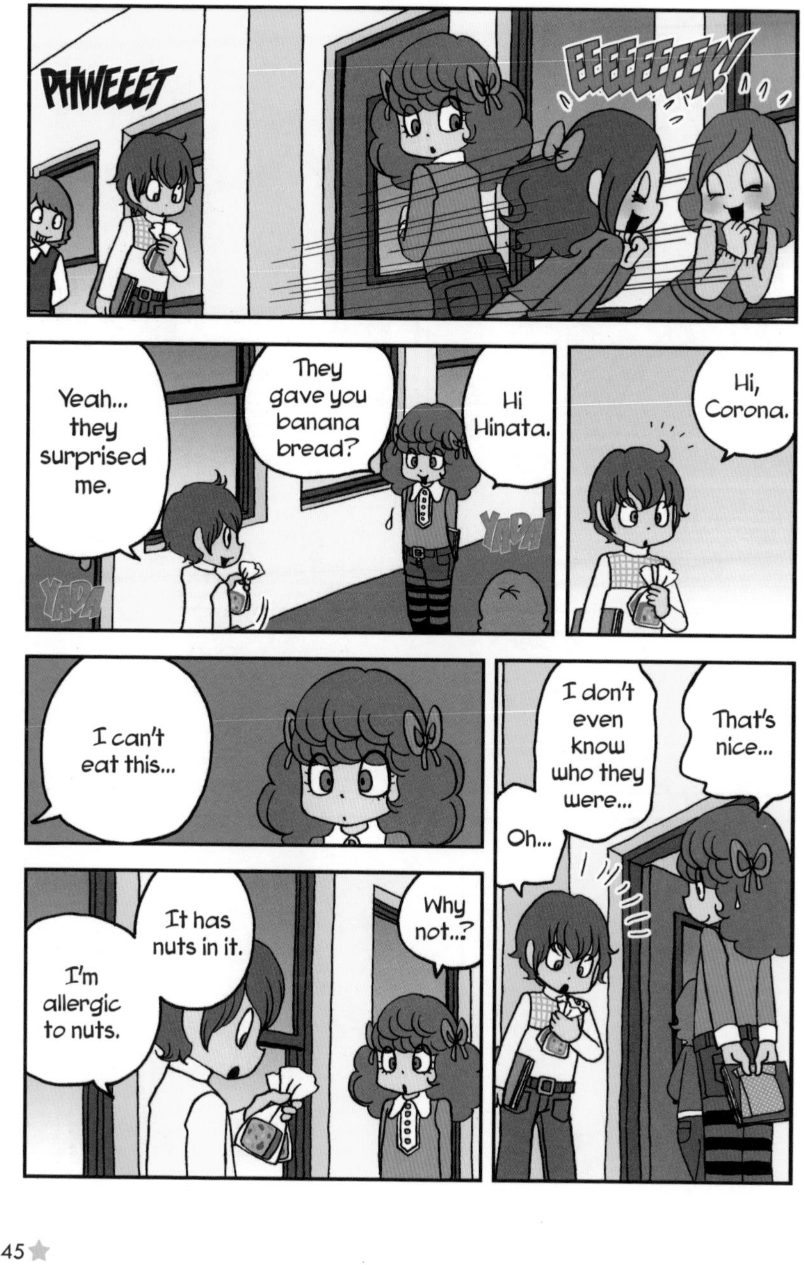
EEEEEEEEK!
PHWEEET
Hi, Corona.
Hi Hinata.
They gave you banana bread?
YADA
Yeah... they surprised me.
YADA
That's nice...
I don't even know who they were...
Oh...
I can't eat this...
Why not..?
It has nuts in it.
I'm allergic to nuts.

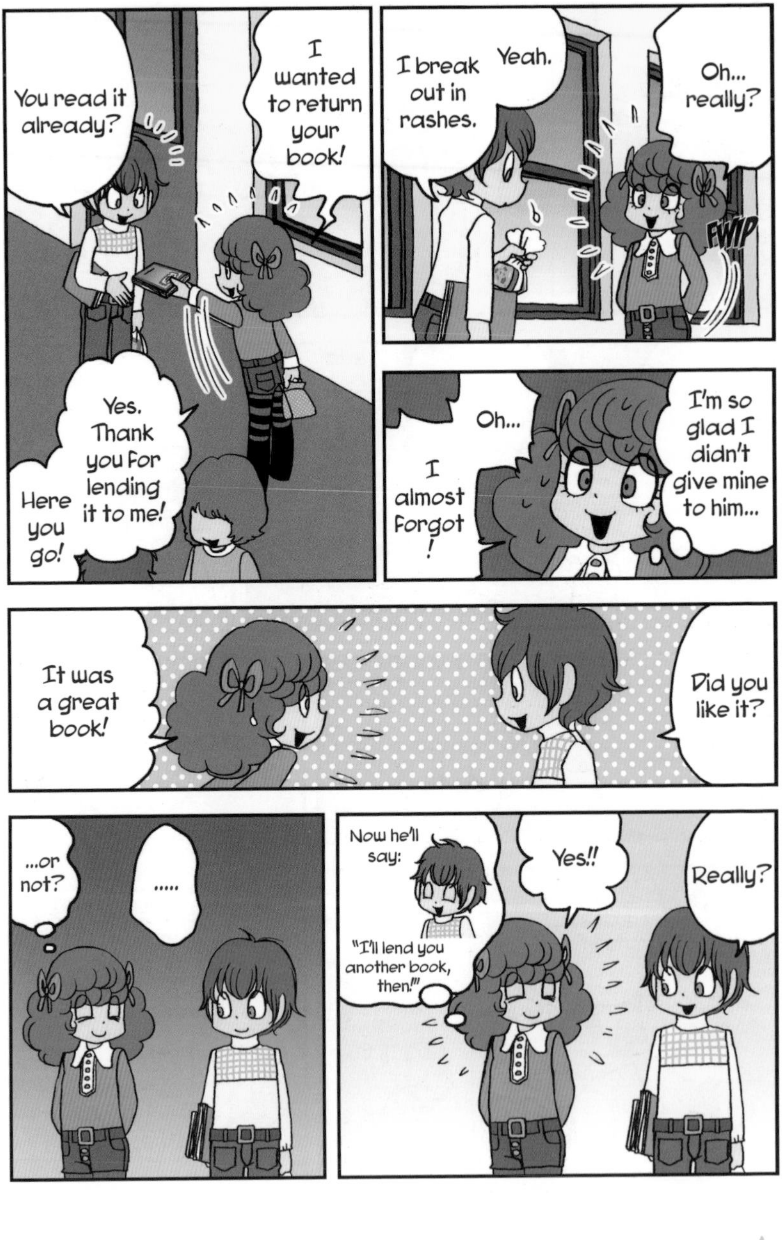
Oh... really?
Yeah.
I break out in rashes.
FWIP
I'm so glad I didn't give mine to him...
Oh...
I almost forgot!
I wanted to return your book!
You read it already?
Yes. Thank you for lending it to me!
Here you go!
Did you like it?
It was a great book!
Really?
Yes!!
Now he'll say:
"I'll lend you another book, then!"
.....
...or not?

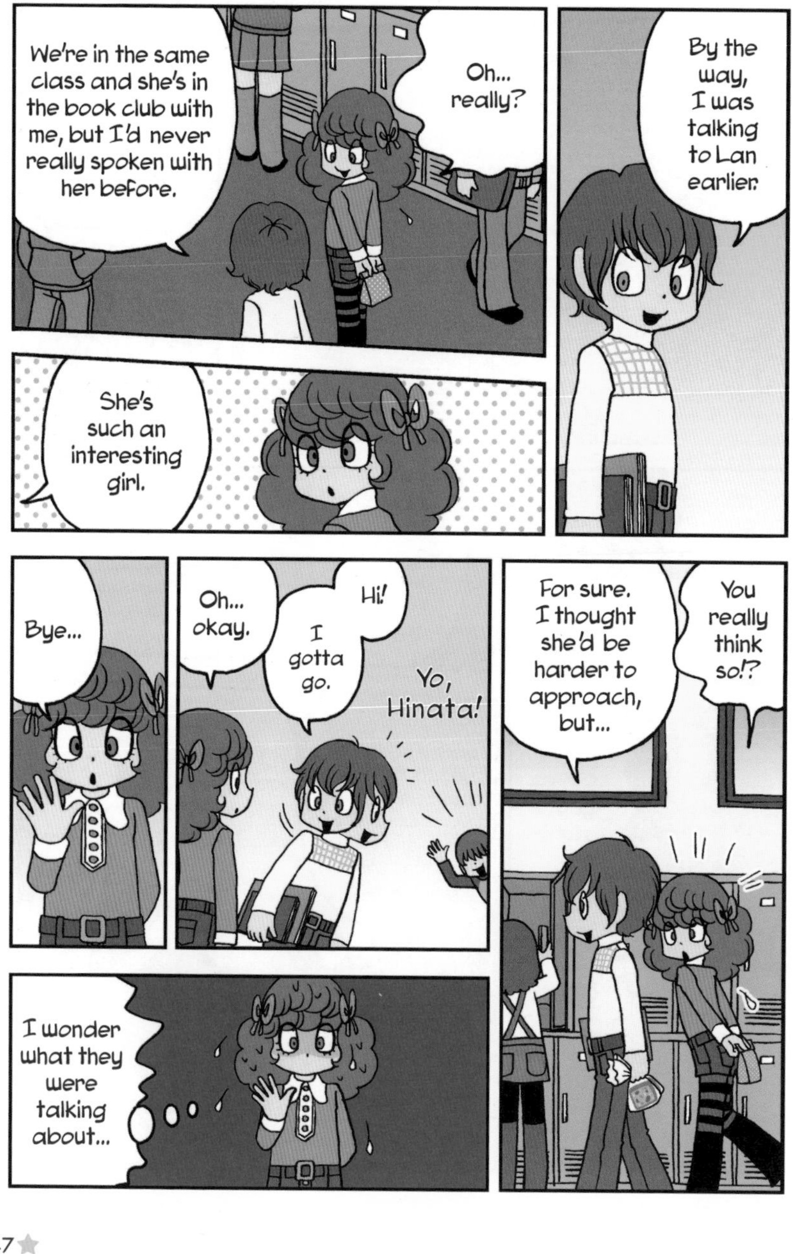
By the way, I was talking to Lan earlier.
Oh... really?
We're in the same class and she's in the book club with me, but I'd never really spoken with her before.
She's such an interesting girl.
You really think so!?
For sure. I thought she'd be harder to approach, but...
Yo, Hinata!
Hi!
I gotta go.
Oh... okay.
Bye...
I wonder what they were talking about...

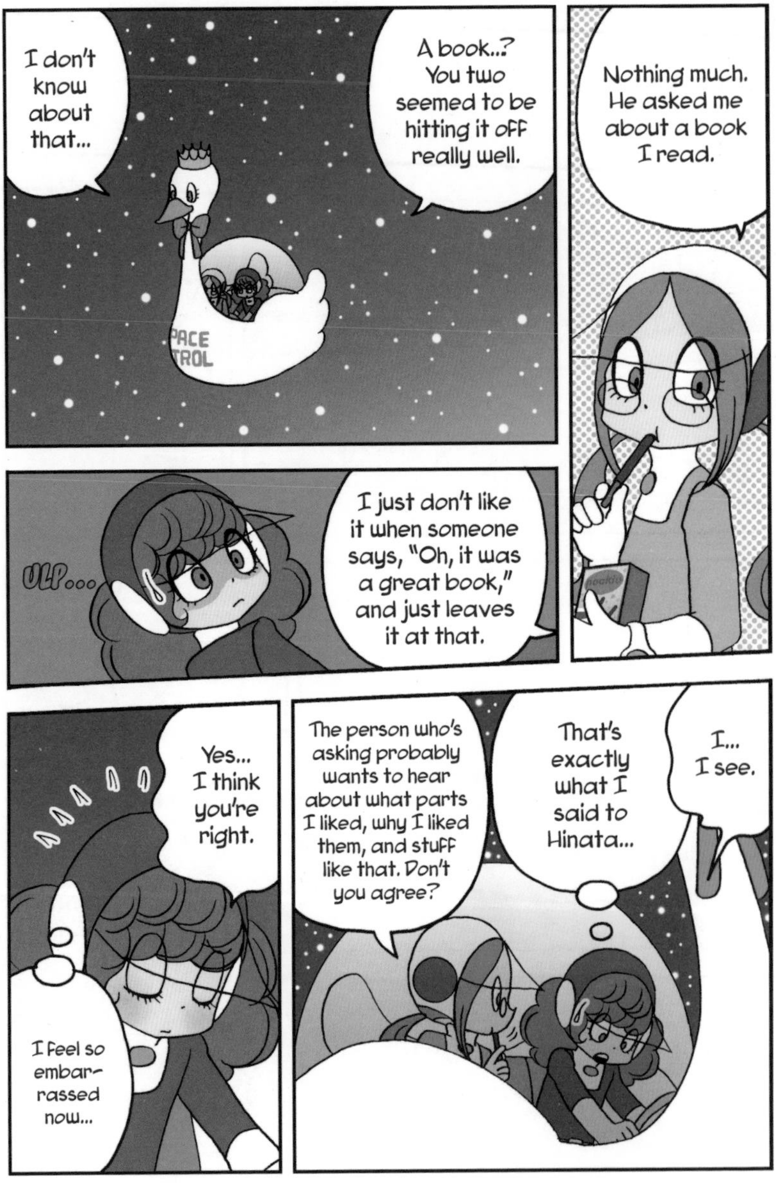
Nothing much. He asked me about a book I read.
A book...? You two seemed to be hitting it off really well.
I don't know about that...
PACE TROL
I just don't like it when someone says, "Oh, it was a great book," and just leaves it at that.
ULP...
I... I see.
That's exactly what I said to Hinata...
The person who's asking probably wants to hear about what parts I liked, why I liked them, and stuff like that. Don't you agree?
Yes... I think you're right.
I feel so embar-rassed now...

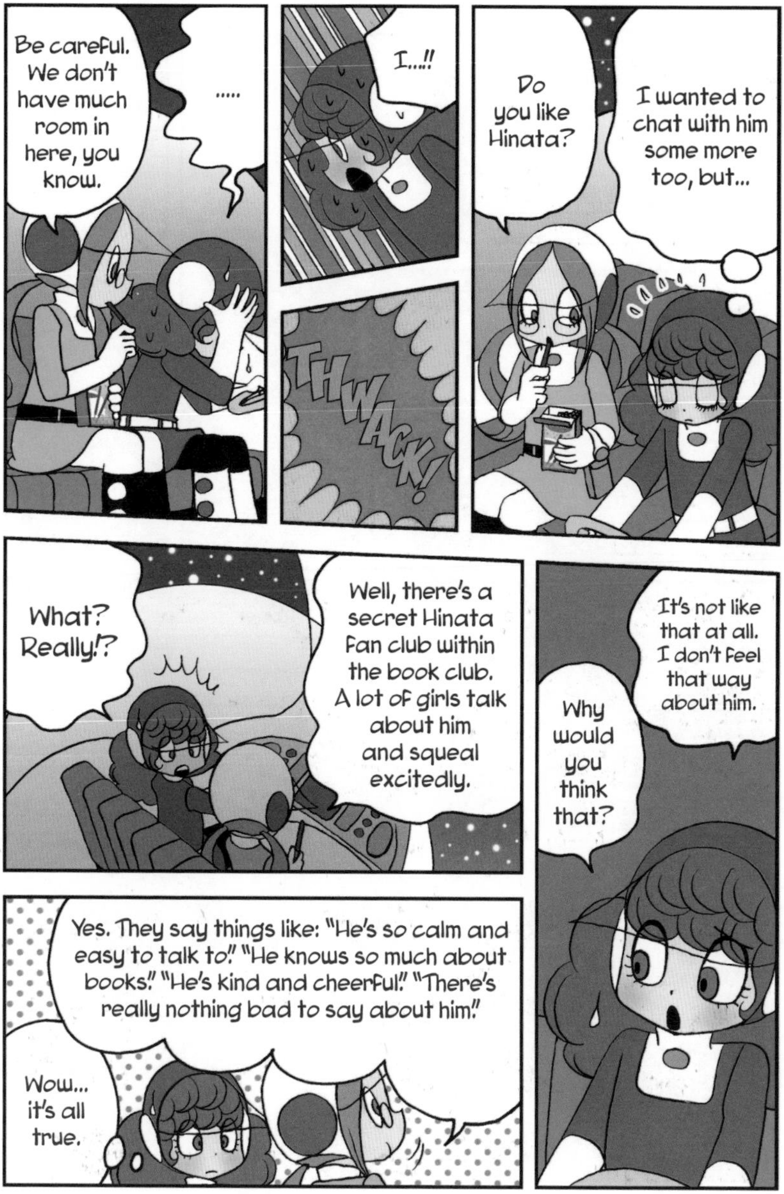
I wanted to chat with him some more too, but...
Do you like Hinata?
I...!!
THWACK!
Be careful. We don't have much room in here, you know.
.....
It's not like that at all. I don't feel that way about him.
Why would you think that?
Well, there's a secret Hinata fan club within the book club. A lot of girls talk about him and squeal excitedly.
What? Really!?
Yes. They say things like: "He's so calm and easy to talk to." "He knows so much about books." "He's kind and cheerful." "There's really nothing bad to say about him."
Wow... it's all true.

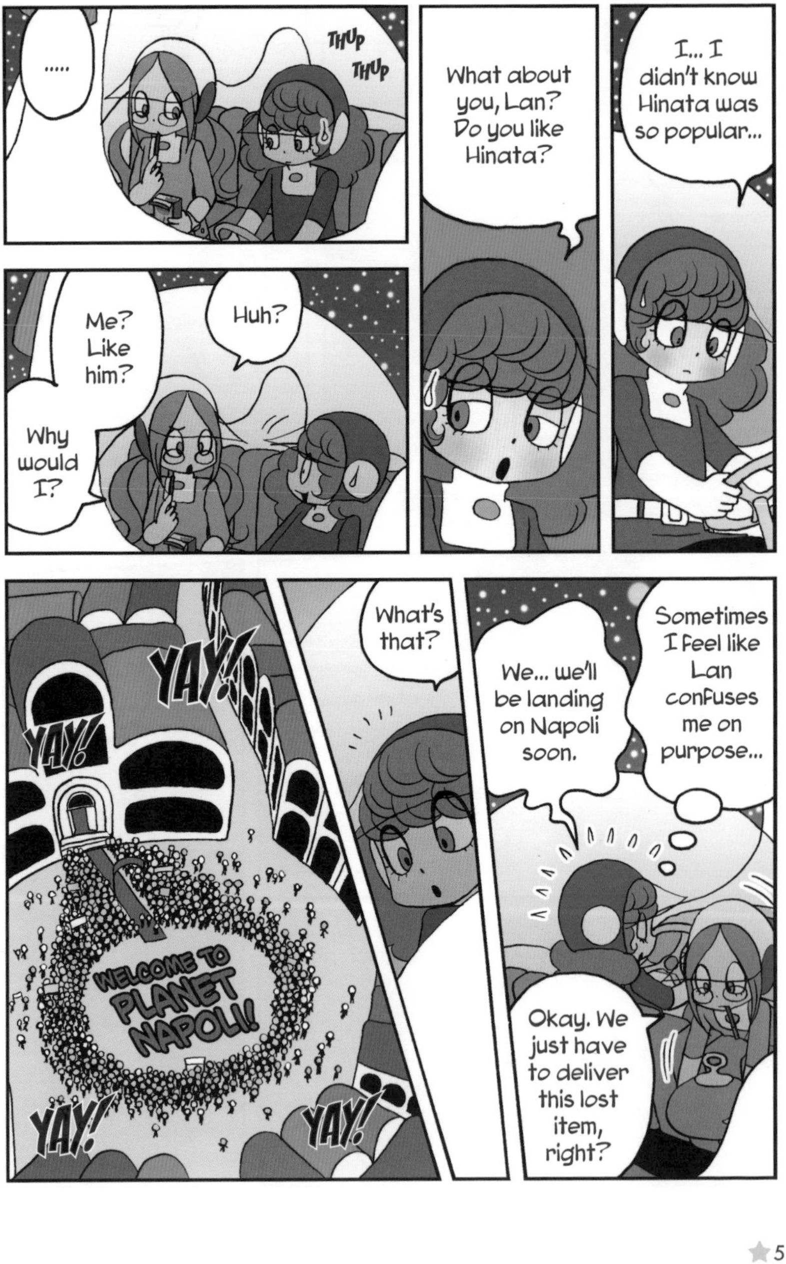
I... I didn't know Hinata was so popular...
What about you, Lan? Do you like Hinata?
.....
THUP THUP
Huh?
Me? Like him?
Why would I?
Sometimes I feel like Lan confuses me on purpose...
We... we'll be landing on Napoli soon.
Okay. We just have to deliver this lost item, right?
What's that?
YAY!
YAY!
WELCOME TO PLANET NAPOLI!
YAY!
YAY!

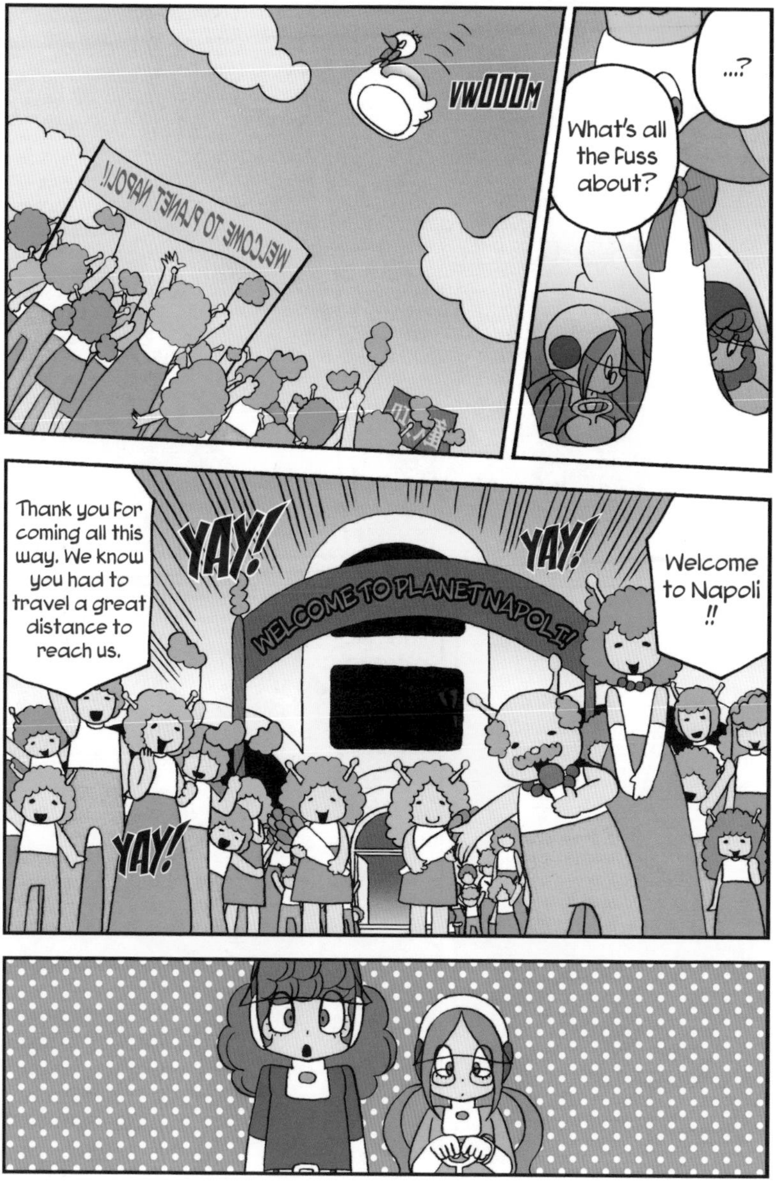
...?
What's all the fuss about?
VWOOOM
WELCOME TO PLANET NAPOLI!
Welcome to Napoli !!
YAY!
WELCOME TO PLANET NAPOLI!
YAY!
Thank you for coming all this way. We know you had to travel a great distance to reach us.
YAY!

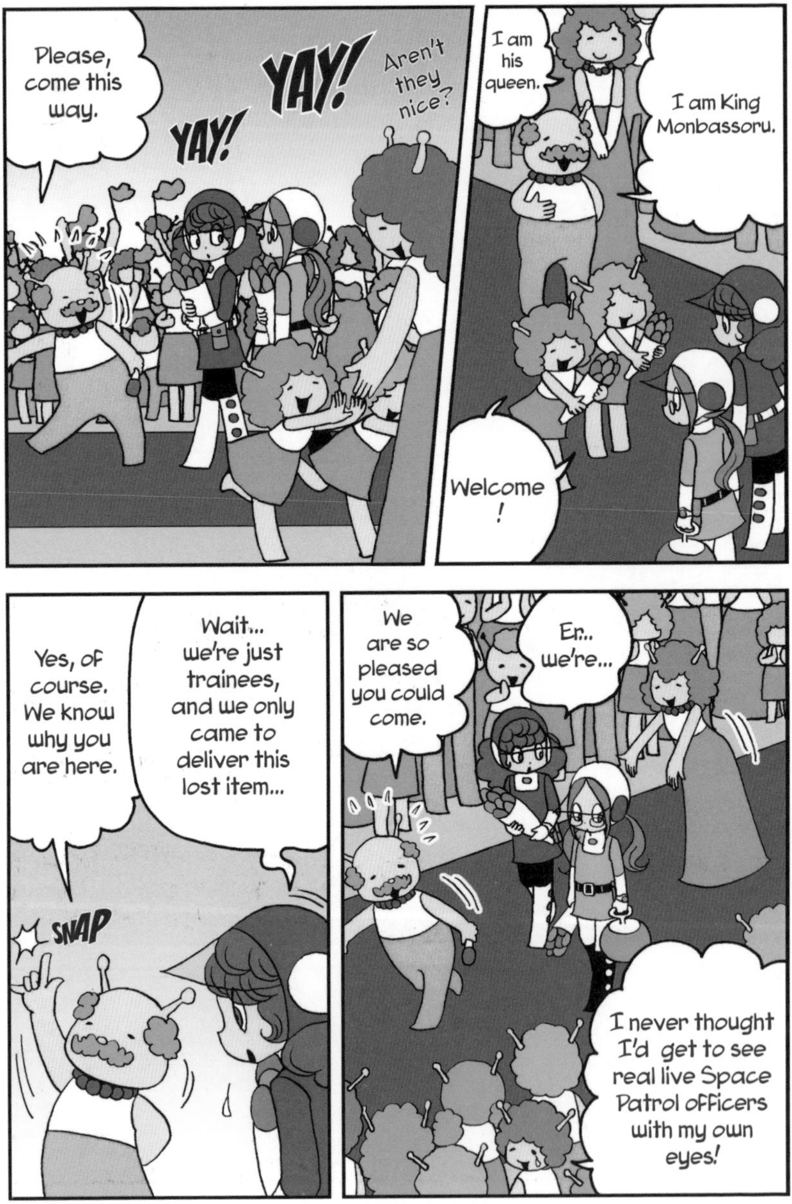
I am King Monbassoru.
I am his queen.
Welcome!
Aren't they nice?
YAY!
YAY!
Please, come this way.
We are so pleased you could come.
Er.. we're...
I never thought I'd get to see real live Space Patrol officers with my own eyes!
Wait... we're just trainees, and we only came to deliver this lost item...
Yes, of course. We know why you are here.
SNAP

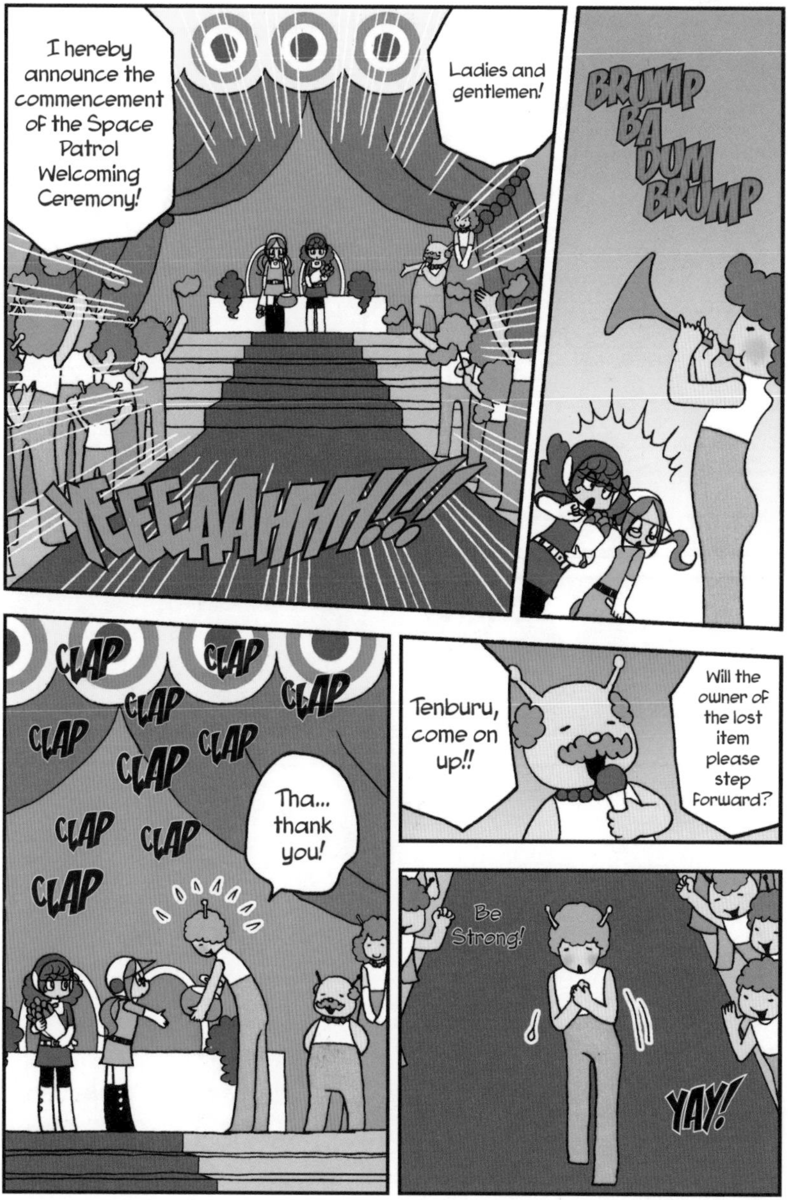

BRUMP BA DUM BRUMP
Ladies and gentlemen!
I hereby announce the commencement of the Space Patrol Welcoming Ceremony!
YEEEAAHHH!!!
Will the owner of the lost item please step forward?
Tenburu, come on up!!
Be Strong!
YAY!
CLAP CLAP CLAP CLAP CLAP CLAP CLAP CLAP CLAP
Tha... thank you!

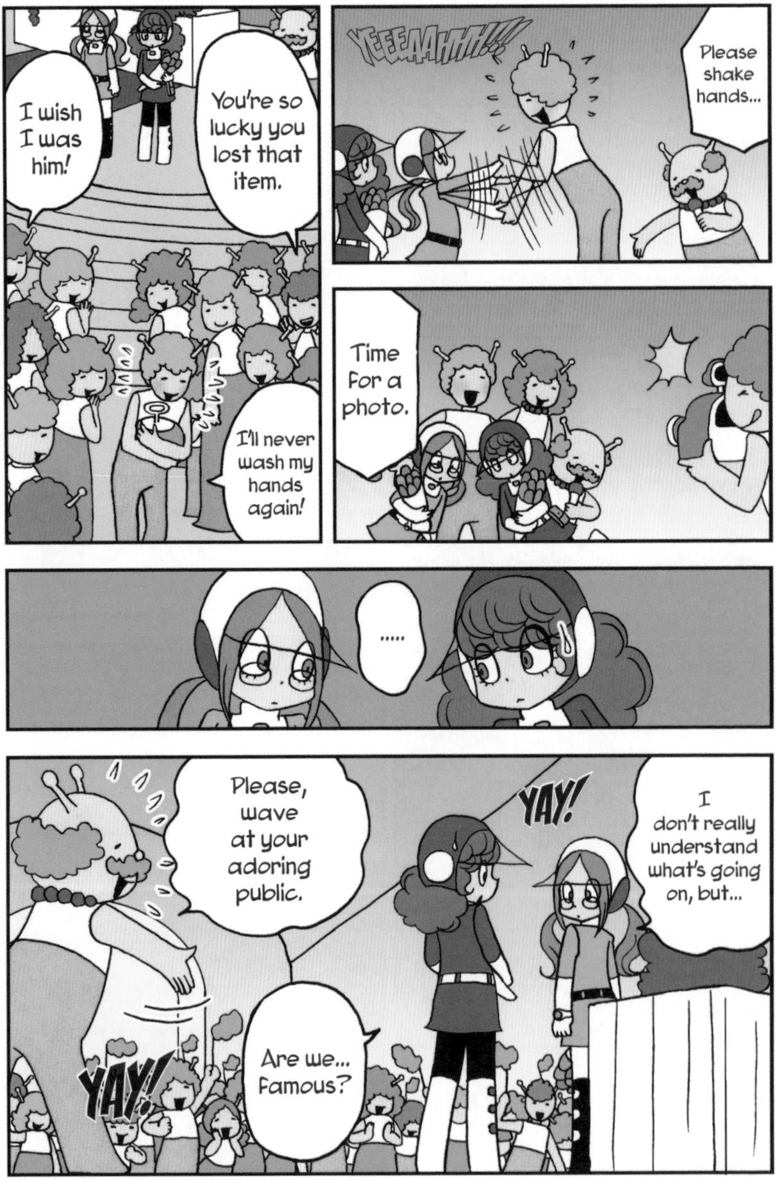
YEEEAAHHH!!!
Please shake hands...
Time for a photo.
You're so lucky you lost that item.
I wish I was him!
I'll never wash my hands again!
.....
I don't really understand what's going on, but...
YAY!
Please, wave at your adoring public.
Are we... famous?
YAY!

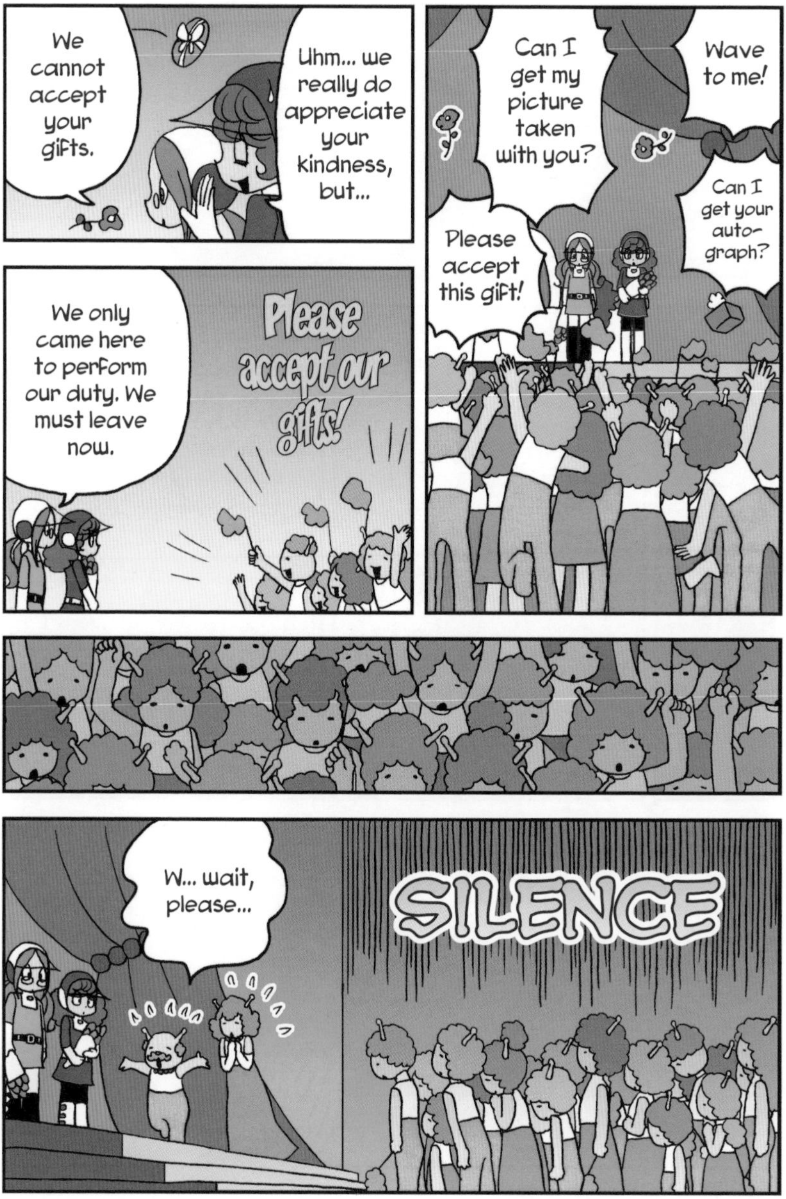

Wave to me!
Can I get my picture taken with you?
Can I get your autograph?
Please accept this gift!
Uhm... we really do appreciate your kindness, but...
We cannot accept your gifts.
Please accept our gifts!
We only came here to perform our duty. We must leave now.
SILENCE
W... wait, please...

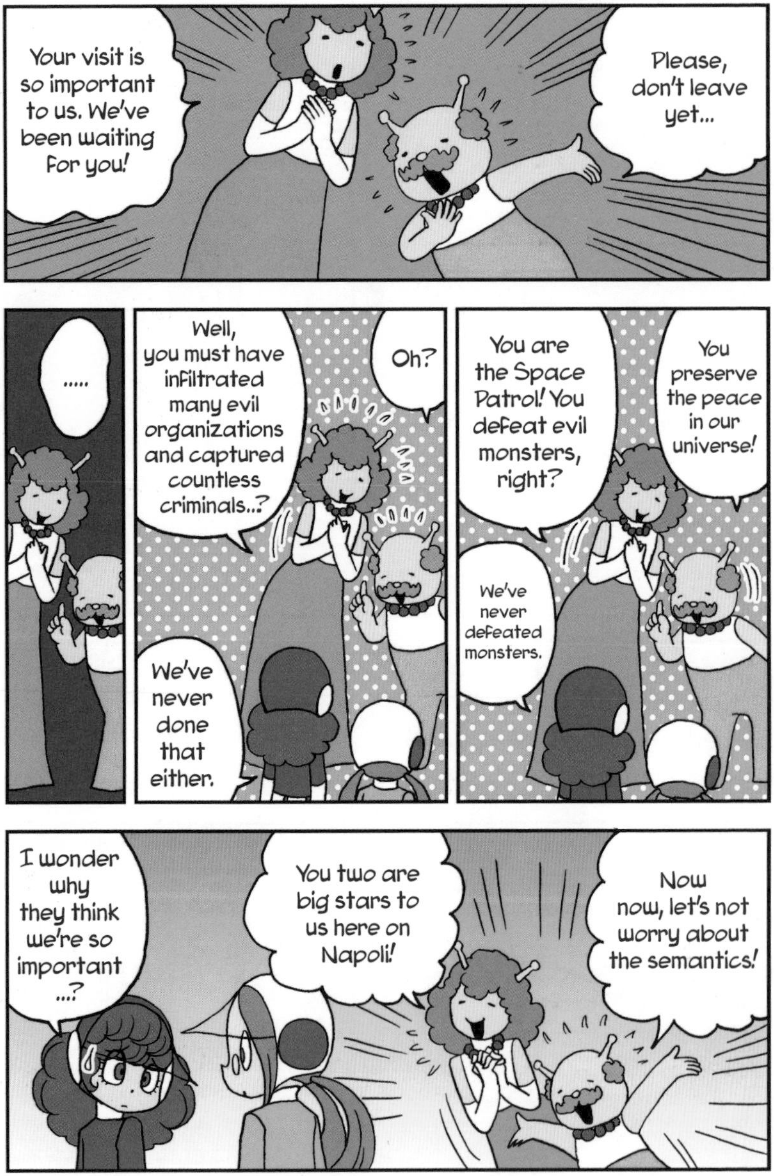
Please, don't leave yet...
Your visit is so important to us. We've been waiting for you!
You preserve the peace in our universe!
You are the Space Patrol! You defeat evil monsters, right?
We've never defeated monsters.
Oh?
Well, you must have infiltrated many evil organizations and captured countless criminals..?
We've never done that either.
.....
Now now, let's not worry about the semantics!
You two are big stars to us here on Napoli!
I wonder why they think we're so important ...?

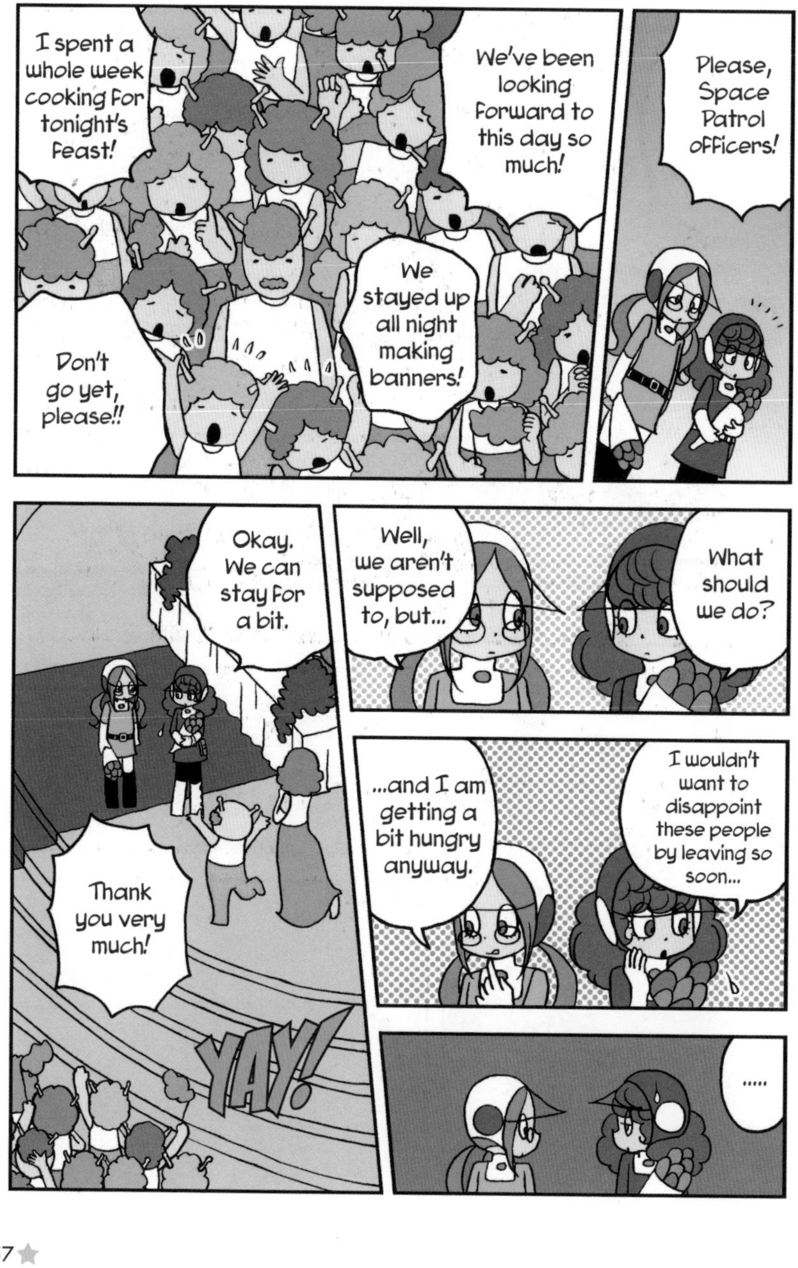
Please, Space Patrol officers!
We've been looking forward to this day so much!
I spent a whole week cooking for tonight's feast!
We stayed up all night making banners!
Don't go yet, please!!
What should we do?
Well, we aren't supposed to, but...
I wouldn't want to disappoint these people by leaving so soon...
...and I am getting a bit hungry anyway.
.....
Okay. We can stay for a bit.
Thank you very much!
YAY!

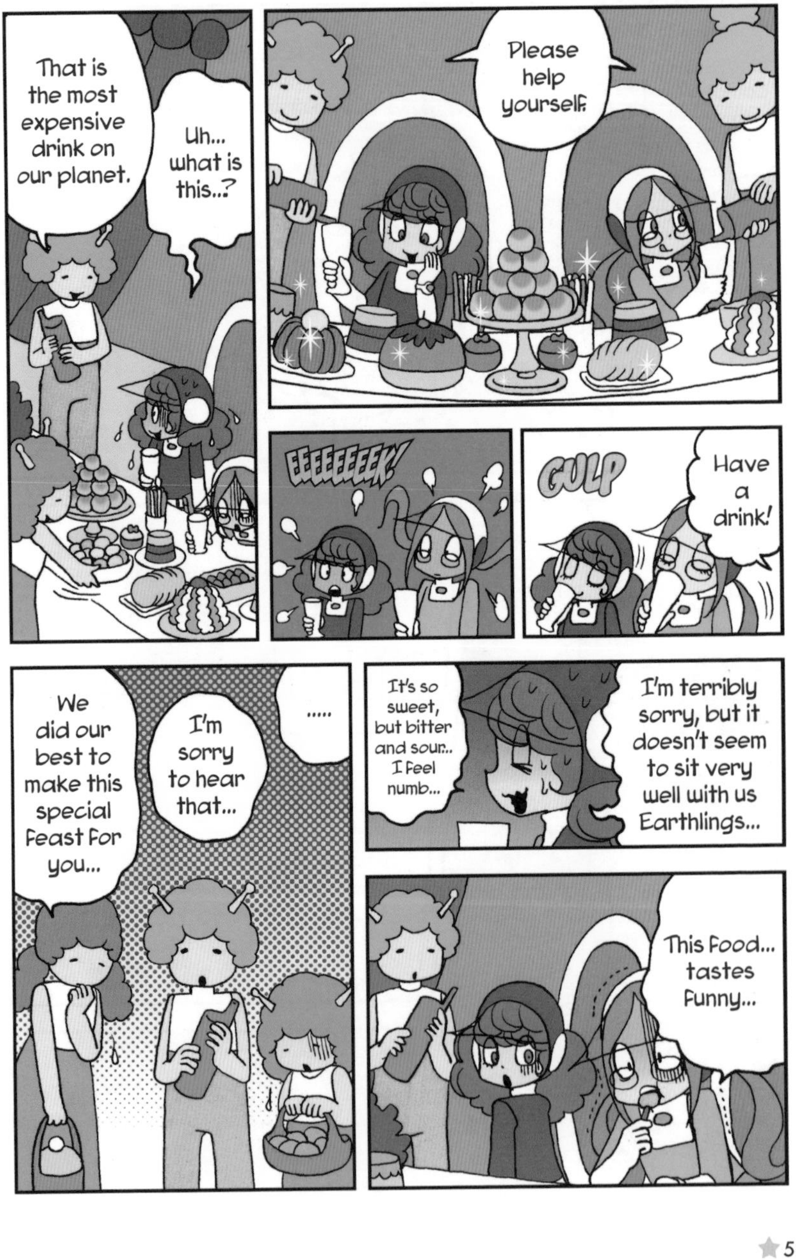
Please help yourself.
GULP
Have a drink!
EEEEEEEEK!
Uh... what is this...?
That is the most expensive drink on our planet.
I'm terribly sorry, but it doesn't seem to sit very well with us Earthlings...
It's so sweet, but bitter and sour... I feel numb...
This food... tastes funny...
.....
I'm sorry to hear that...
We did our best to make this special feast for you...

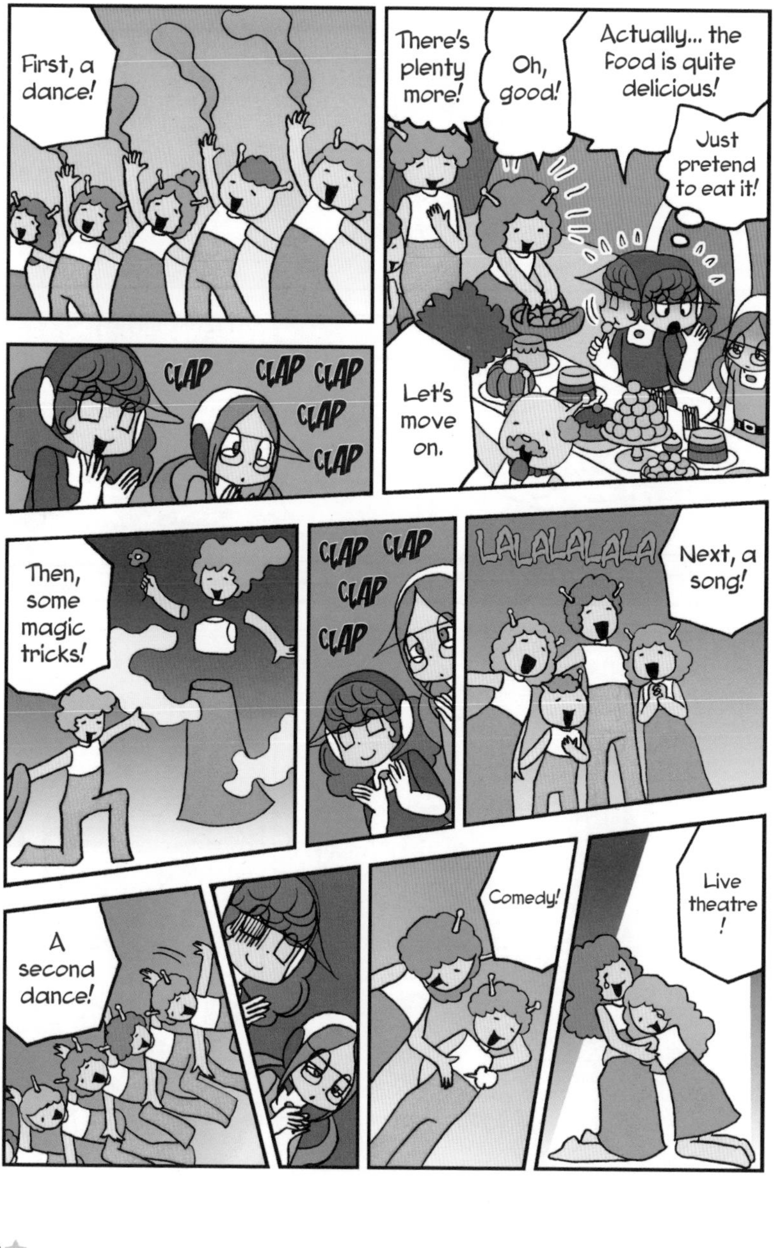
Actually... the food is quite delicious!
Just pretend to eat it!
Oh, good!
There's plenty more!
Let's move on.
First, a dance!
CLAP CLAP CLAP CLAP CLAP
Next, a song!
LALALALALA
CLAP CLAP CLAP CLAP
Then, some magic tricks!
Live theatre !
Comedy!
A second dance!

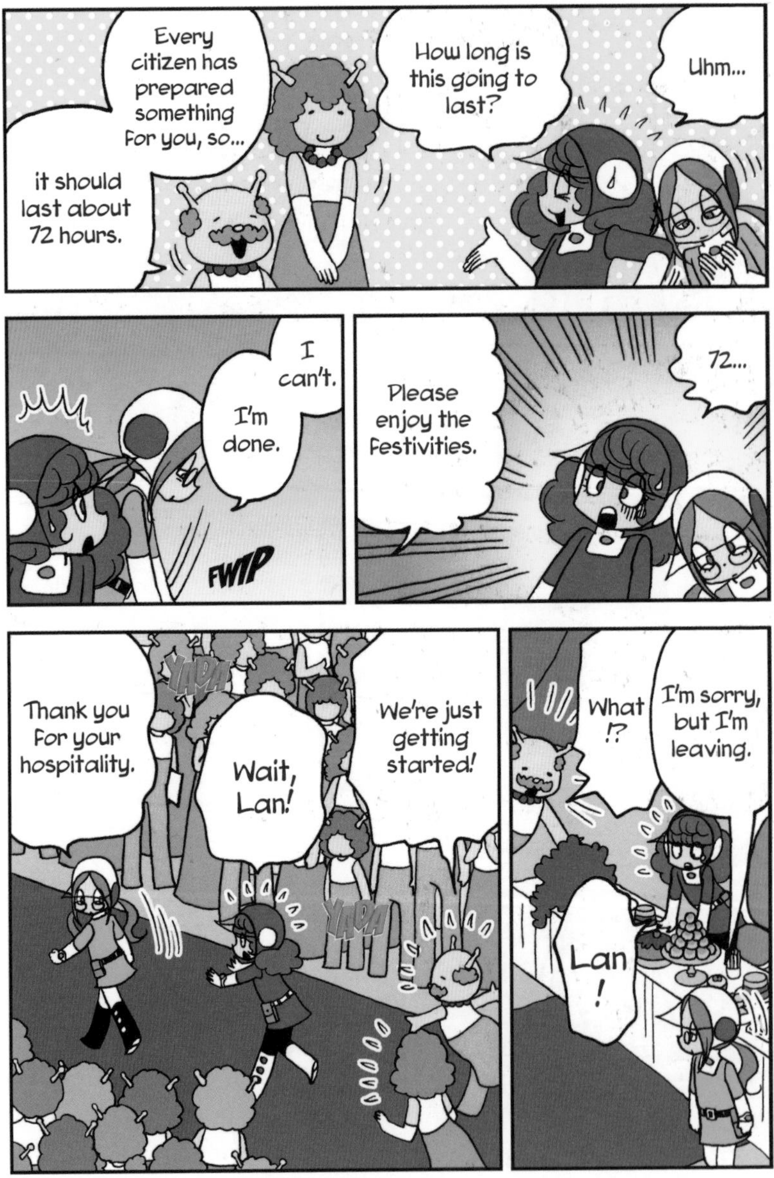

Uhm...
How long is this going to last?
Every citizen has prepared something for you, so...
it should last about 72 hours.
72...
Please enjoy the festivities.
I can't.
I'm done.
FWIP
I'm sorry, but I'm leaving.
What!?
Lan!
We're just getting started!
YADA
Wait, Lan!
Thank you for your hospitality.
YADA

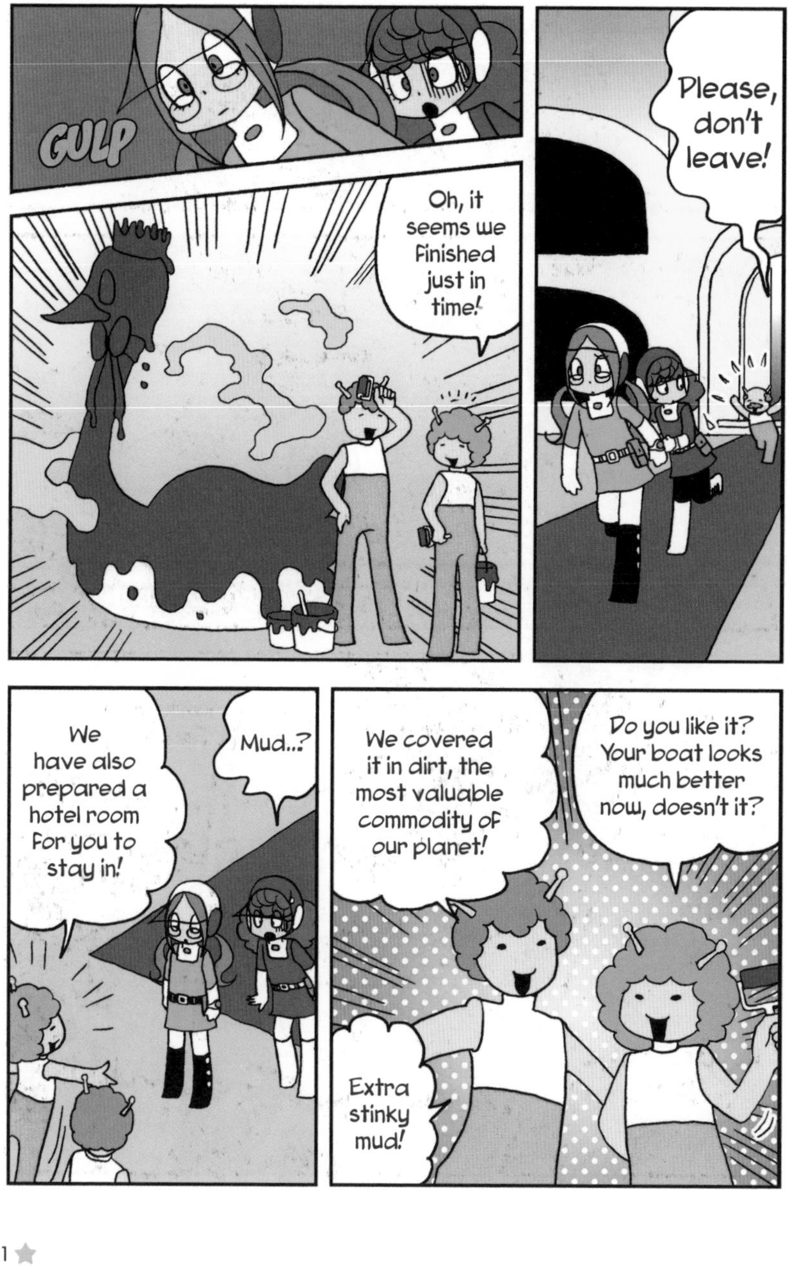
Please, don't leave!
GULP
Oh, it seems we finished just in time!
Do you like it? Your boat looks much better now, doesn't it?
We covered it in dirt, the most valuable commodity of our planet!
Extra stinky mud!
Mud..?
We have also prepared a hotel room for you to stay in!

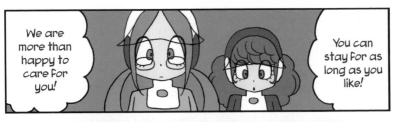

You can stay for as long as you like!
We are more than happy to care for you!
FWUP
Wait!
CLOMP
FWUP
Don't leave!
CLOMP
CLOMP
CLOMP
FWUP
Take this with you!
CLOMP
FWUP
HEY!
HEY!
HEY!
Let's go, Corona.
DASH
Huh!?
Uh... wait...
WOBBLE
CRASH
Oh!
WOBBLE
We caught you!
WAAAH
WAAAH

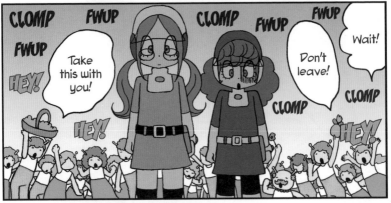

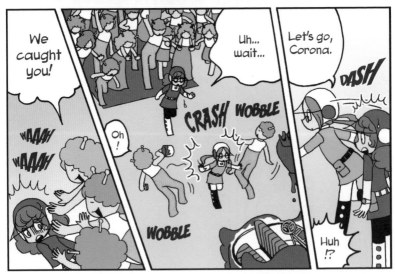

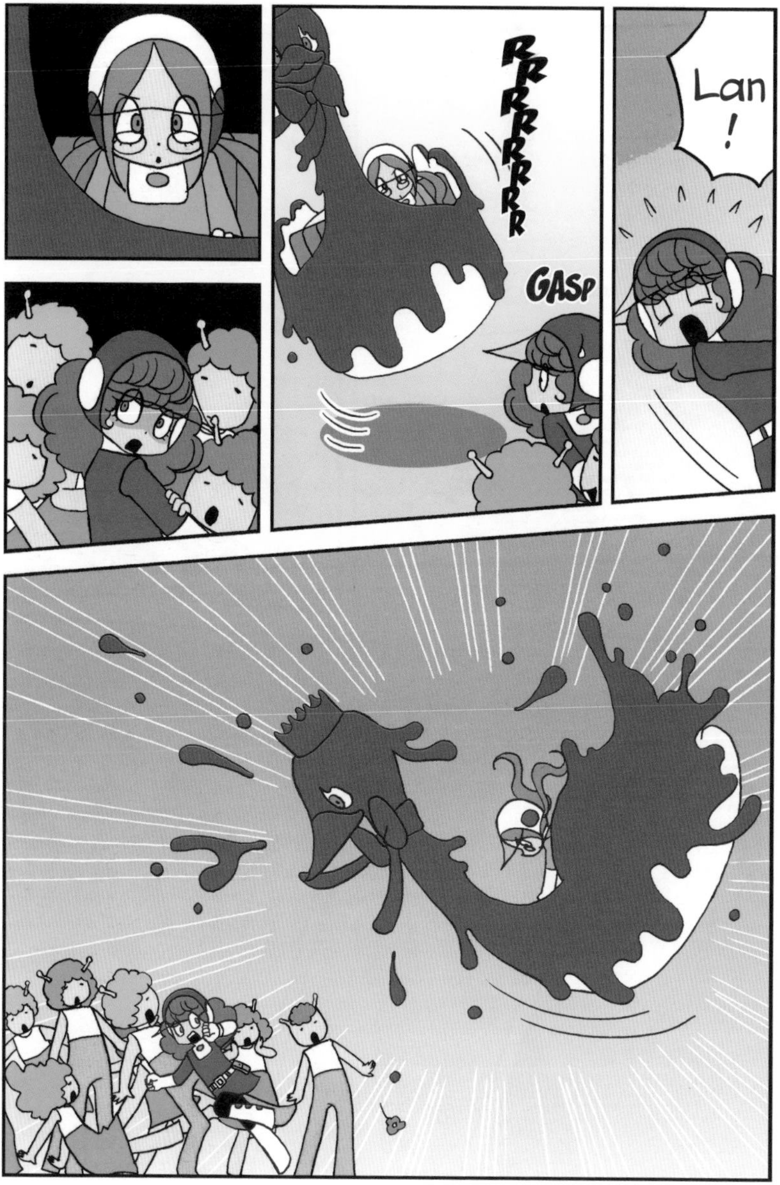
Lan!
RRRRRRRR
GASP

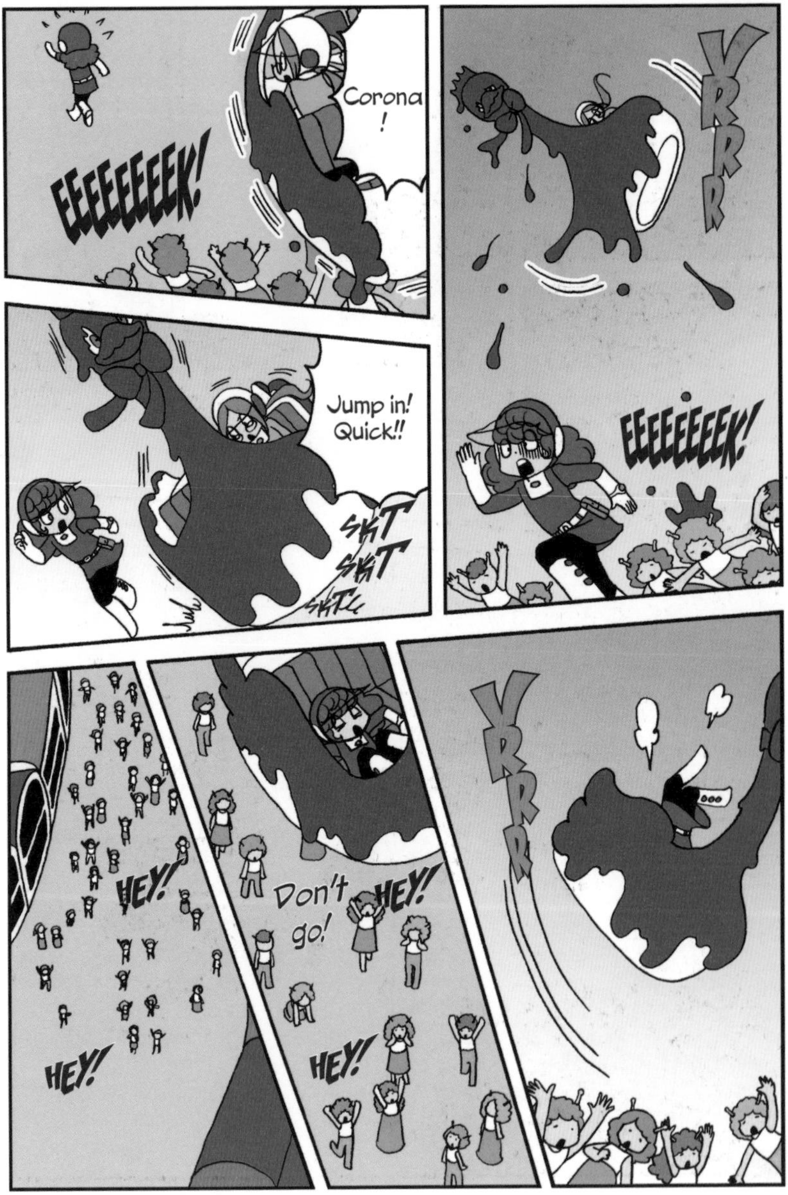
VRRR
EEEEEEEEK!
EEEEEEEEK!
Corona!
Jump in! Quick!!
SKT SKT SKT
VRRR
HEY!
Don't go!
HEY!
HEY!
HEY!

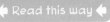

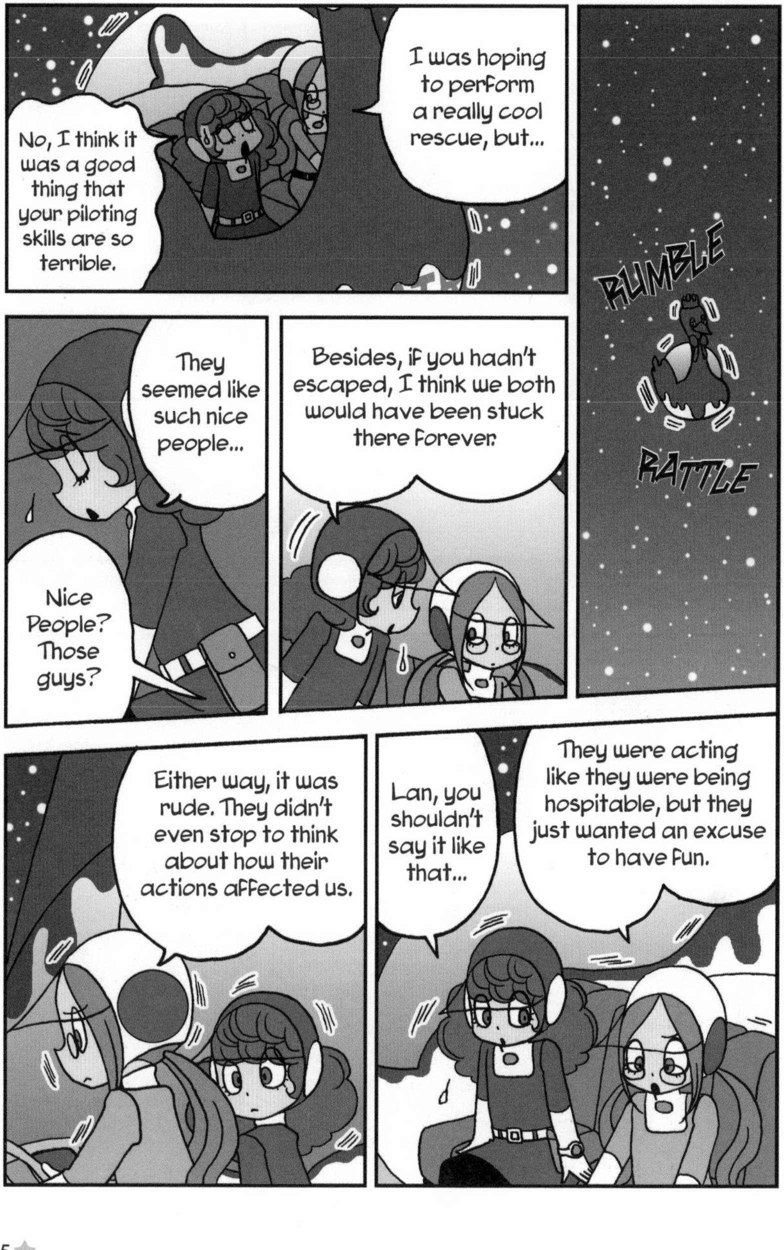
RUMBLE
RATTLE
I was hoping to perform a really cool rescue, but...
No, I think it was a good thing that your piloting skills are so terrible.
Besides, if you hadn't escaped, I think we both would have been stuck there forever.
They seemed like such nice people...
Nice People? Those guys?
They were acting like they were being hospitable, but they just wanted an excuse to have fun.
Lan, you shouldn't say it like that...
Either way, it was rude. They didn't even stop to think about how their actions affected us.

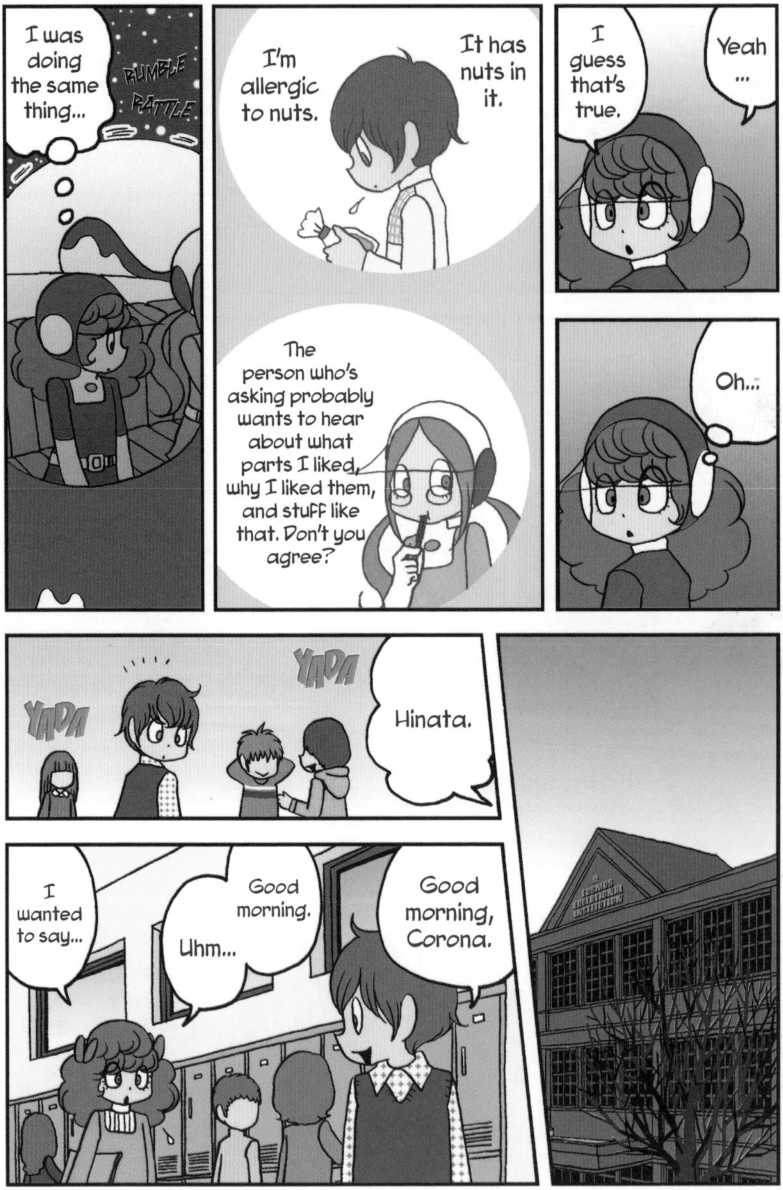
Yeah ...
I guess that's true.
Oh...
It has nuts in it.
I'm allergic to nuts.
The person who's asking probably wants to hear about what parts I liked, why I liked them, and stuff like that. Don't you agree?
I was doing the same thing...
RUMBLE
RATTLE
YADA
Hinata.
YADA
Good morning, Corona.
Good morning.
Uhm...
I wanted to say...

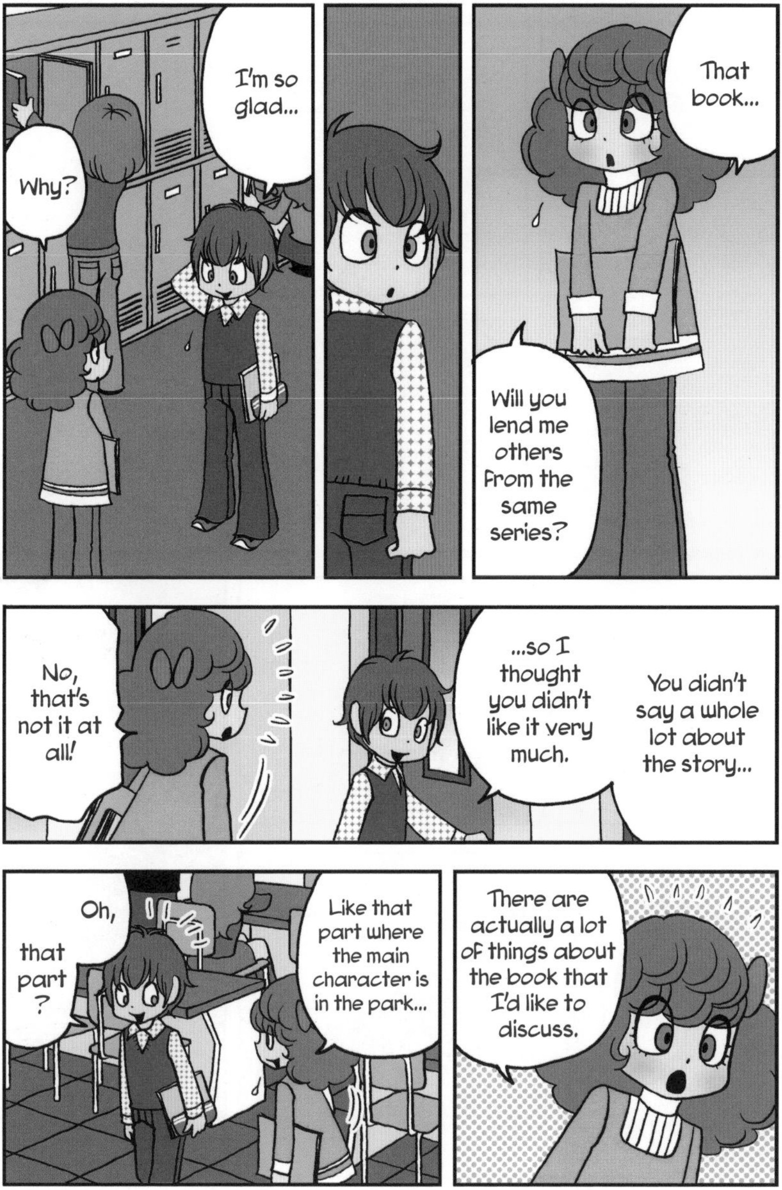
That book...
Will you lend me others from the same series?
I'm so glad...
Why?
You didn't say a whole lot about the story...
...so I thought you didn't like it very much.
No, that's not it at all!
There are actually a lot of things about the book that I'd like to discuss.
Like that part where the main character is in the park...
Oh,
that part ?

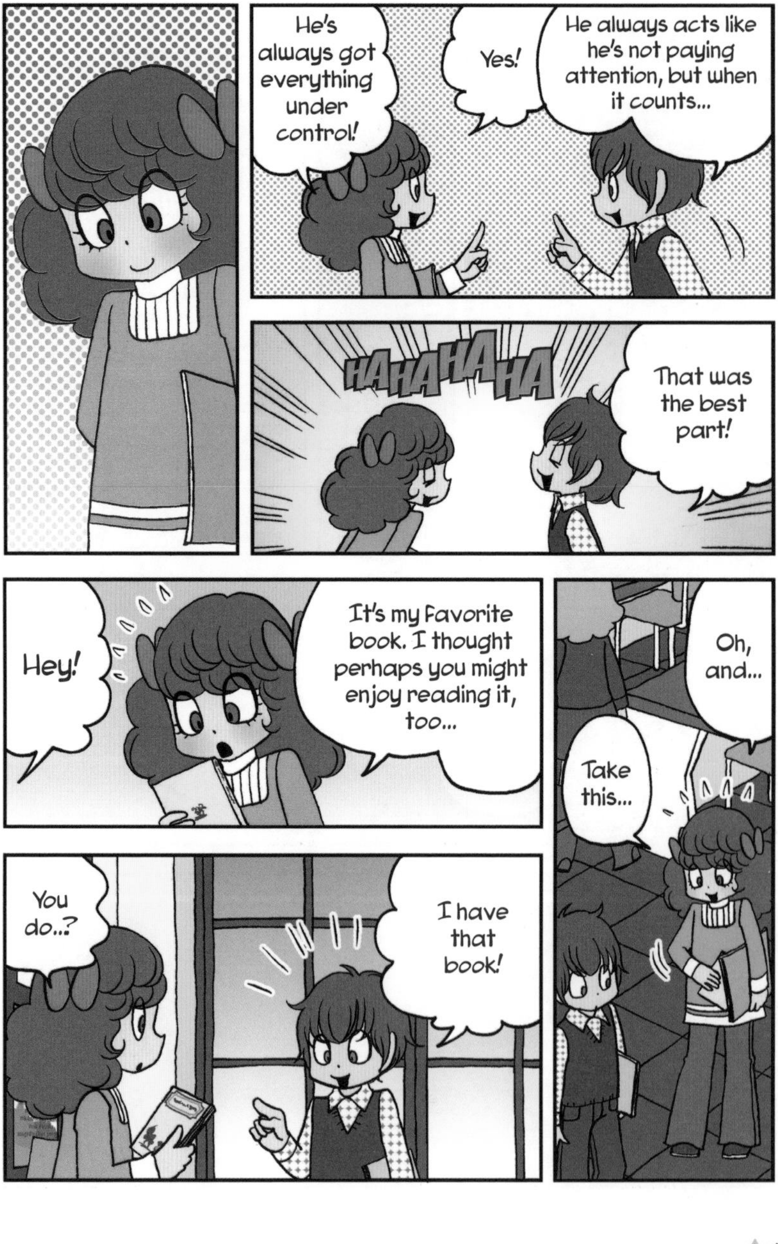
He always acts like he's not paying attention, but when it counts...
Yes!
He's always got everything under control!
That was the best part!
HAHAHAHA
Oh, and...
Take this...
It's my favorite book. I thought perhaps you might enjoy reading it, too...
Hey!
I have that book!
You do..?

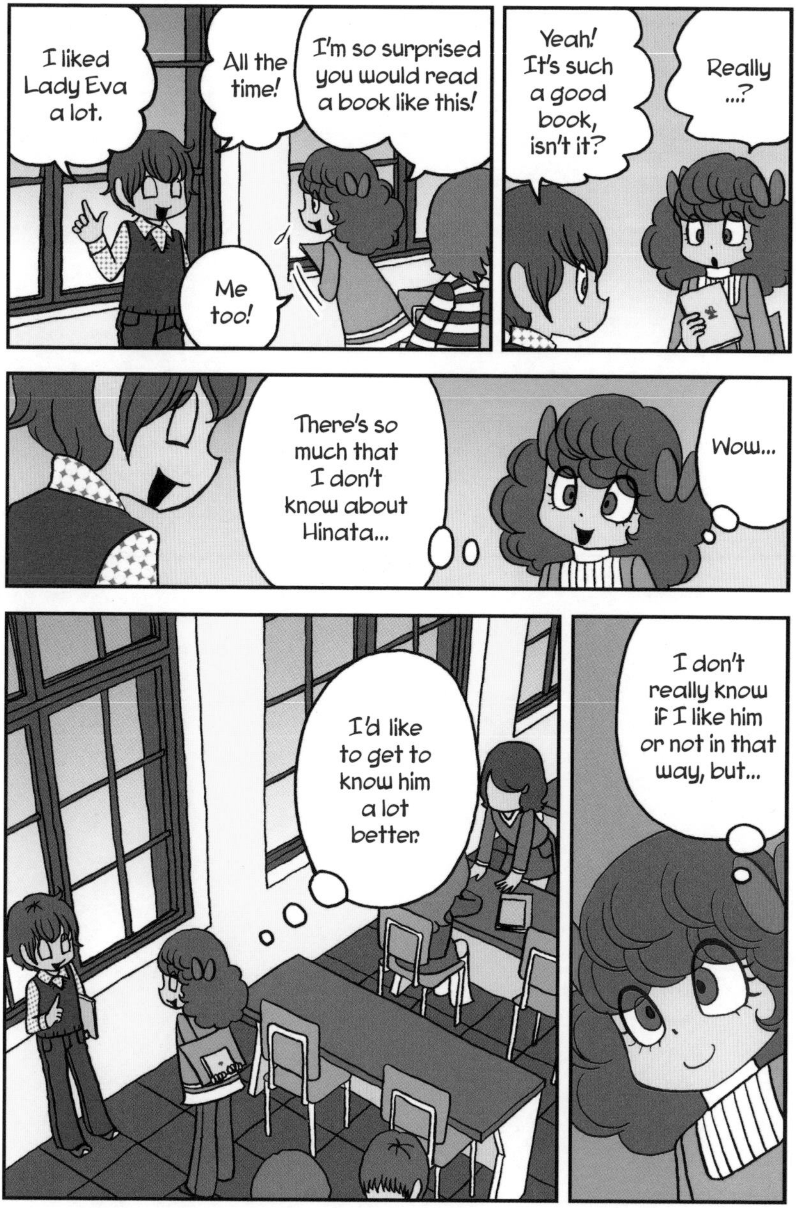

Really ...?
Yeah! It's such a good book, isn't it?
I'm so surprised you would read a book like this!
All the time!
I liked Lady Eva a lot.
Me too!
Wow...
There's so much that I don't know about Hinata...
I don't really know if I like him or not in that way, but...
I'd like to get to know him a lot better.

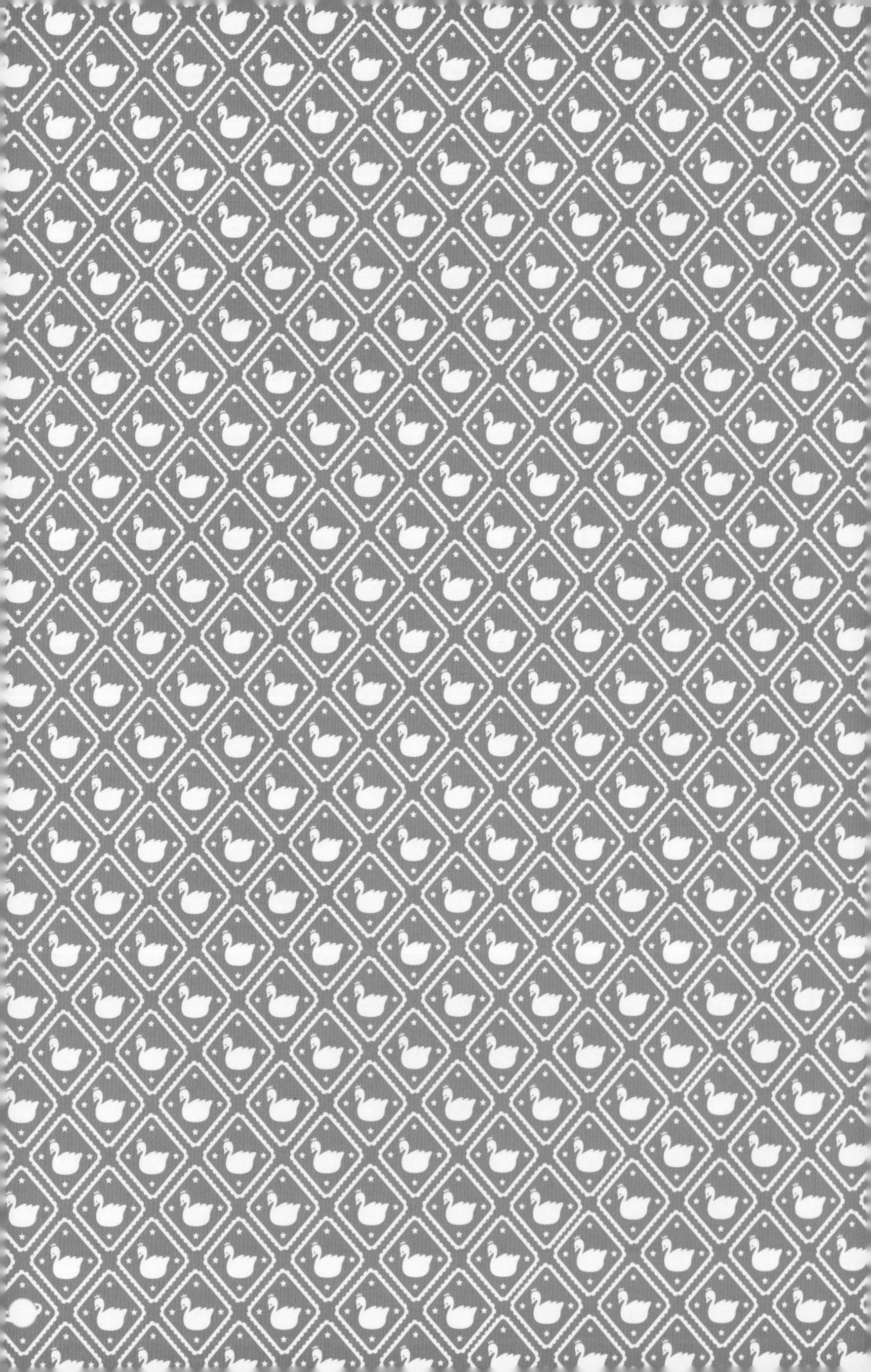

SWANS IN SPACE

CHAPTER 7
PETTSIE THE MOMU

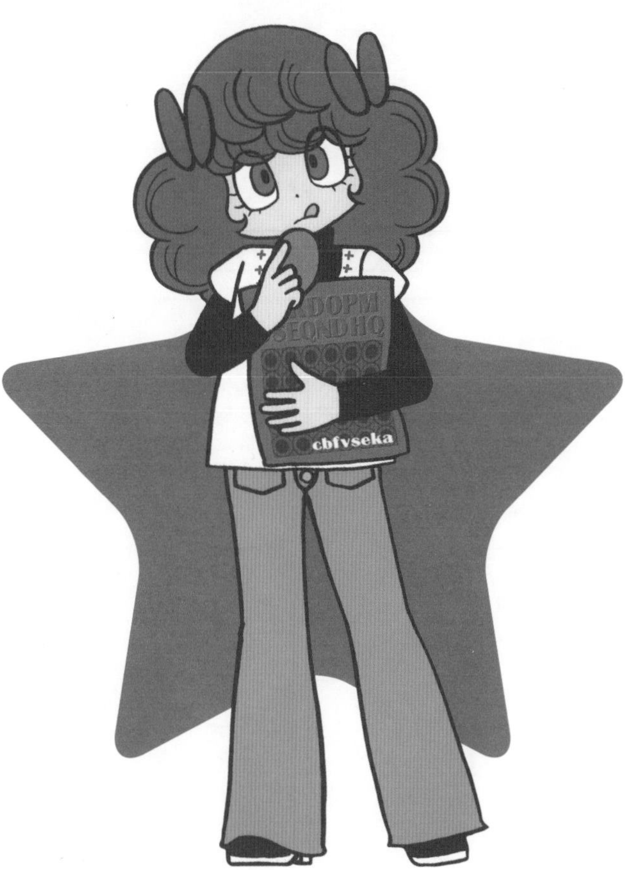
cbfvseka

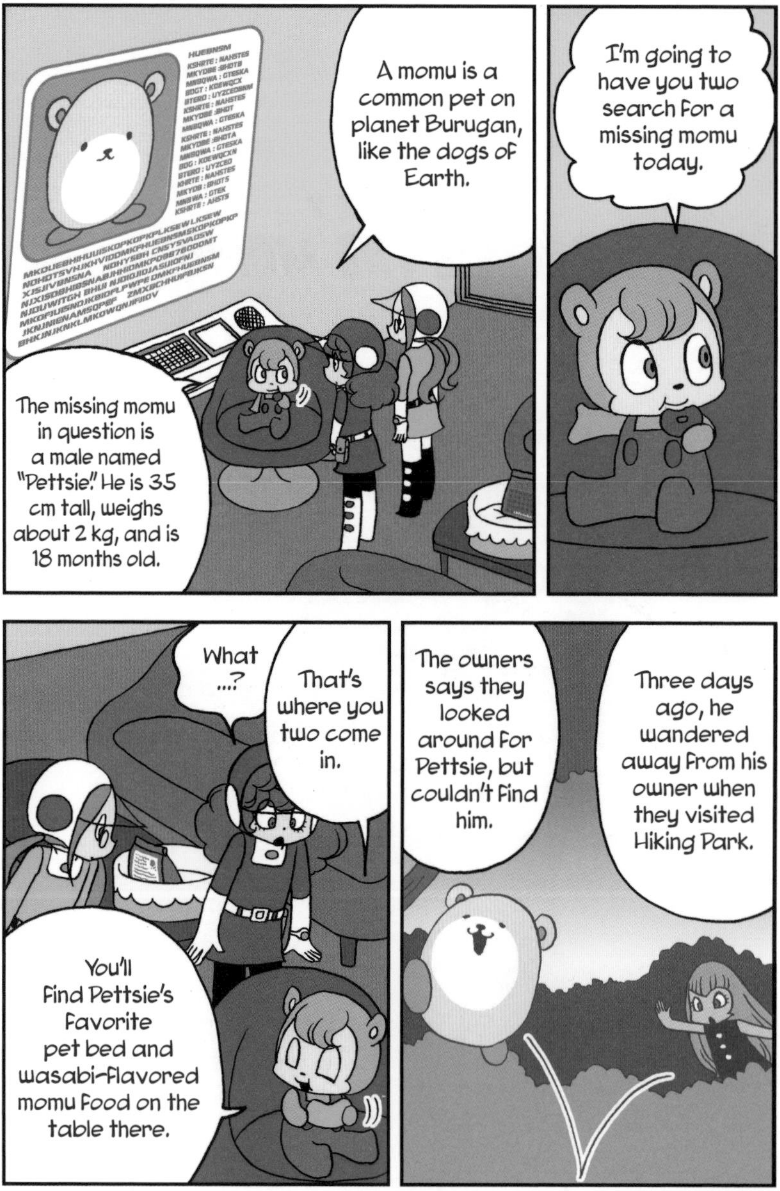
I'm going to have you two search for a missing momu today.
A momu is a common pet on planet Burugan, like the dogs of Earth.
The missing momu in question is a male named "Pettsie." He is 35 cm tall, weighs about 2 kg, and is 18 months old.
Three days ago, he wandered away from his owner when they visited Hiking Park.
The owners says they looked around for Pettsie, but couldn't find him.
That's where you two come in.
What ...?
You'll find Pettsie's favorite pet bed and wasabi-flavored momu food on the table there.

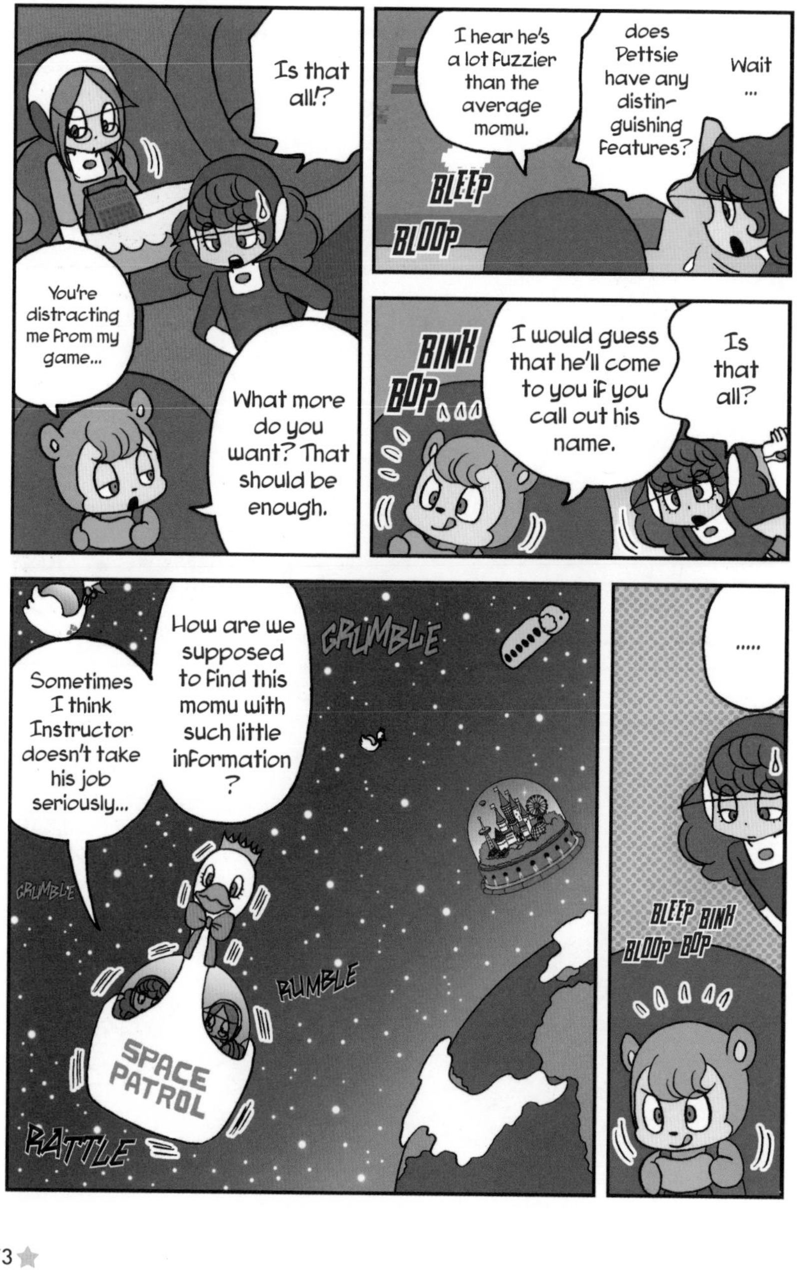
Wait ...
does Pettsie have any distinguishing features?
I hear he's a lot fuzzier than the average momu.
BLEEP
BLOOP
Is that all?
I would guess that he'll come to you if you call out his name.
BINK
BOP
Is that all!?
What more do you want? That should be enough.
You're distracting me from my game...
.....
BLEEP BINK
BLOOP BOP
GRUMBLE
How are we supposed to find this momu with such little information?
Sometimes I think Instructor doesn't take his job seriously...
GRUMBLE
RUMBLE
SPACE PATROL
RATTLE

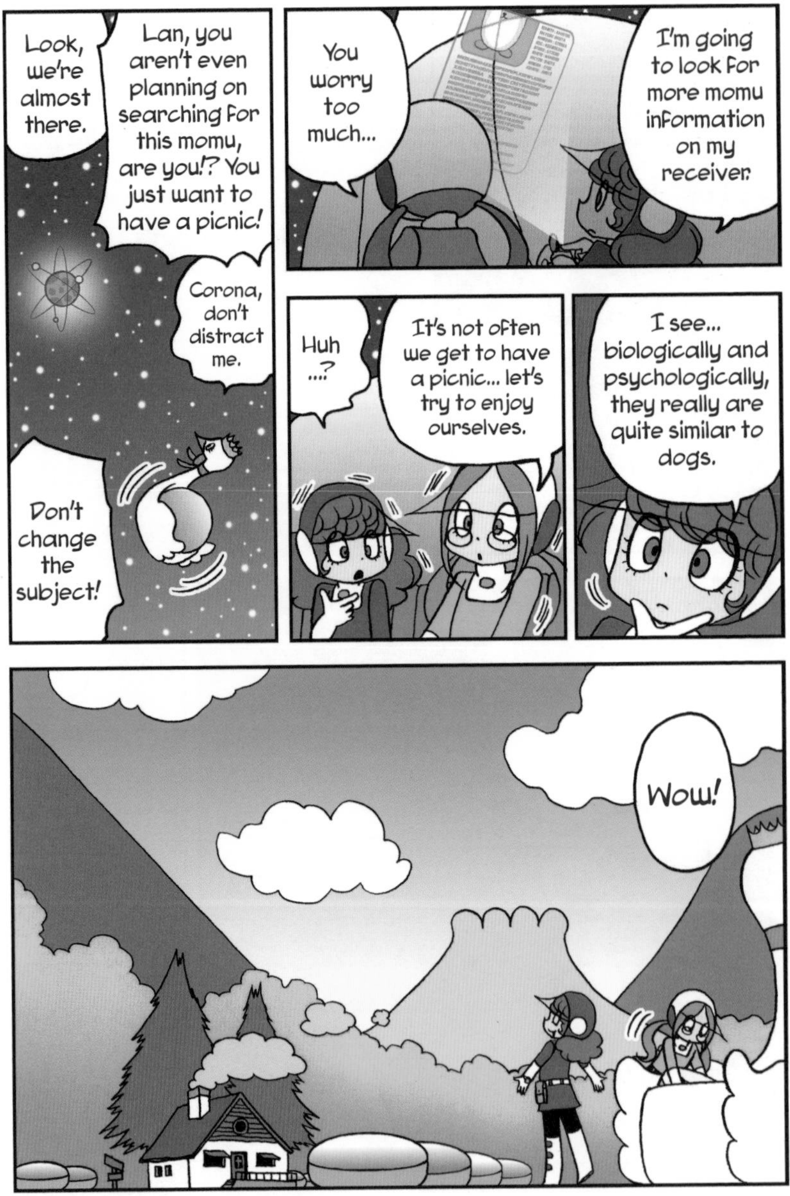
I'm going to look for more momu information on my receiver.
You worry too much...
I see... biologically and psychologically, they really are quite similar to dogs.
It's not often we get to have a picnic... let's try to enjoy ourselves.
Huh ...?
Lan, you aren't even planning on searching for this momu, are you!? You just want to have a picnic!
Look, we're almost there.
Corona, don't distract me.
Don't change the subject!
Wow!

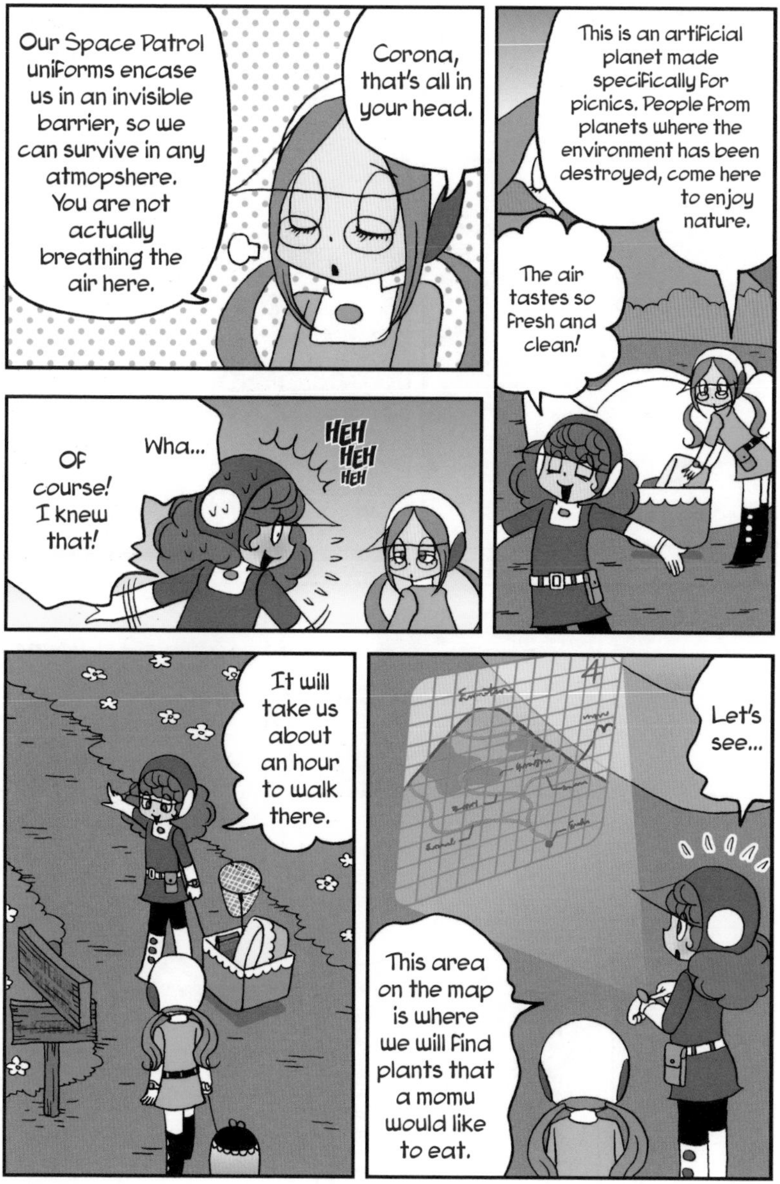
This is an artificial planet made specifically for picnics. People from planets where the environment has been destroyed, come here to enjoy nature.
The air tastes so fresh and clean!
Corona, that's all in your head.
Our Space Patrol uniforms encase us in an invisible barrier, so we can survive in any atmopshere. You are not actually breathing the air here.
HEH HEH HEH
Wha...
Of course! I knew that!
Let's see...
This area on the map is where we will find plants that a momu would like to eat.
It will take us about an hour to walk there.

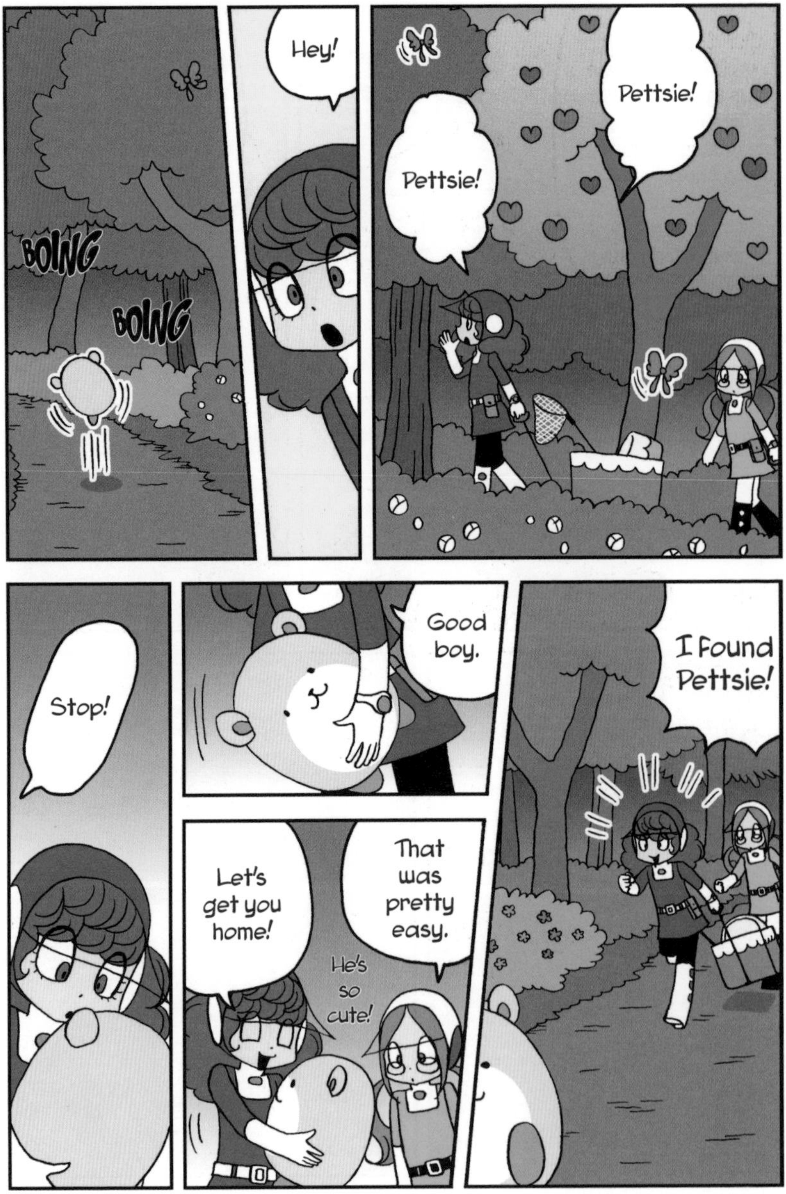
Pettsie!
Pettsie!
Hey!
BOING
BOING
I Found Pettsie!
Good boy.
That was pretty easy.
Let's get you home!
He's so cute!
Stop!

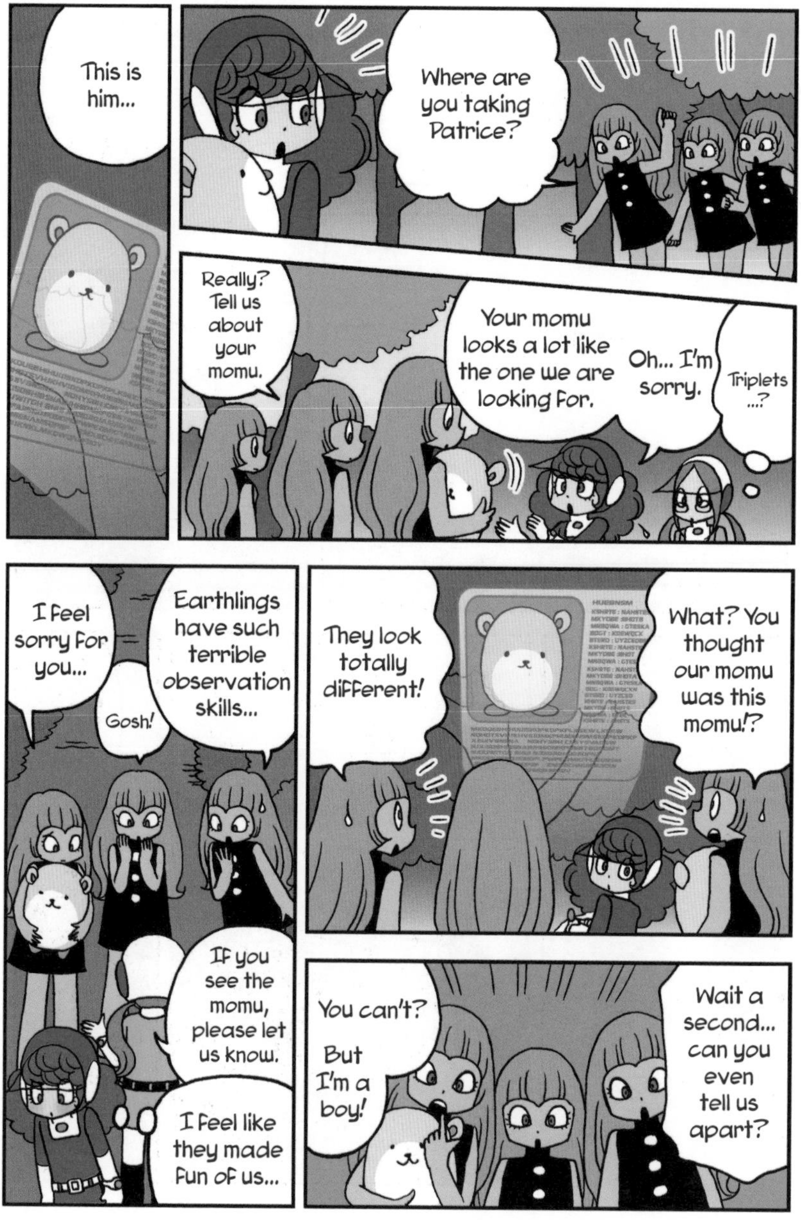
Where are you taking Patrice?
Triplets ...?
Oh... I'm sorry.
Your momu looks a lot like the one we are looking for.
Really? Tell us about your momu.
This is him...
What? You thought our momu was this momu!?
They look totally different!
Wait a second... can you even tell us apart?
You can't?
But I'm a boy!
Earthlings have such terrible observation skills...
I feel sorry for you...
Gosh!
If you see the momu, please let us know.
I feel like they made fun of us...

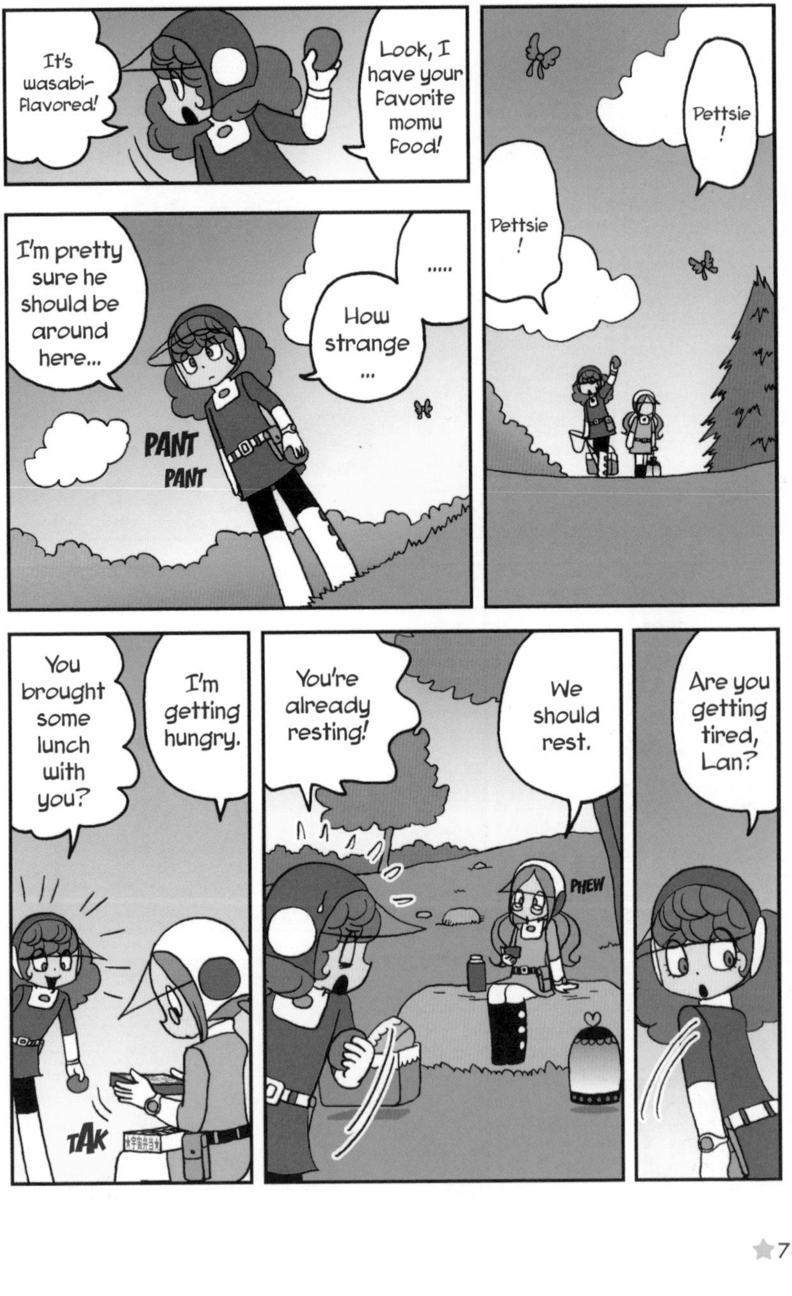
Pettsie!
Pettsie!
Look, I have your favorite momu food!
It's wasabi-flavored!
.....
How strange ...
I'm pretty sure he should be around here...
PANT PANT
Are you getting tired, Lan?
We should rest.
PHEW
You're already resting!
I'm getting hungry.
You brought some lunch with you?
TAK

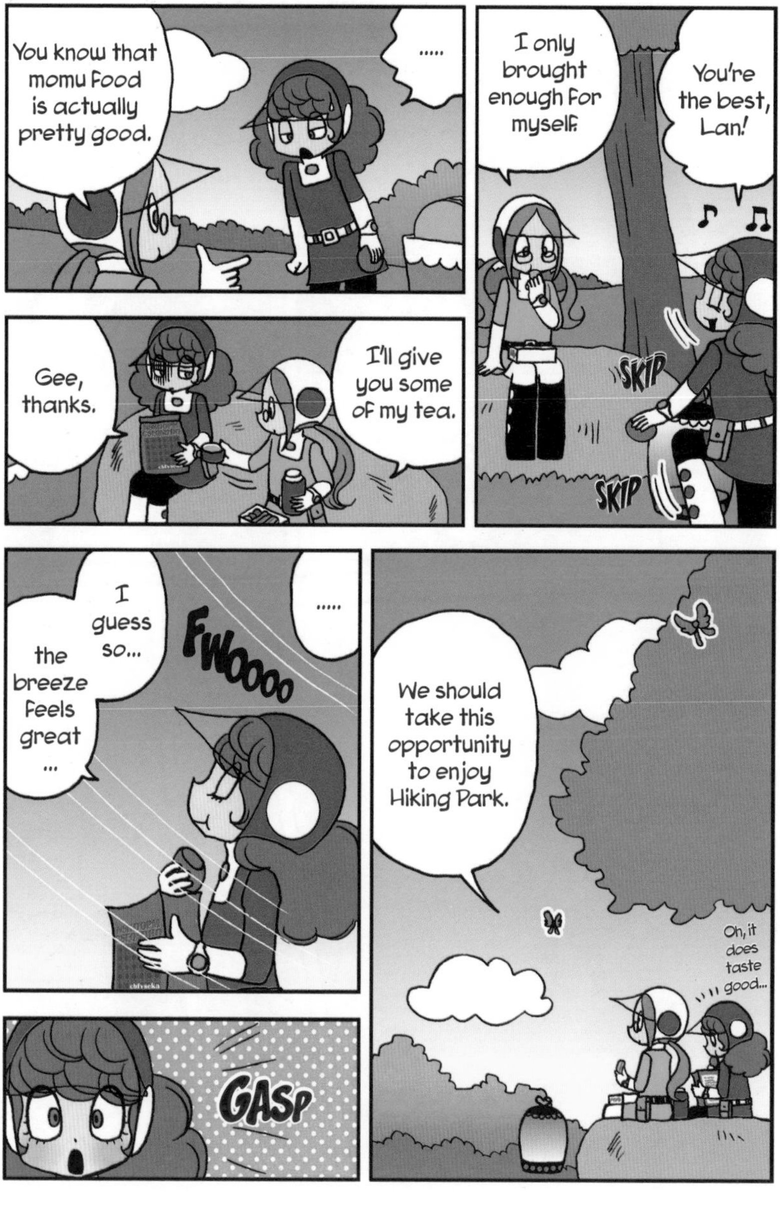
You're the best, Lan!
I only brought enough for myself.
SKIP
SKIP
.....
You know that momu food is actually pretty good.
I'll give you some of my tea.
Gee, thanks.
We should take this opportunity to enjoy Hiking Park.
Oh, it does taste good...
.....
FWOOOO
I guess so...
the breeze feels great ...
GASP

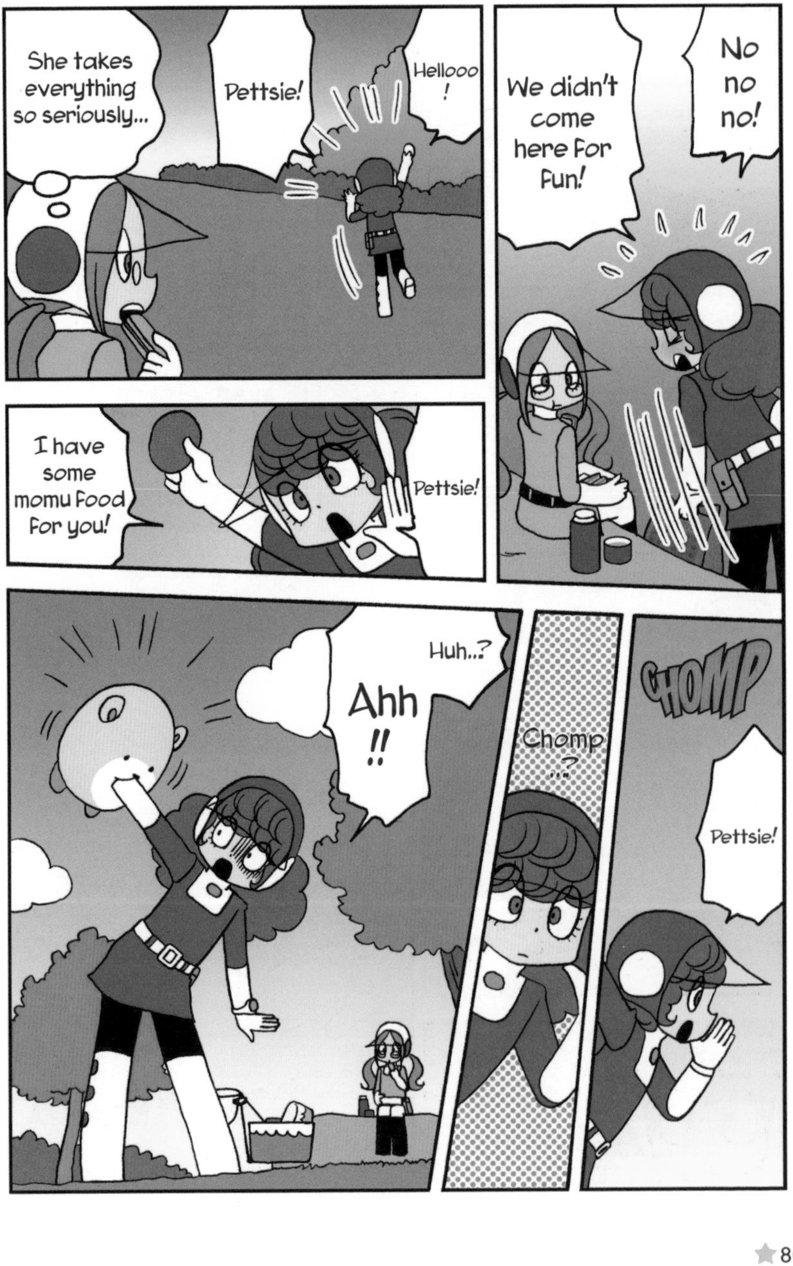
No no no!
We didn't come here for fun!
Hellooo!
Pettsie!
She takes everything so seriously...
Pettsie!
I have some momu food for you!
CHOMP
Pettsie!
Champ ..?
Huh..?
Ahh!!

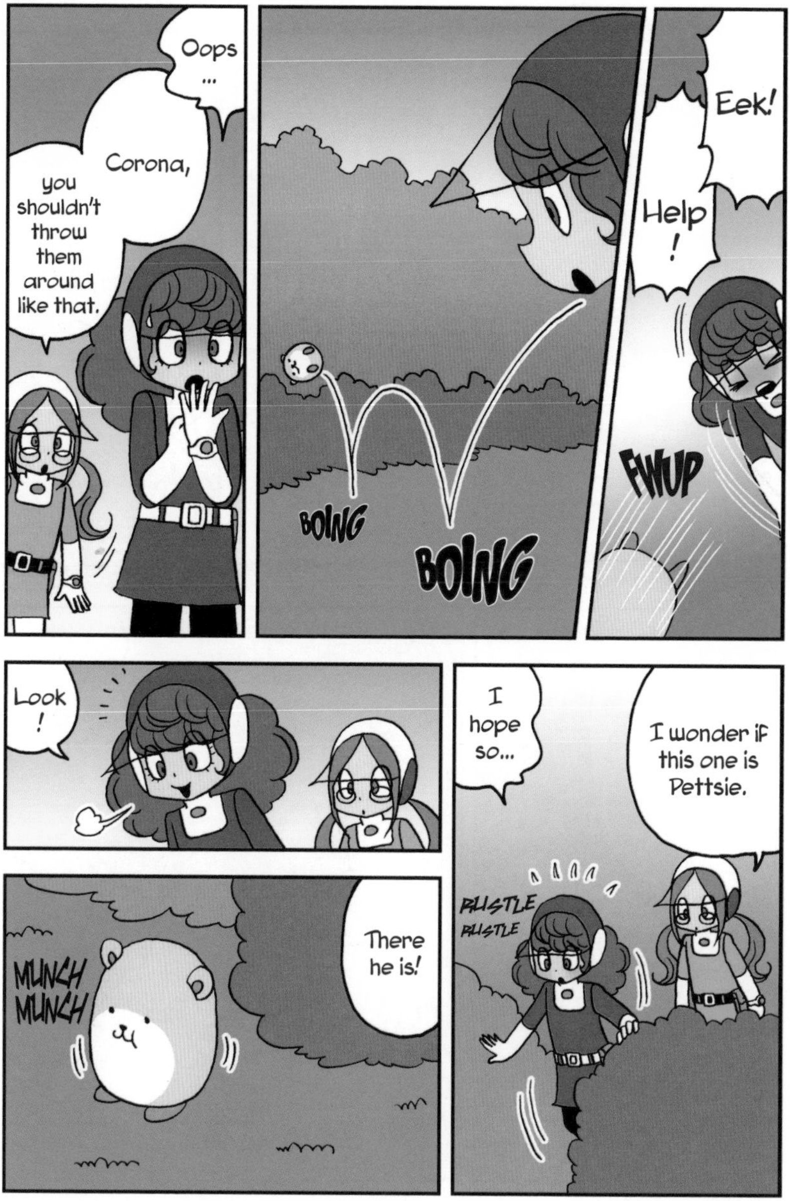
Eek!
Help!
FWUP
BOING
BOING
Oops ...
Corona, you shouldn't throw them around like that.
I wonder if this one is Pettsie.
I hope so...
RUSTLE RUSTLE
Look!
There he is!
MUNCH MUNCH

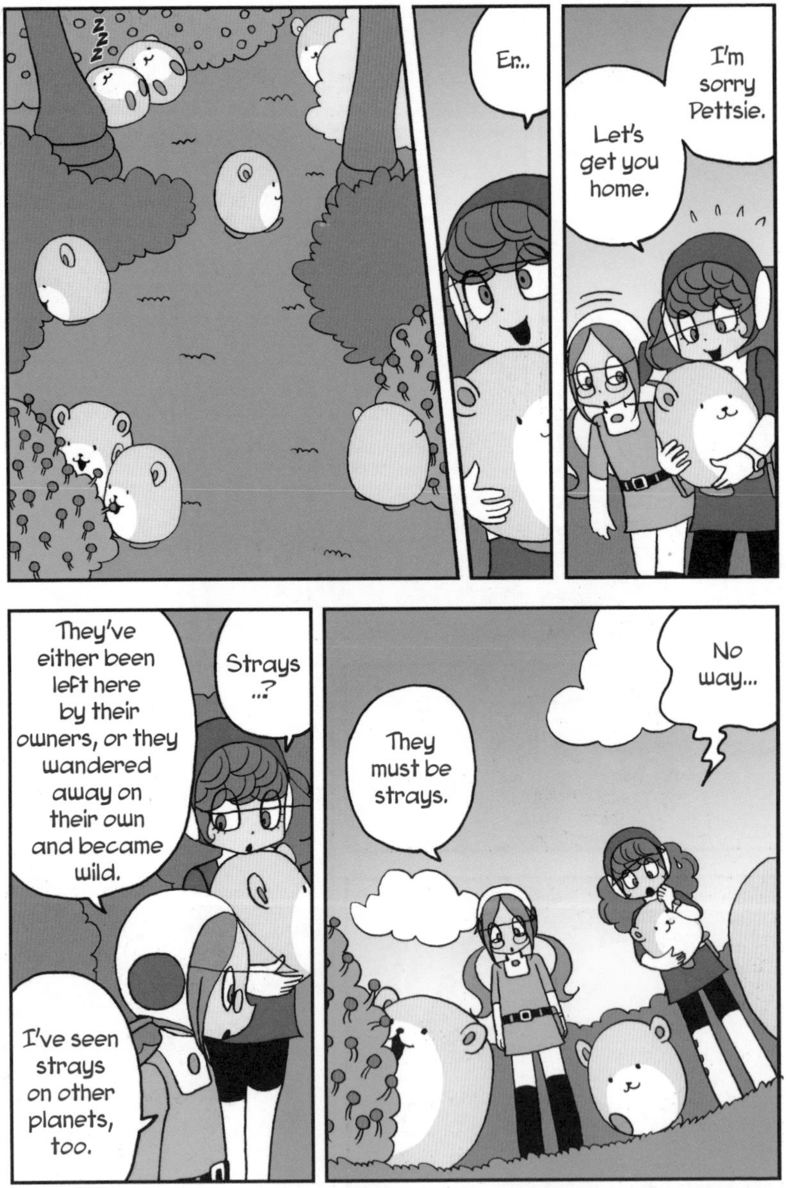
I'm sorry Pettsie.
Let's get you home.
Er..
ZZZ
No way...
They must be strays.
Strays ...?
They've either been left here by their owners, or they wandered away on their own and became wild.
I've seen strays on other planets, too.

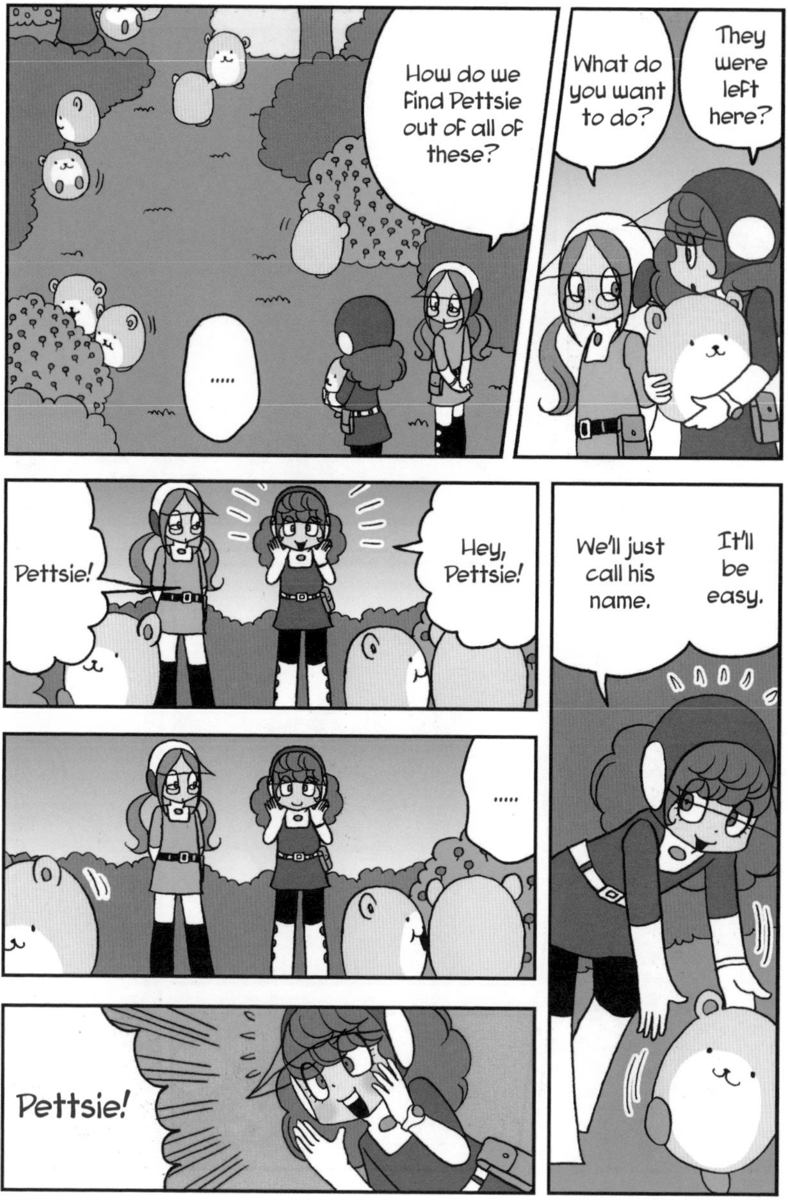
They were left here?
What do you want to do?
How do we find Pettsie out of all of these?
.....
It'll be easy.
We'll just call his name.
Hey, Pettsie!
Pettsie!
.....
Pettsie!

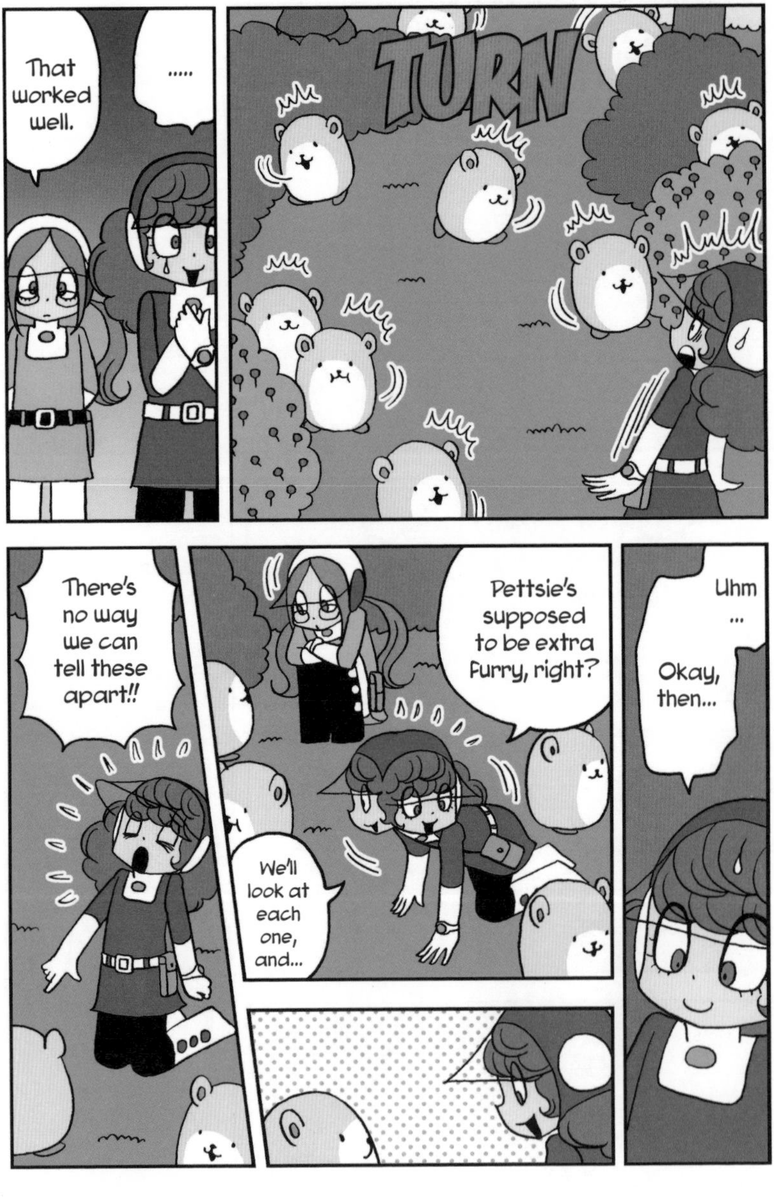
TURN
.....
That worked well.
Uhm ...
Okay, then...
Pettsie's supposed to be extra furry, right?
We'll look at each one, and...
There's no way we can tell these apart!!

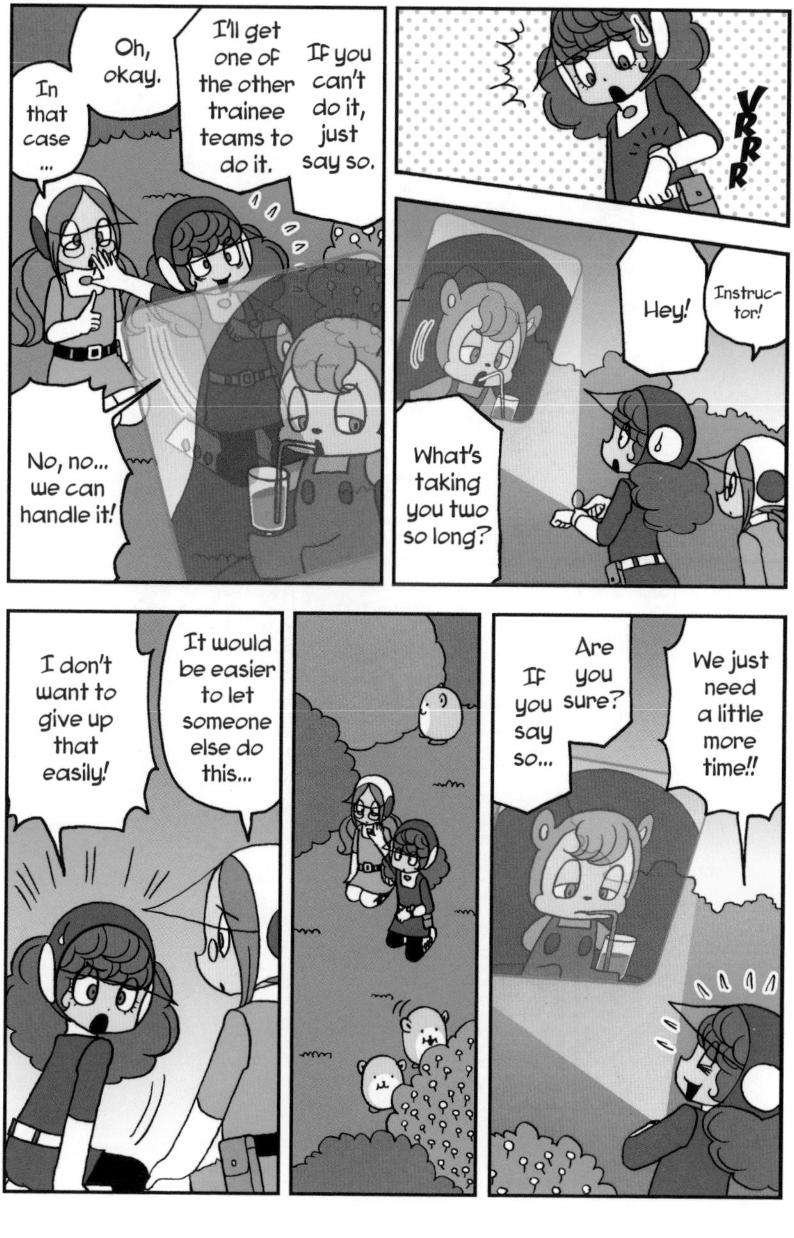
VRRR
Instructor!
Hey!
What's taking you two so long?
If you can't do it, just say so.
I'll get one of the other trainee teams to do it.
Oh, okay.
In that case ...
No, no... we can handle it!
We just need a little more time!!
Are you sure?
If you say so...
It would be easier to let someone else do this...
I don't want to give up that easily!

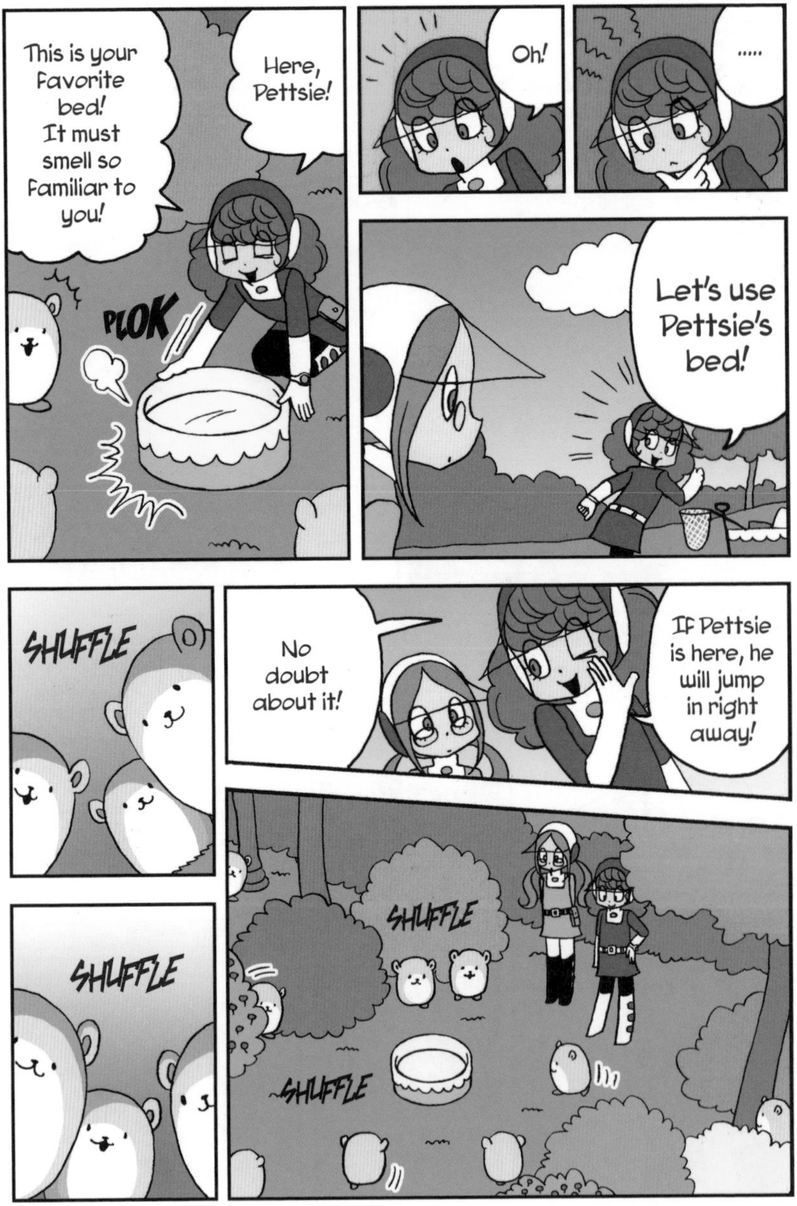
.....
Oh!
Let's use Pettsie's bed!
Here, Pettsie!
This is your favorite bed! It must smell so familiar to you!
PLOK
If Pettsie is here, he will jump in right away!
No doubt about it!
SHUFFLE
SHUFFLE
SHUFFLE
SHUFFLE

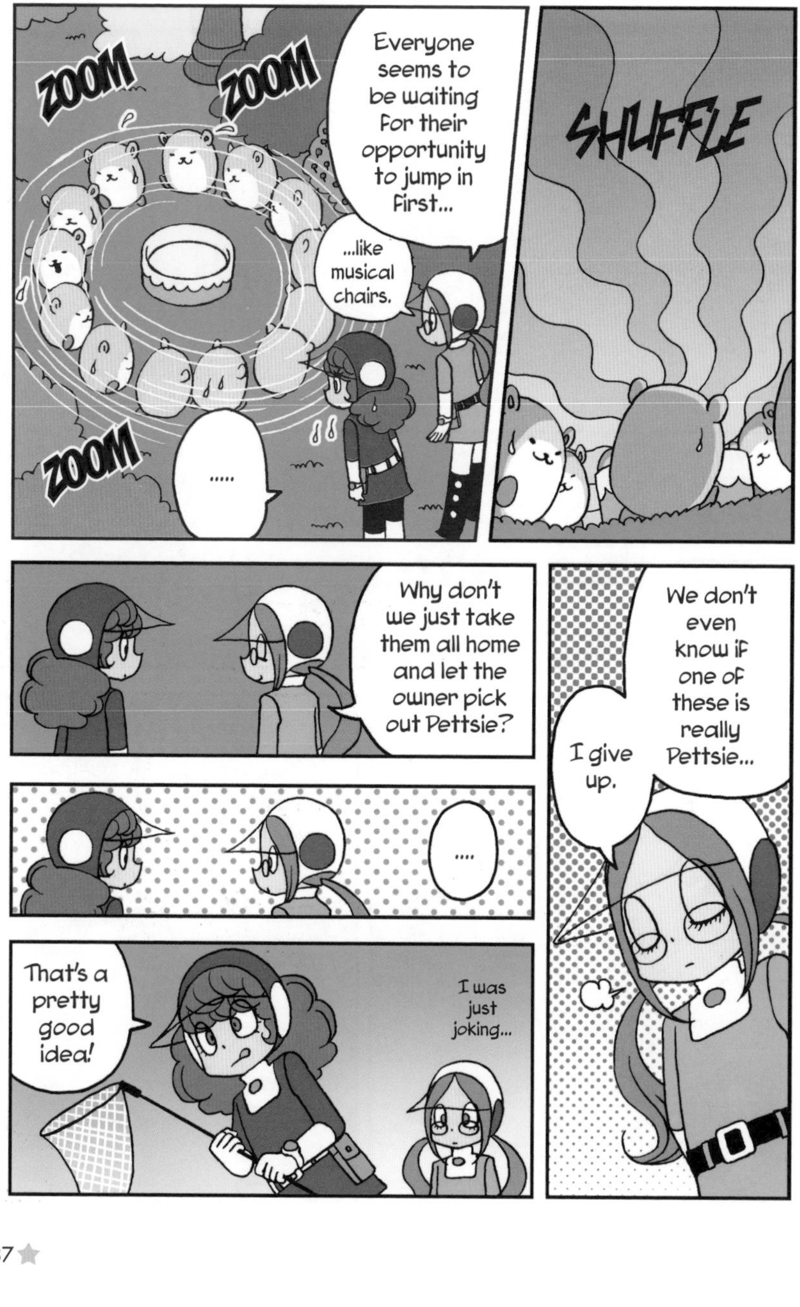
SHUFFLE
Everyone seems to be waiting for their opportunity to jump in first...
ZOOM
ZOOM
...like musical chairs.
......
ZOOM
We don't even know if one of these is really Pettsie...
I give up.
Why don't we just take them all home and let the owner pick out Pettsie?
....
I was just joking...
That's a pretty good idea!

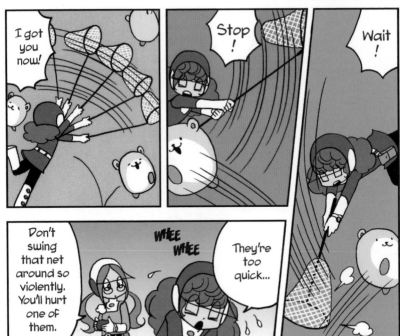

Wait!
Stop!
I got you now!
WHEE WHEE
They're too quick...
Don't swing that net around so violently. You'll hurt one of them.
Then you do it, Lan!
No way.
I'm not as athletic as you, Corona.
SIP
BOING
BOING
Are you ready to give up yet?
No!!

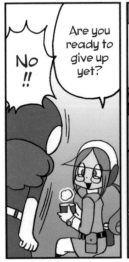

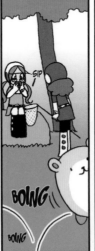

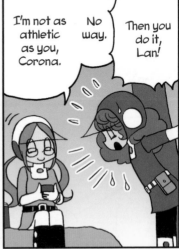

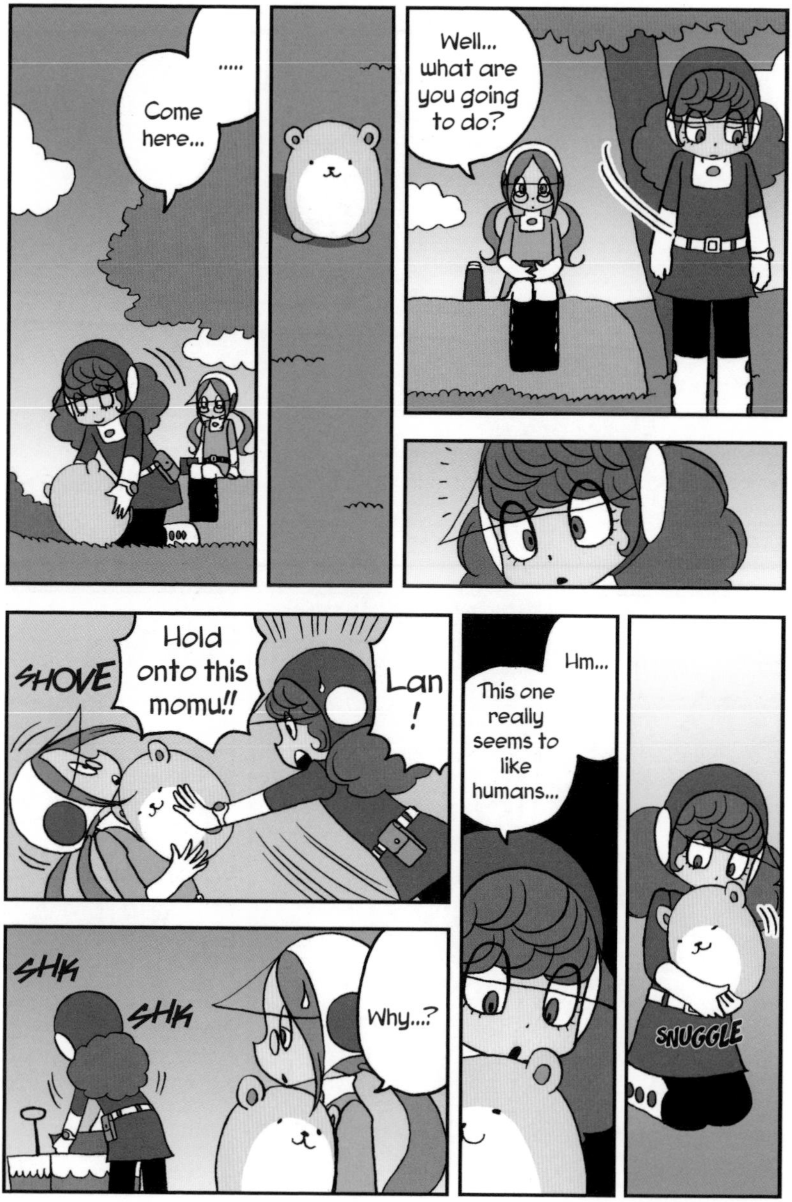
Well... what are you going to do?
.....
Come here...
SNUGGLE
Hm...
This one really seems to like humans...
Lan!
Hold onto this momu!!
SHOVE
Why...?
SHK
SHK

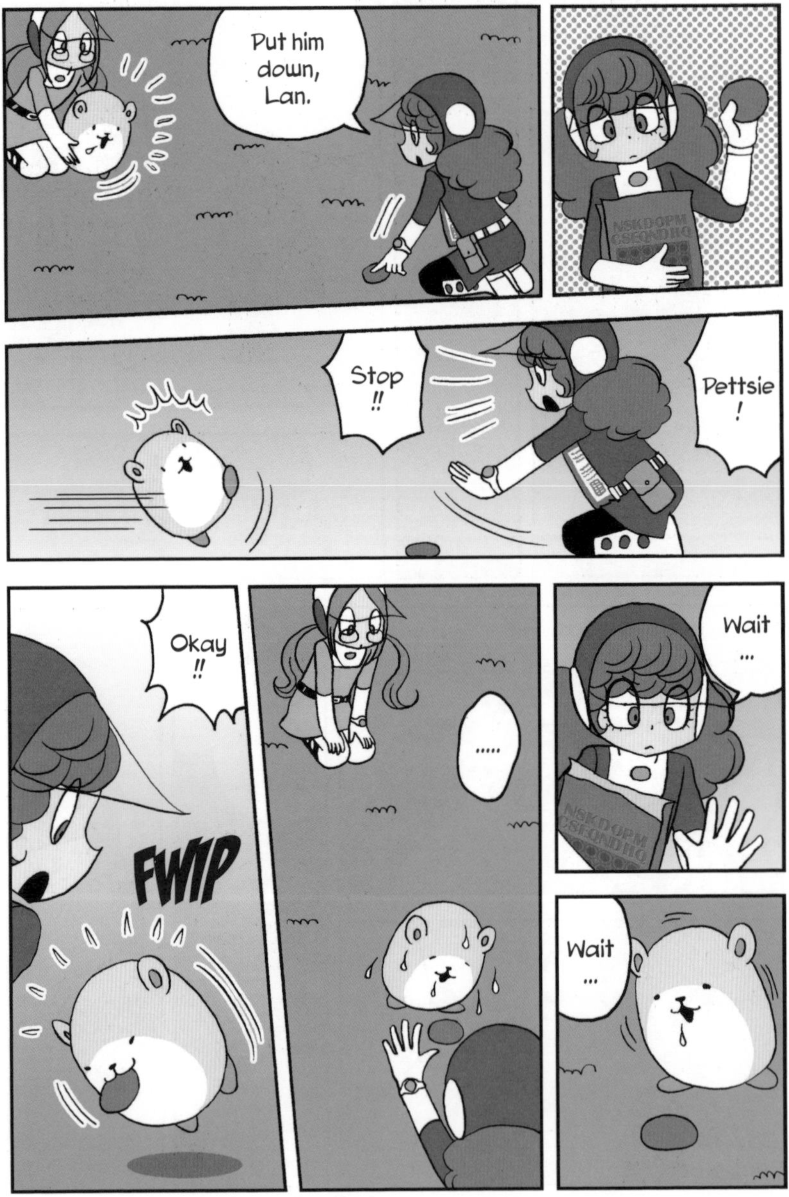
Put him down, Lan.
Pettsie !
Stop !!
Wait ...
Wait ...
.....
Okay !!
FWIP

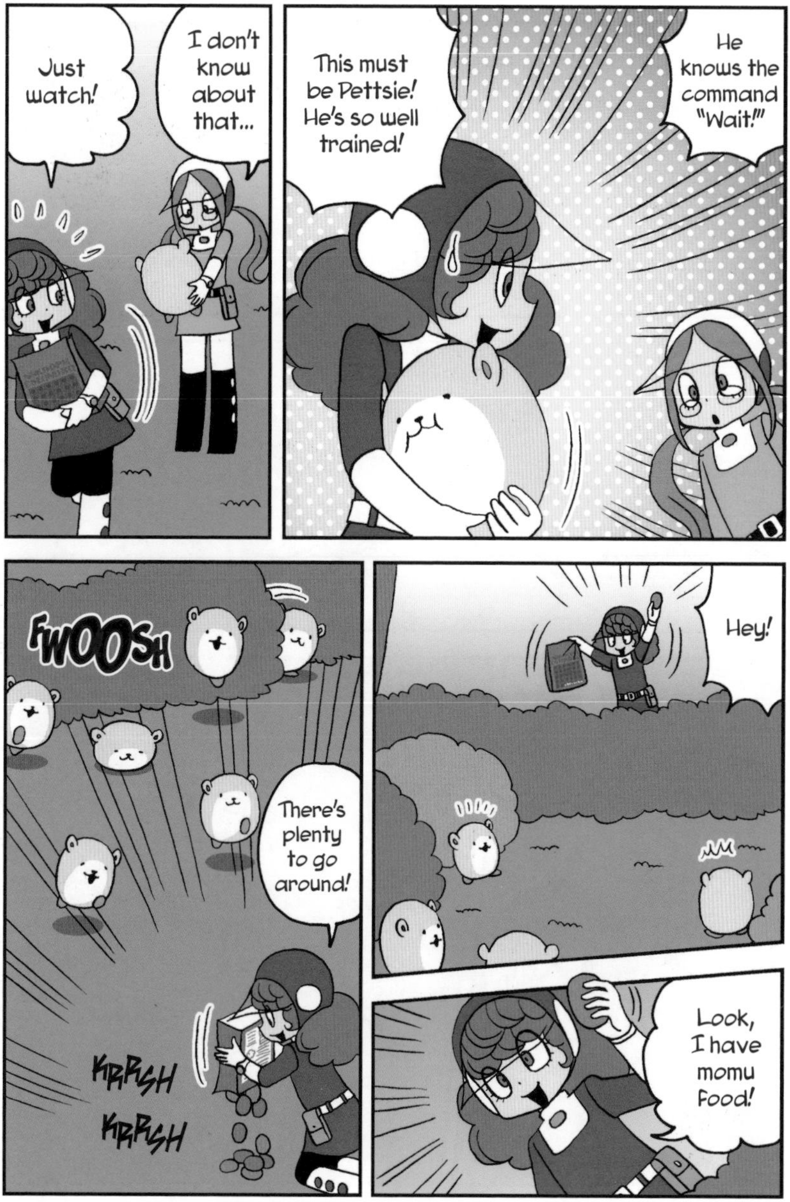
He knows the command "Wait!"
This must be Pettsie! He's so well trained!
I don't know about that...
Just watch!
Hey!
Look, I have momu Food!
FWOOSH
There's plenty to go around!
KRRSH
KRRSH

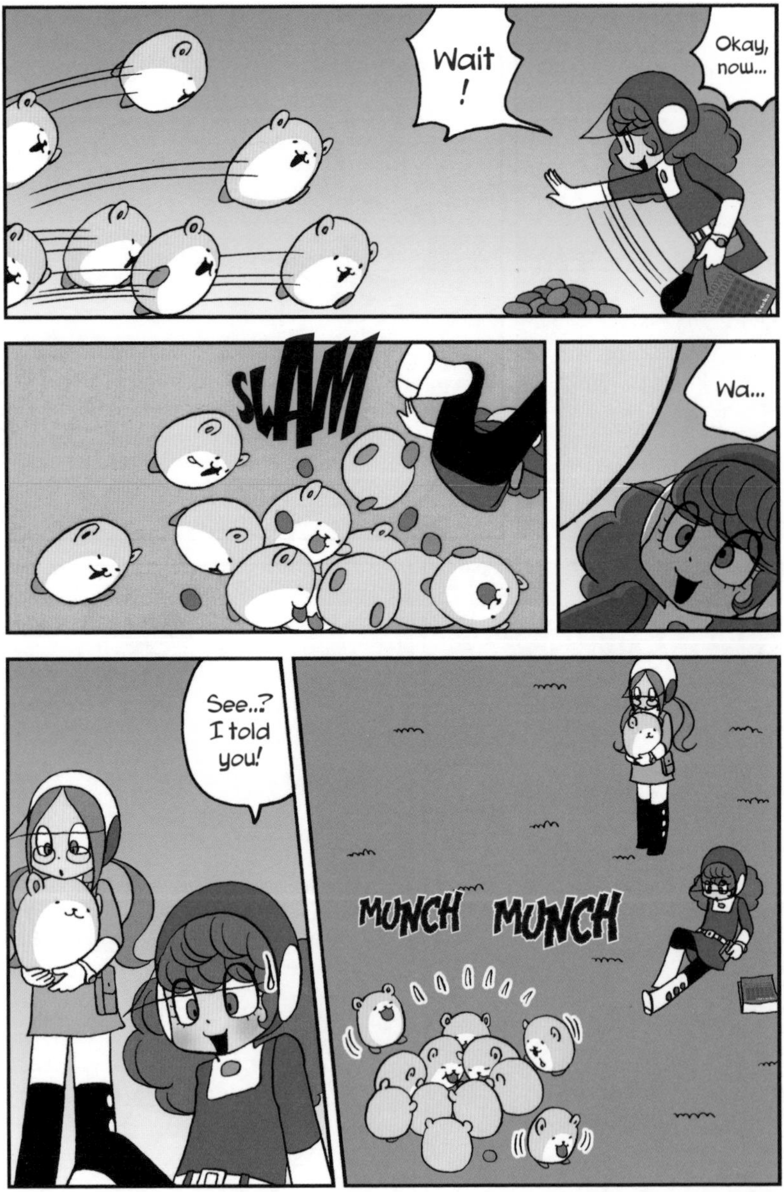
Okay, now...
Wait!
Wa...
SLAM
MUNCH MUNCH
See..? I told you!

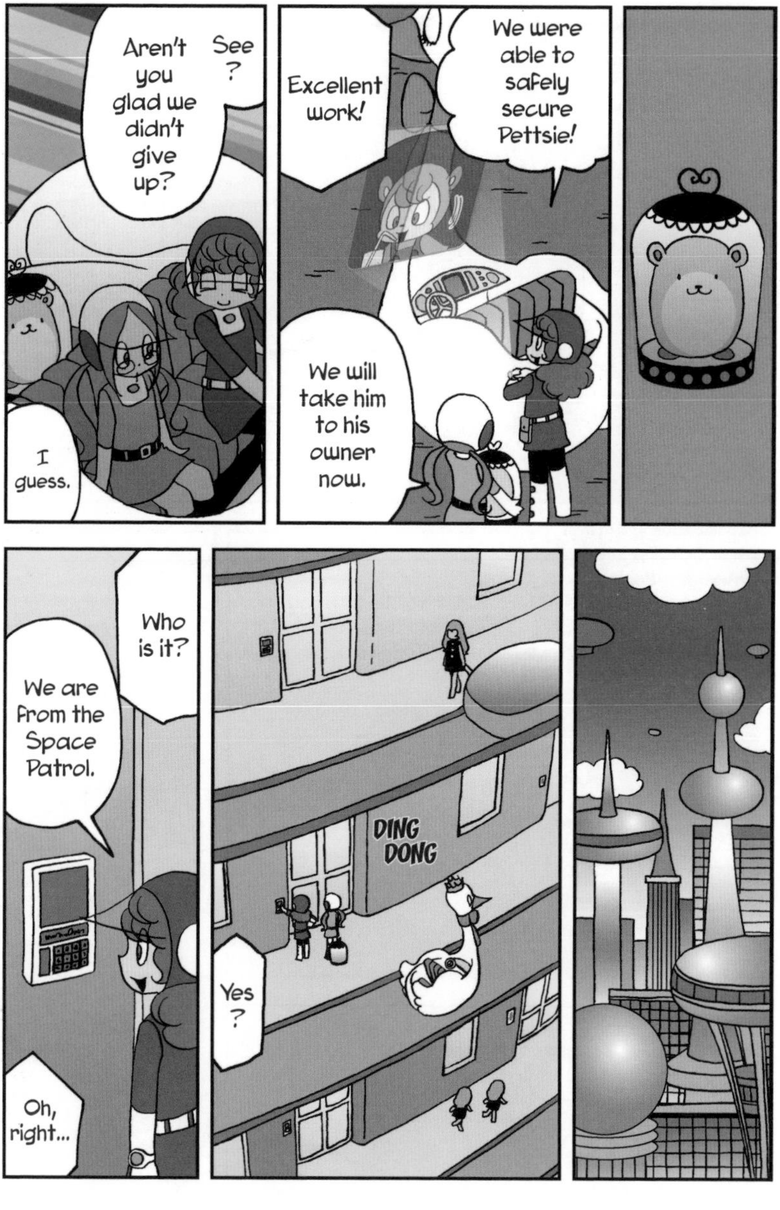
We were able to safely secure Pettsie!
Excellent work!
We will take him to his owner now.
See?
Aren't you glad we didn't give up?
I guess.
DING DONG
Yes?
Who is it?
We are from the Space Patrol.
Oh, right...

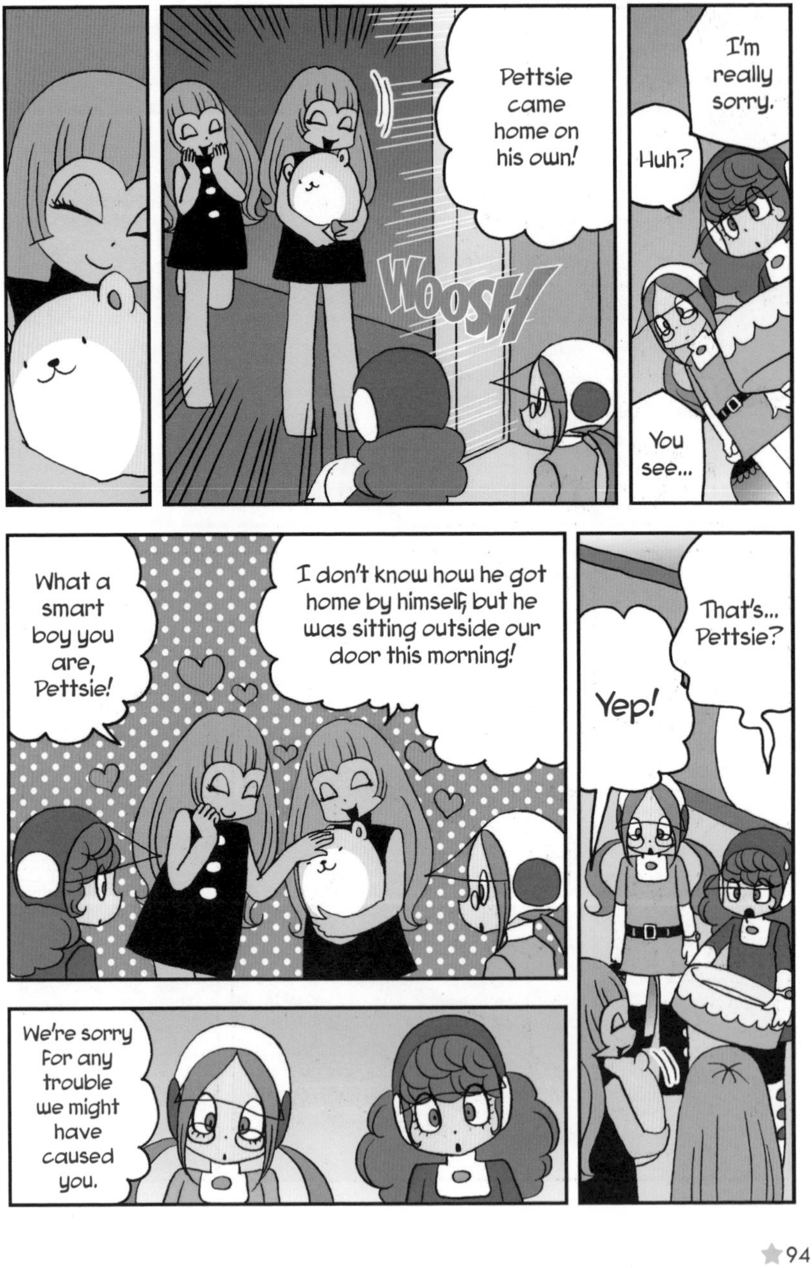
I'm really sorry.
Huh?
You see...
Pettsie came home on his own!
WOOSH
That's... Pettsie?
Yep!
I don't know how he got home by himself, but he was sitting outside our door this morning!
What a smart boy you are, Pettsie!
We're sorry for any trouble we might have caused you.

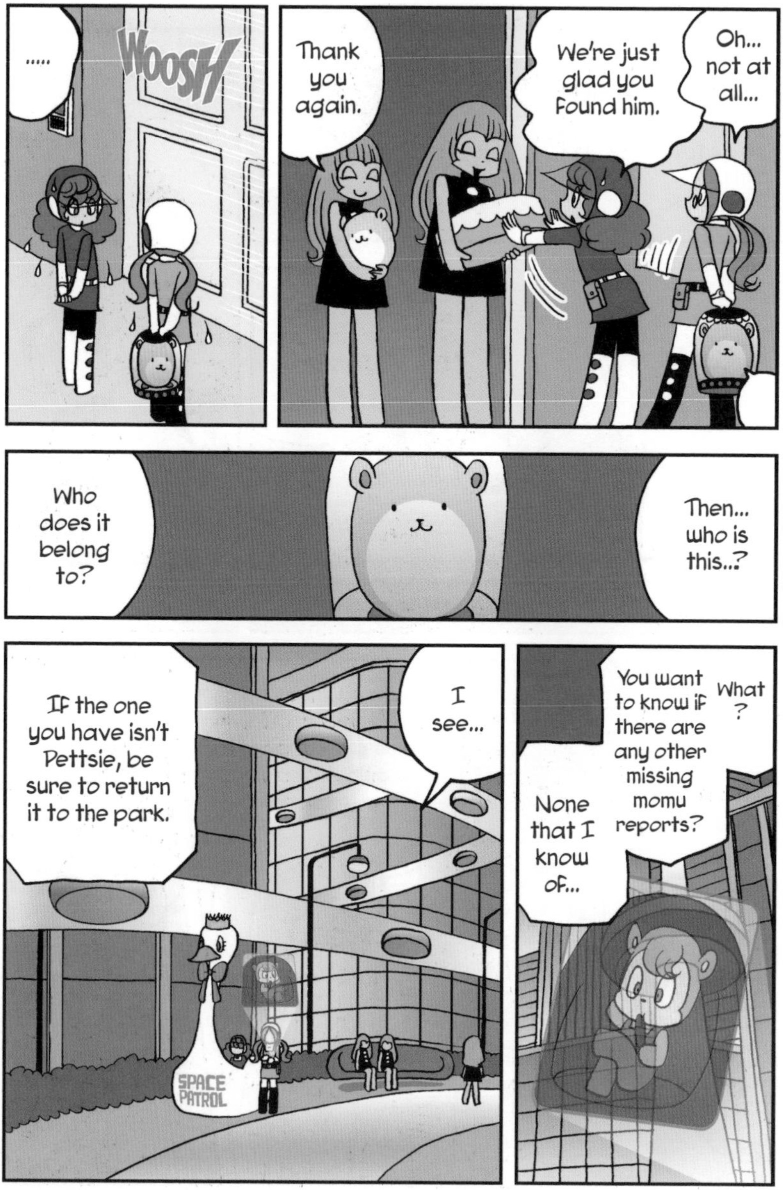
Oh... not at all...
We're just glad you found him.
Thank you again.
WOOSH
.....
Then... who is this..?
Who does it belong to?
What?
You want to know if there are any other missing momu reports?
None that I know of...
I see...
If the one you have isn't Pettsie, be sure to return it to the park.
SPACE PATROL

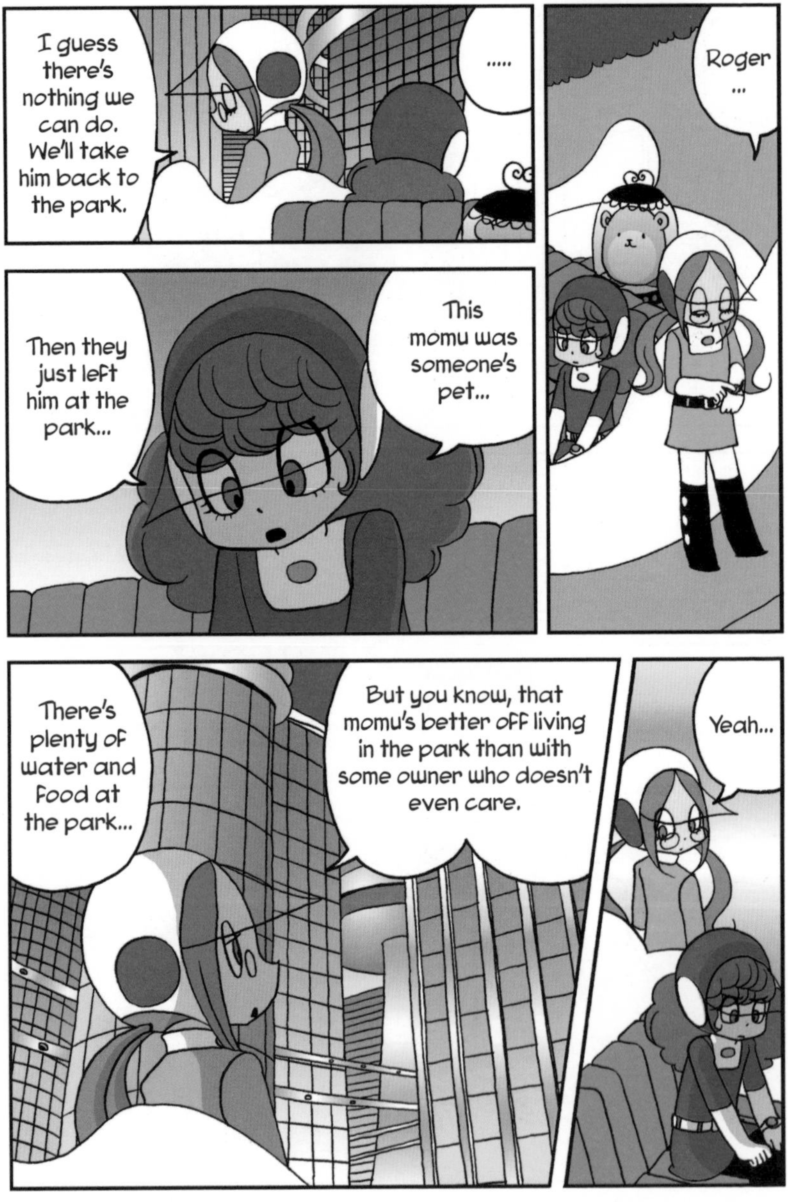
Roger ...
.....
I guess there's nothing we can do. We'll take him back to the park.
This momu was someone's pet...
Then they just left him at the park...
Yeah...
But you know, that momu's better off living in the park than with some owner who doesn't even care.
There's plenty of water and food at the park...

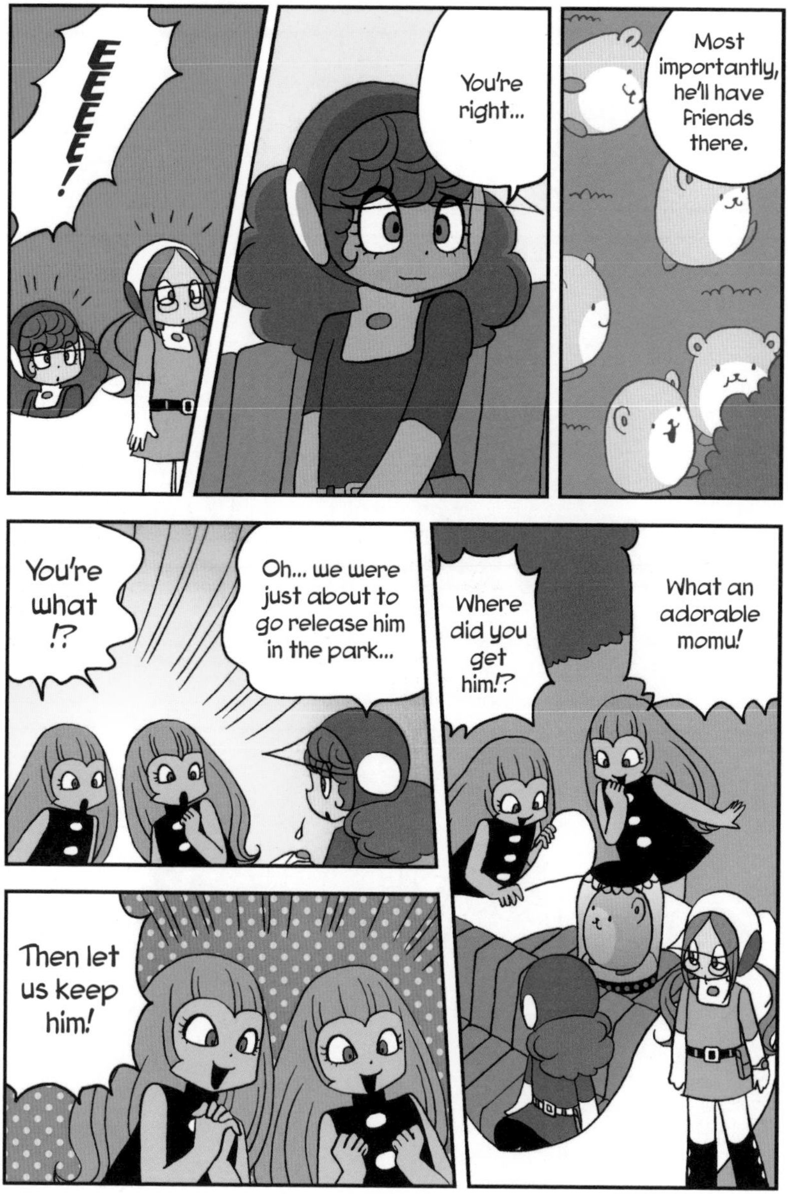

Most importantly, he'll have friends there.
You're right...
EEEEE!
What an adorable momu!
Where did you get him!?
Oh... we were just about to go release him in the park...
You're what!?
Then let us keep him!

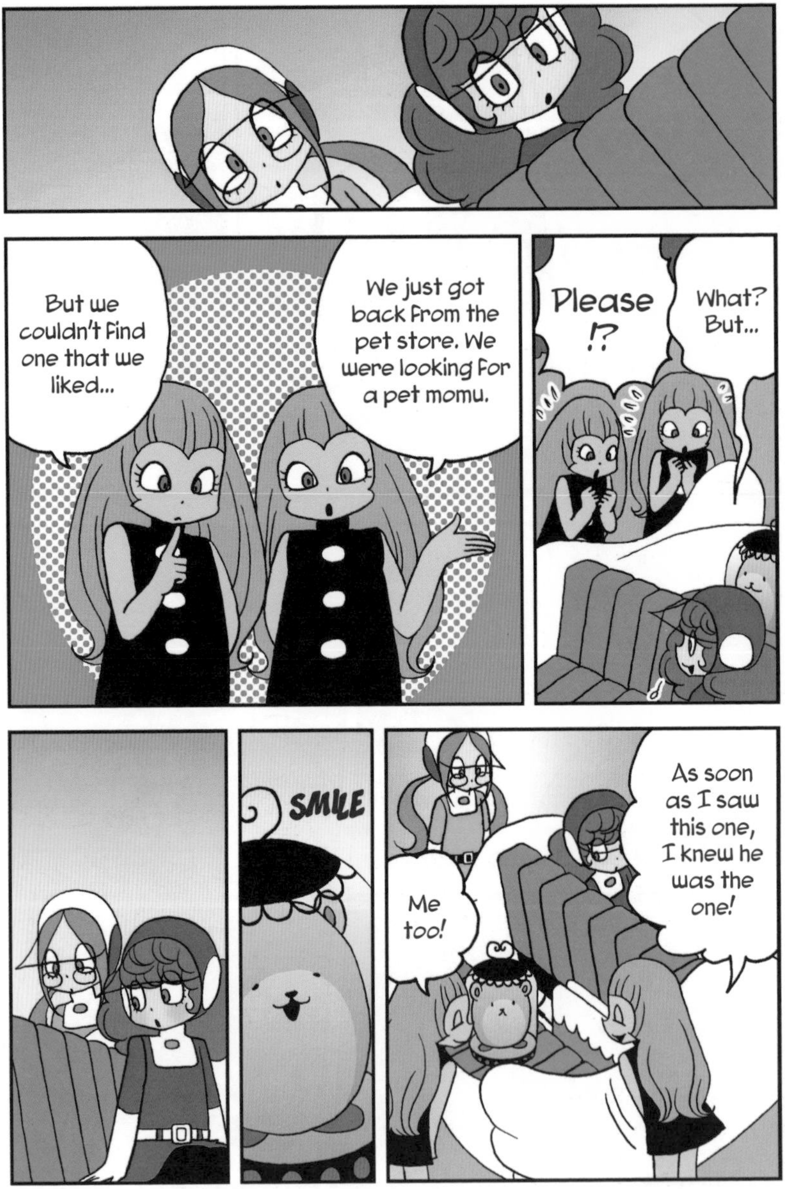
What? But...
Please !?
We just got back from the pet store. We were looking for a pet momu.
But we couldn't find one that we liked...
As soon as I saw this one, I knew he was the one!
Me too!
SMILE

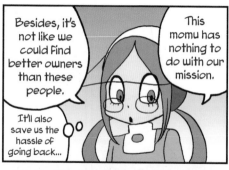

Okay, hold on. I will get permission from our instructor first...
There's no need for that.
This momu has nothing to do with our mission.
Besides, it's not like we could find better owners than these people.
It'll also save us the hassle of going back...
I... I guess so...
So we can have him!?
Yay!!
Please register your pet with the local office.
We will!
Also be sure to get it checked out and vaccinated.
Thank you so much!
Bye!
Hey... wait!!

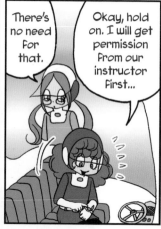

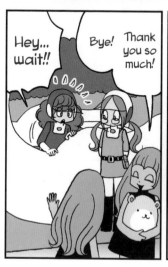

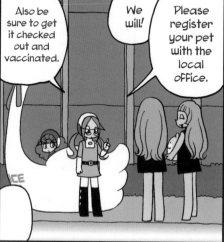

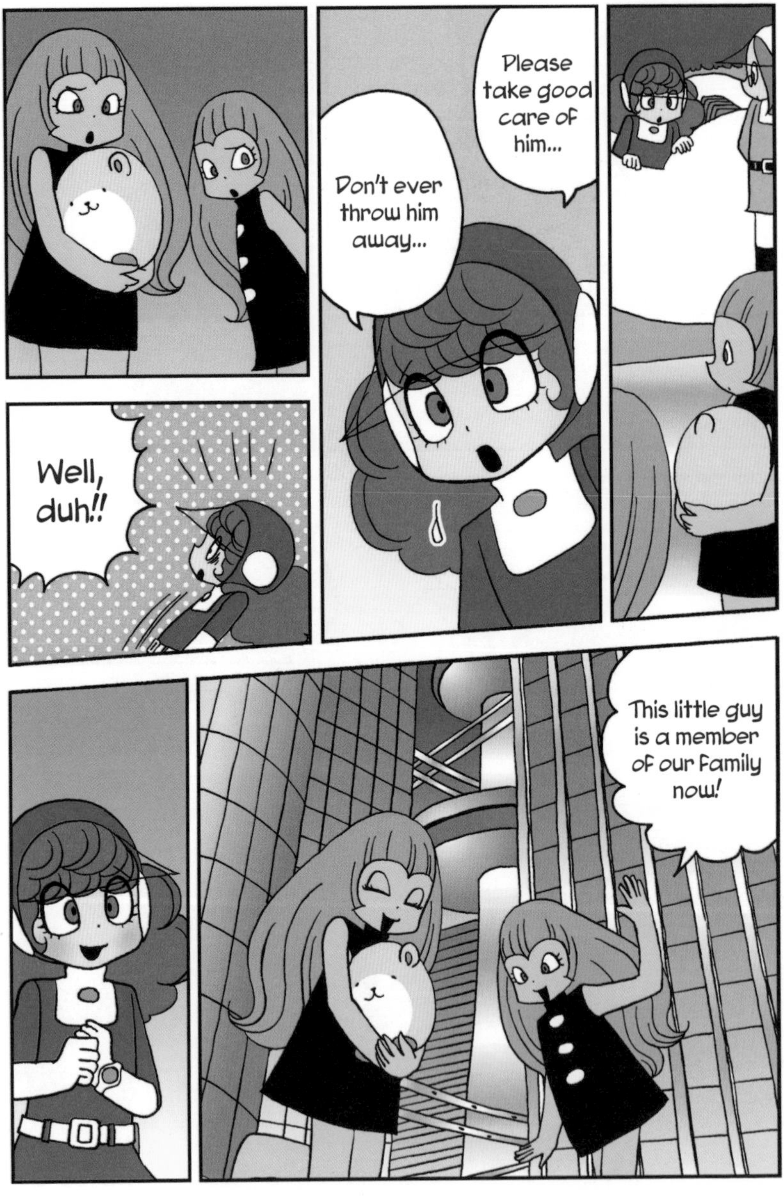
Please take good care of him...
Don't ever throw him away...
Well, duh!!
This little guy is a member of our family now!

SPACE PATROL
Well... that turned out better than we expected...
Though we won't get any points for this mission since we didn't catch Pettsie.
Our planets are so different, yet so similar..
Hm?
Nothing.
Never-mind.
I just miss home all of a sudden.

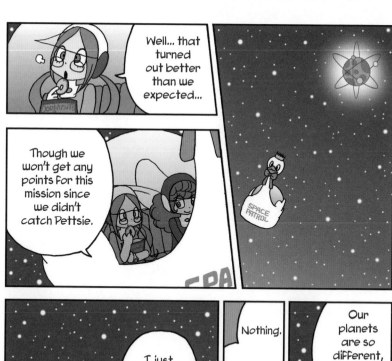

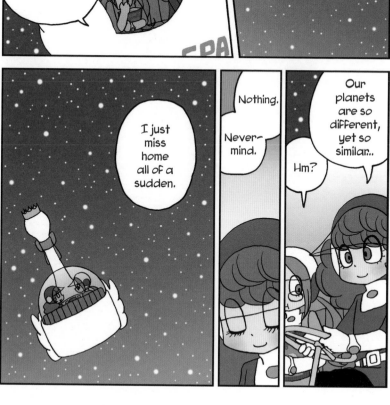

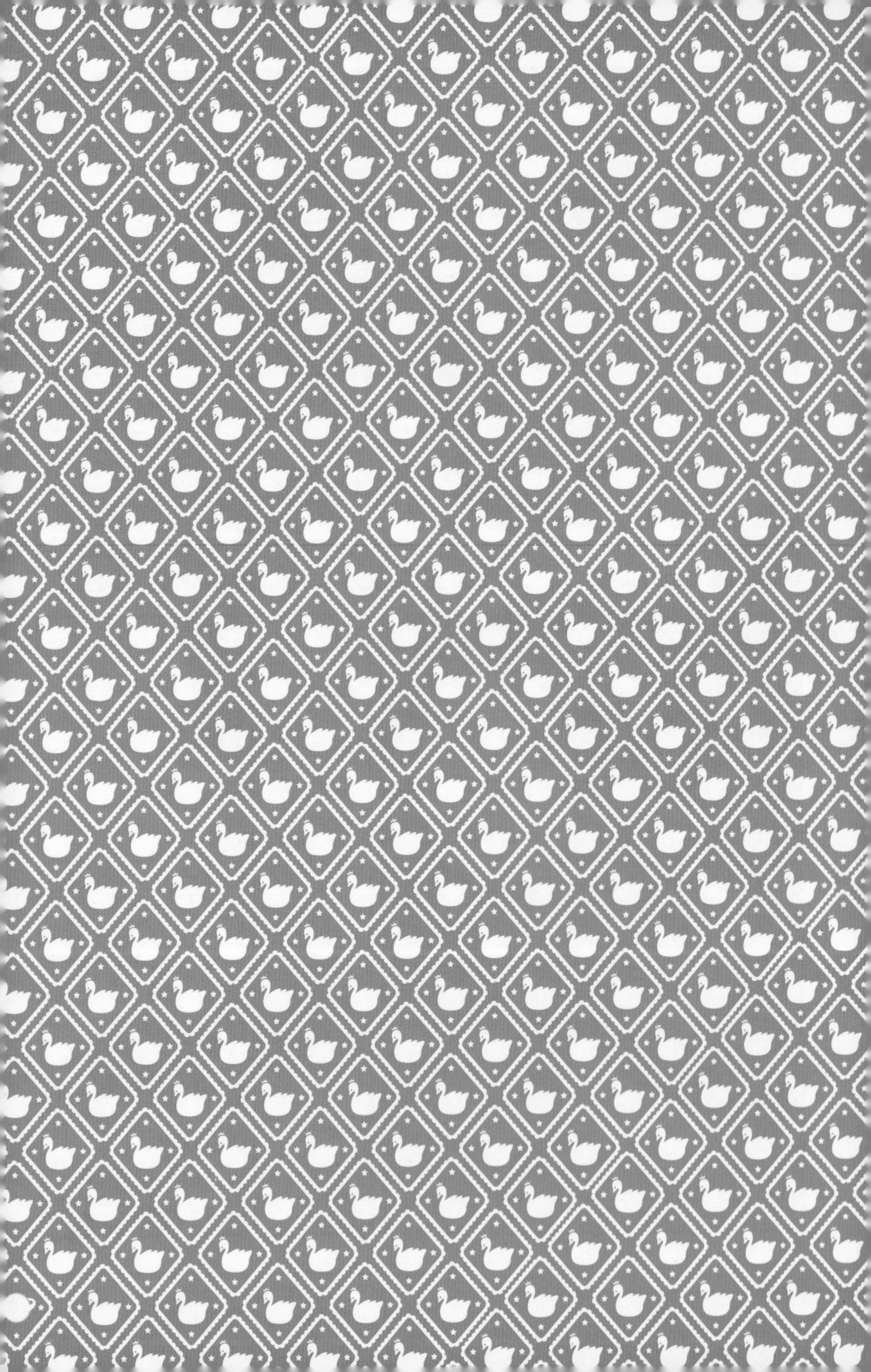

SWANS IN SPACE

CHAPTER 8
IS THE STUDENT COUNCIL PRESIDENT A BAD GUY?

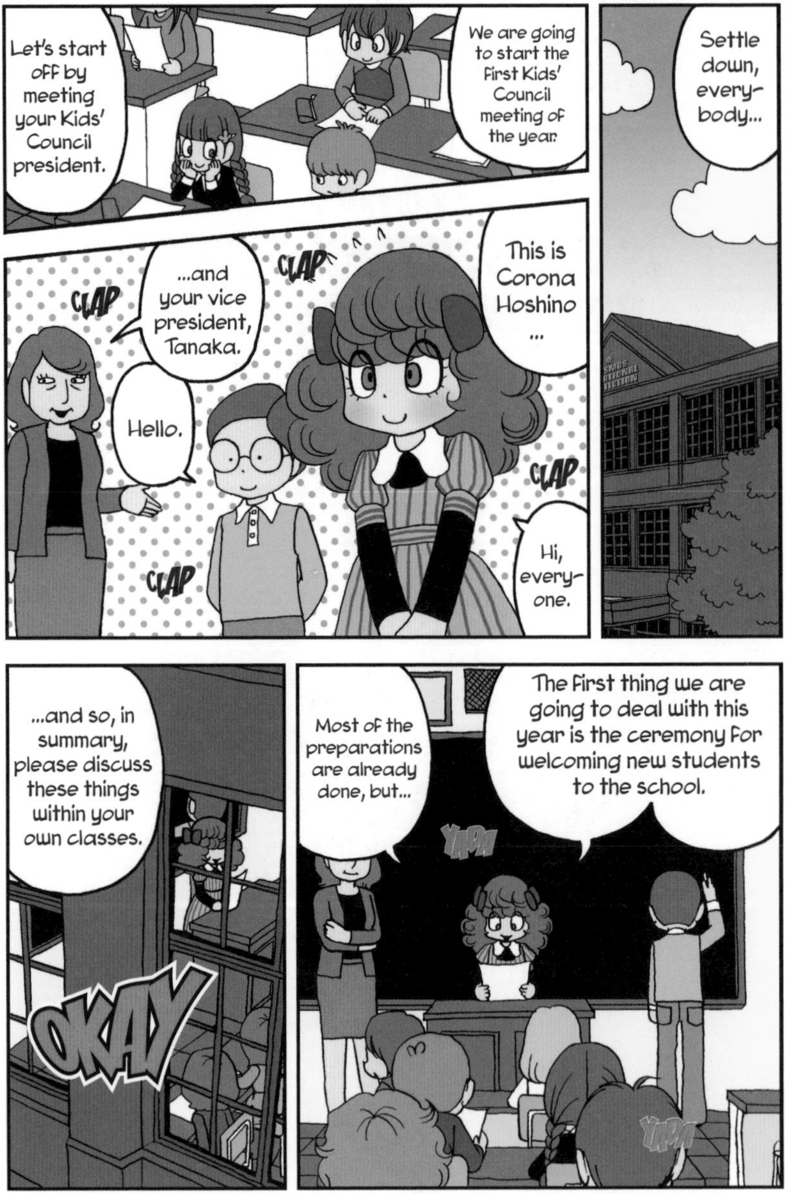
Settle down, everybody...
We are going to start the first Kids' Council meeting of the year.
Let's start off by meeting your Kids' Council president.
This is Corona Hoshino ...
CLAP
...and your vice president, Tanaka.
CLAP
Hello.
CLAP
Hi, everyone.
CLAP
The first thing we are going to deal with this year is the ceremony for welcoming new students to the school.
Most of the preparations are already done, but...
YADA
YADA
...and so, in summary, please discuss these things within your own classes.
OKAY

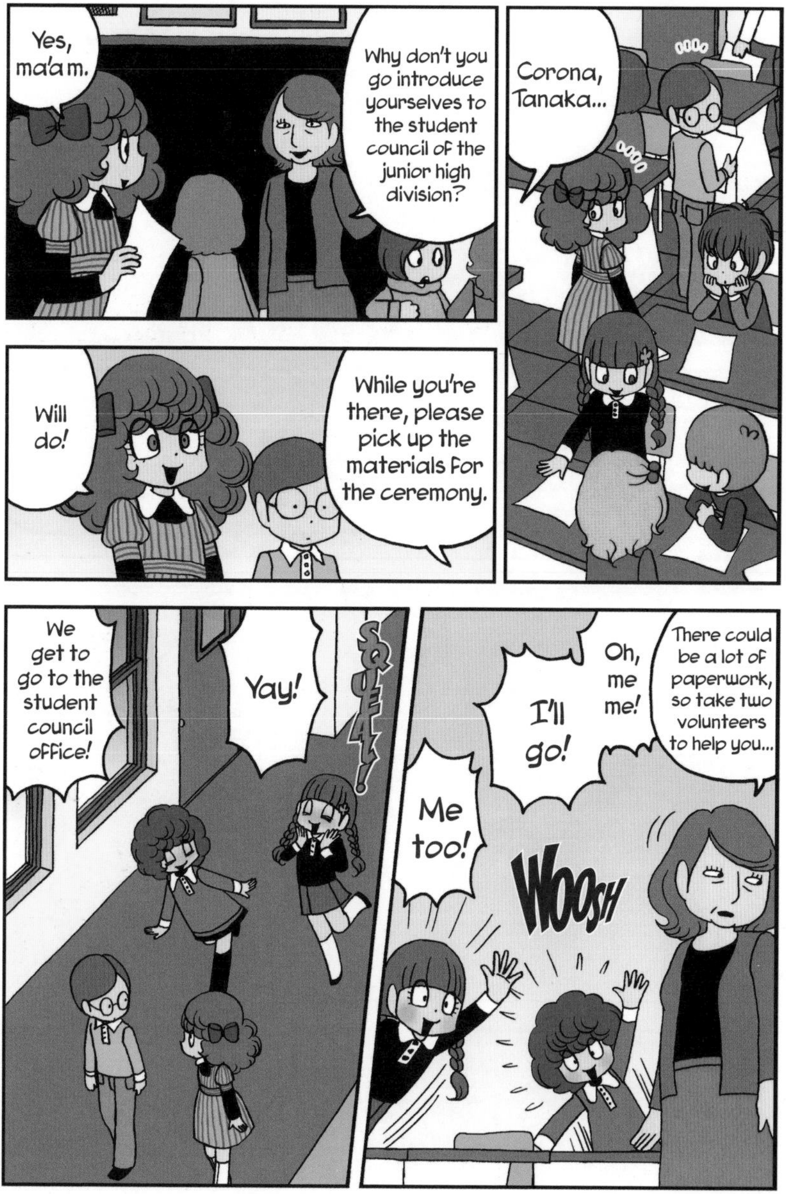
Corona, Tanaka...
Why don't you go introduce yourselves to the student council of the junior high division?
Yes, ma'am.
While you're there, please pick up the materials for the ceremony.
Will do!
There could be a lot of paperwork, so take two volunteers to help you...
Oh, me me!
I'll go!
Me too!
WOOSH
SQUEAL!
Yay!
We get to go to the student council office!

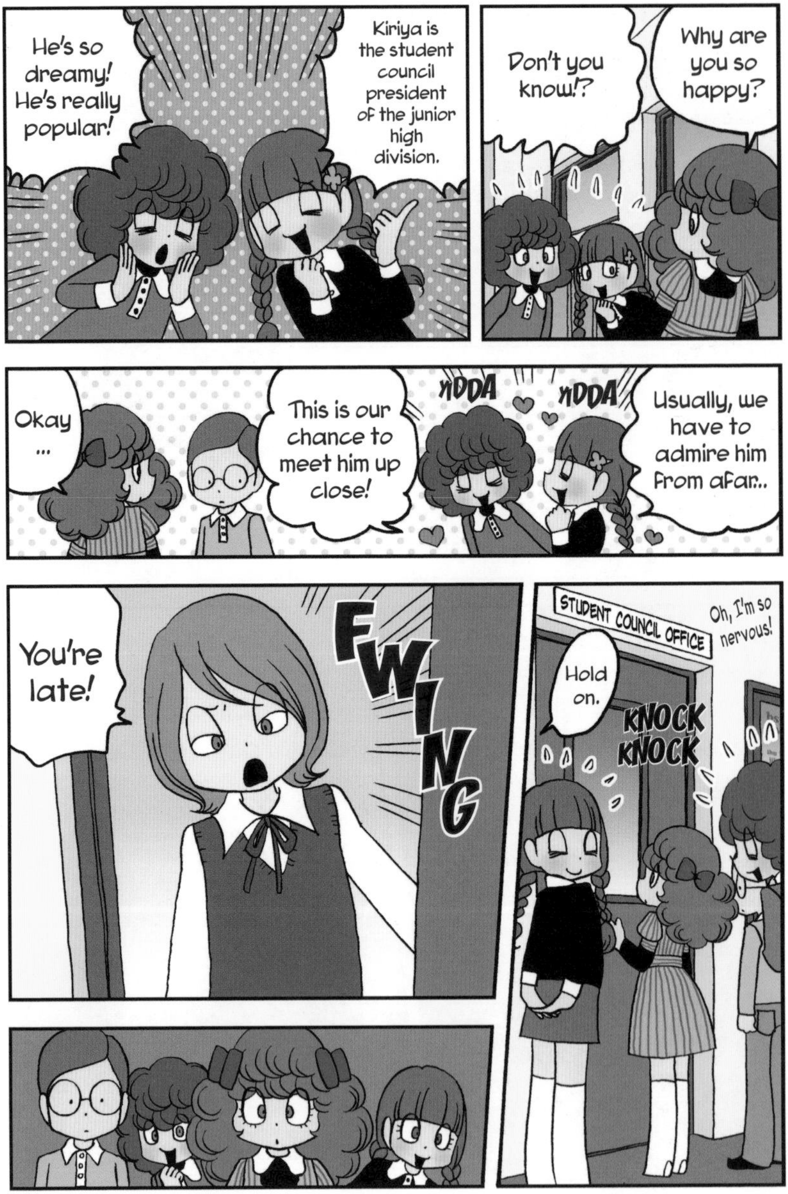
Why are you so happy?
Don't you know!?
Kiriya is the student council president of the junior high division.
He's so dreamy! He's really popular!
Usually, we have to admire him from afar...
This is our chance to meet him up close!
Okay ...
Oh, I'm so nervous!
STUDENT COUNCIL OFFICE
Hold on.
KNOCK KNOCK
FWING
You're late!

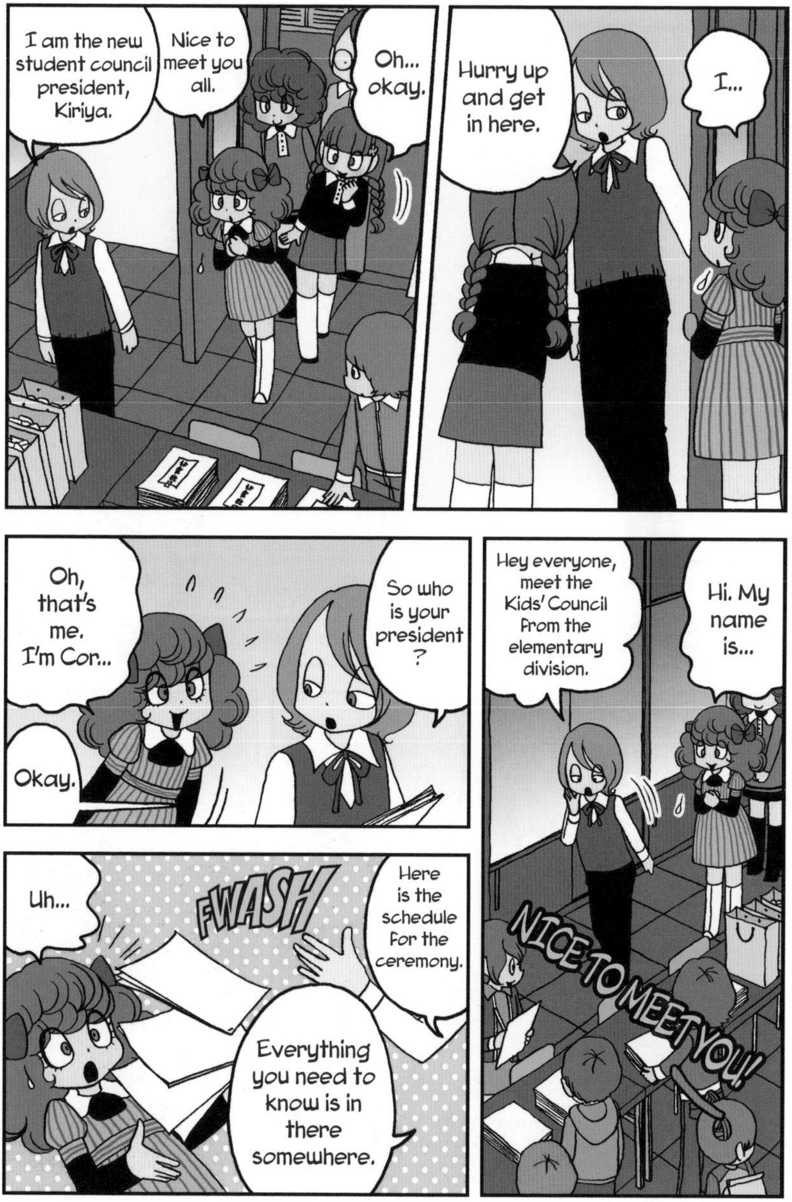
I...
Hurry up and get in here.
Oh... okay.
Nice to meet you all.
I am the new student council president, Kiriya.
Hi. My name is...
Hey everyone, meet the Kids' Council from the elementary division.
NICE TO MEET YOU!
So who is your president?
Oh, that's me. I'm Cor...
Okay.
Here is the schedule for the ceremony.
FWASH
Everything you need to know is in there somewhere.
Uh...

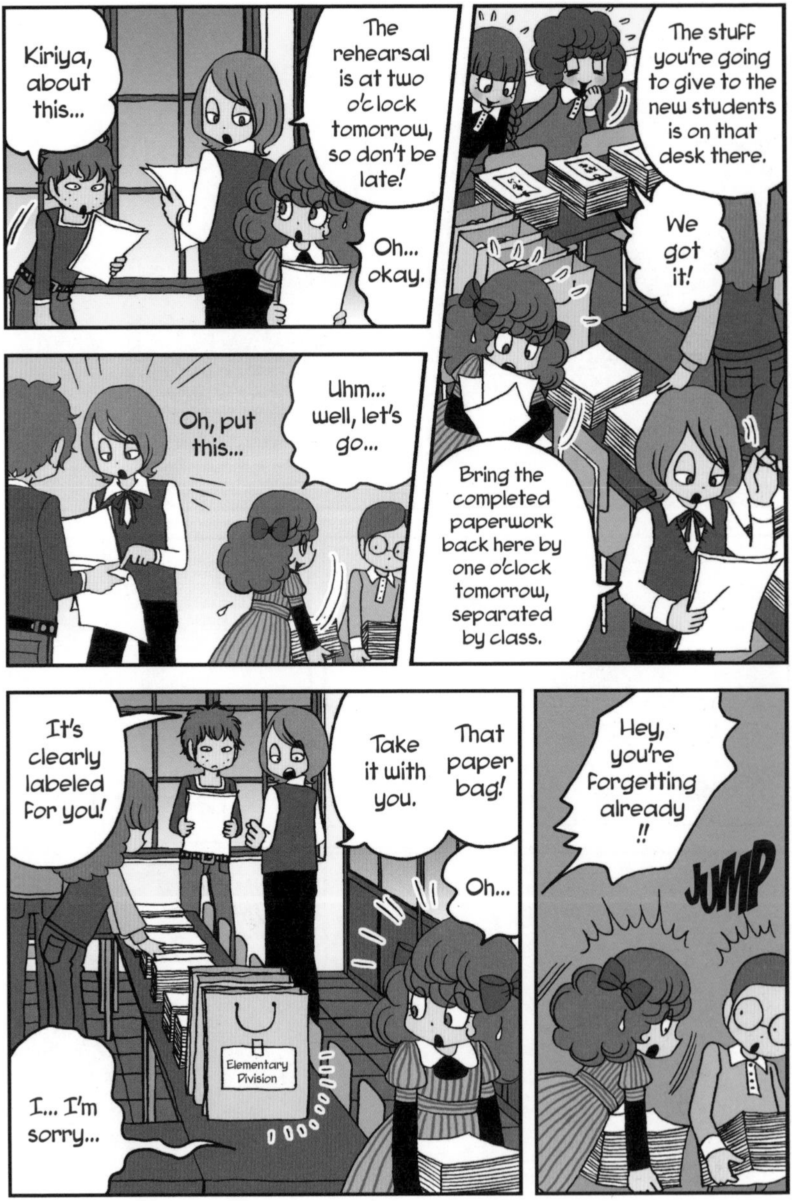
The stuff you're going to give to the new students is on that desk there.
We got it!
Bring the completed paperwork back here by one o'clock tomorrow, separated by class.
The rehearsal is at two o'clock tomorrow, so don't be late!
Oh... okay.
Kiriya, about this...
Uhm... well, let's go...
Oh, put this...
Hey, you're forgetting already !!
JUMP
That paper bag!
Take it with you.
It's clearly labeled for you!
Oh...
Elementary Division
I... I'm sorry...

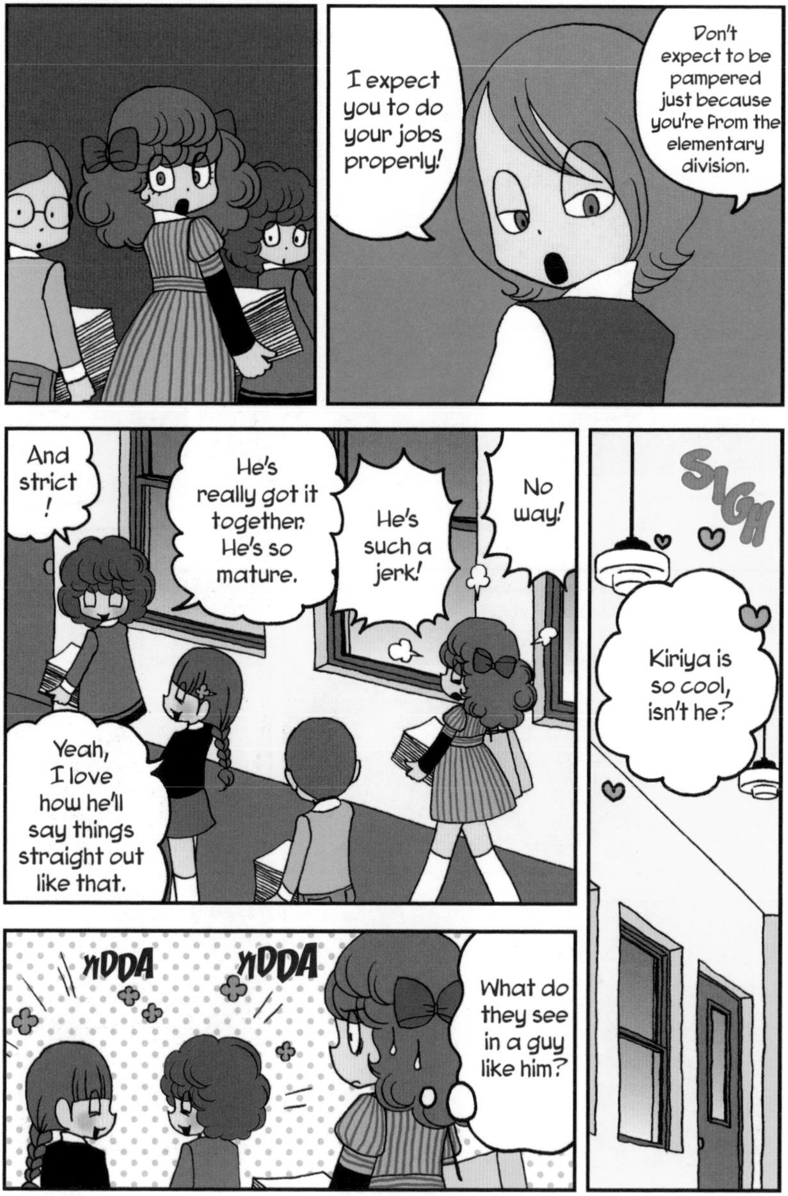
Don't expect to be pampered just because you're from the elementary division.
I expect you to do your jobs properly!
SIGH
Kiriya is so cool, isn't he?
No way!
He's such a jerk!
He's really got it together. He's so mature.
And strict!
Yeah, I love how he'll say things straight out like that.
What do they see in a guy like him?
YADDA
YADDA

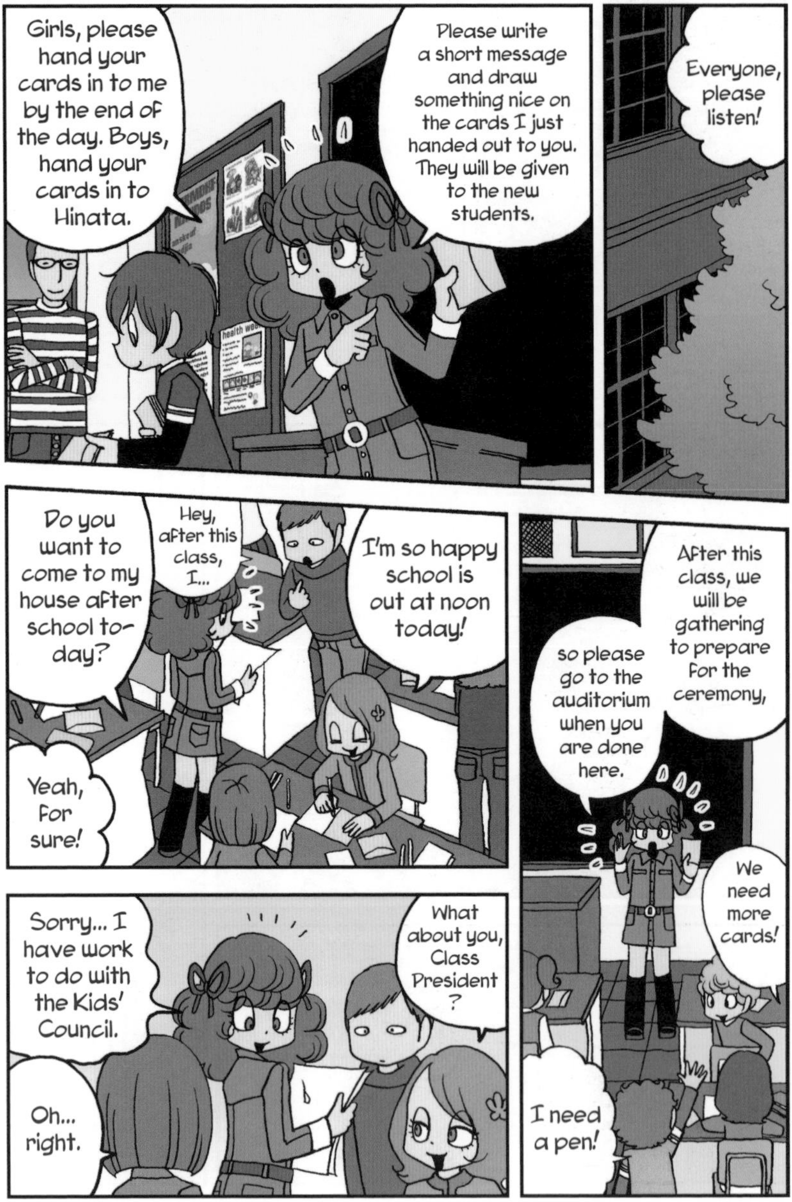
Everyone, please listen!
Please write a short message and draw something nice on the cards I just handed out to you. They will be given to the new students.
Girls, please hand your cards in to me by the end of the day. Boys, hand your cards in to Hinata.
After this class, we will be gathering to prepare for the ceremony,
so please go to the auditorium when you are done here.
We need more cards!
I need a pen!
I'm so happy school is out at noon today!
Hey, after this class, I...
Do you want to come to my house after school to-day?
Yeah, for sure!
What about you, Class President?
Sorry... I have work to do with the Kids' Council.
Oh... right.

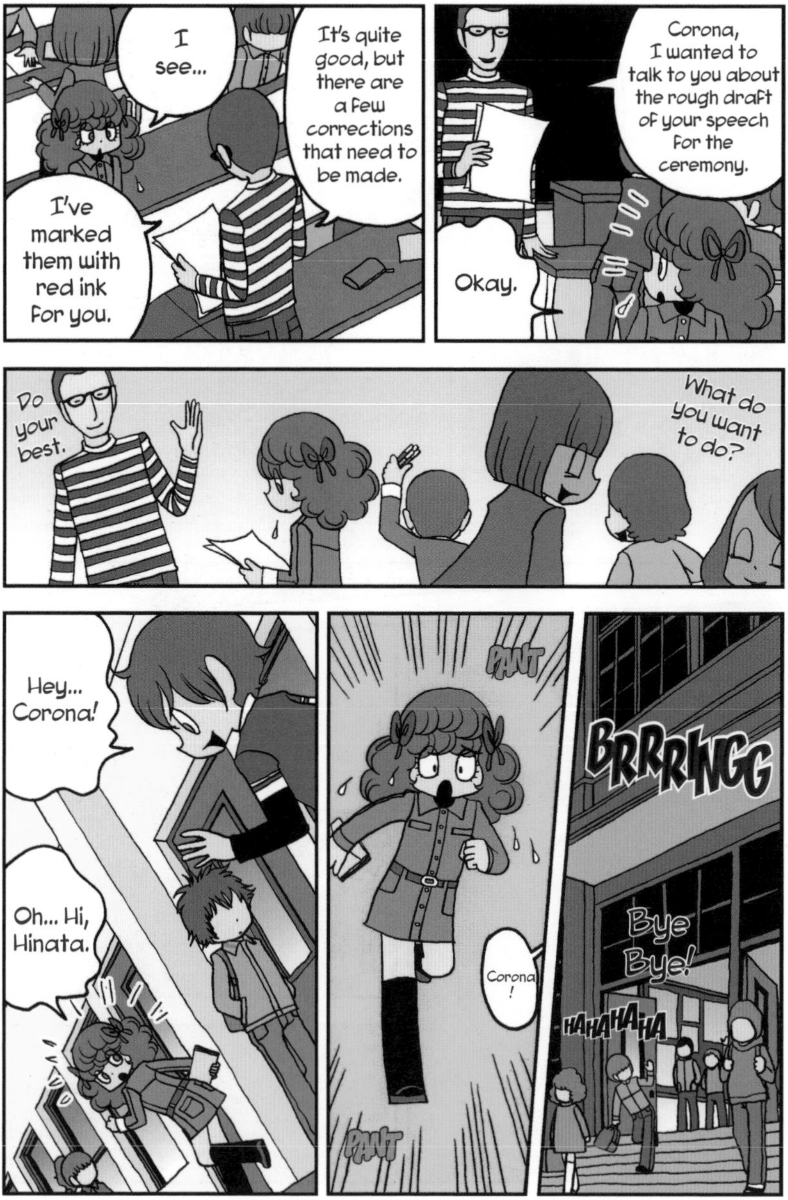
Corona, I wanted to talk to you about the rough draft of your speech for the ceremony.
Okay.
It's quite good, but there are a few corrections that need to be made.
I see...
I've marked them with red ink for you.
What do you want to do?
Do your best.
BRRRINGG
Bye Bye!
HAHAHAHA
PANT
Corona!
PANT
Hey... Corona!
Oh... Hi, Hinata.

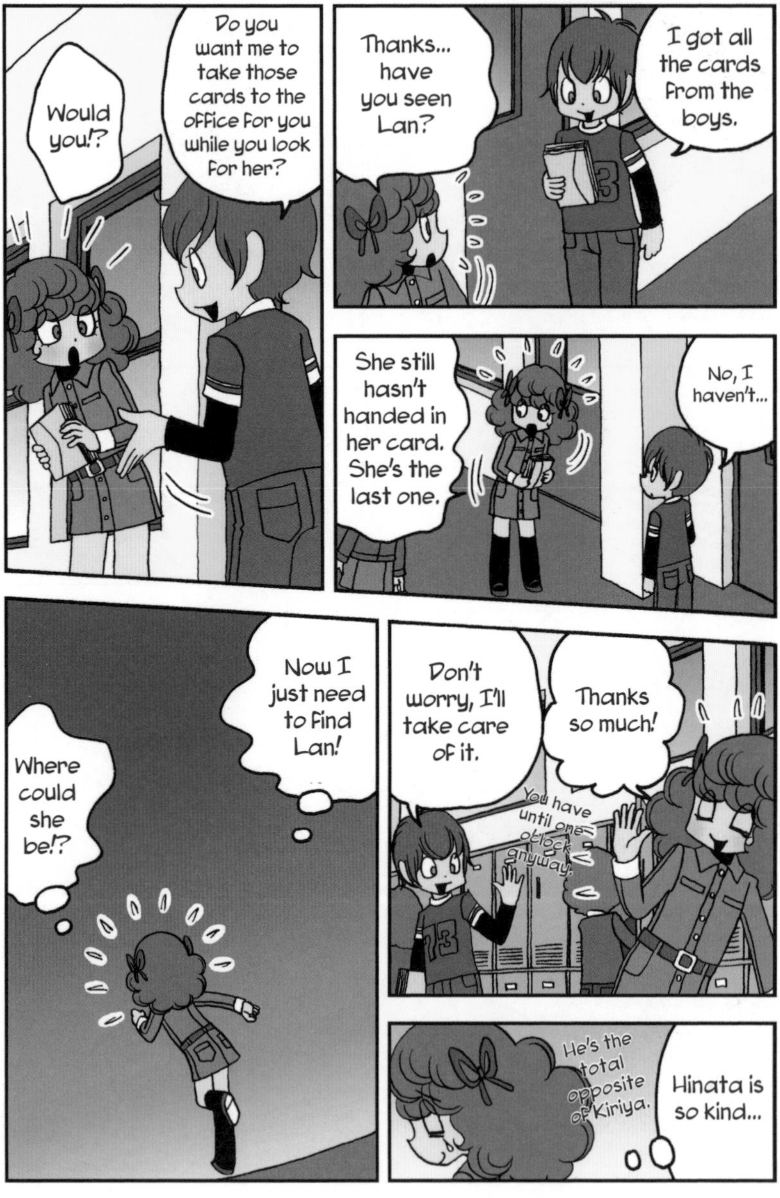
I got all the cards from the boys.
Thanks... have you seen Lan?
No, I haven't...
She still hasn't handed in her card. She's the last one.
Do you want me to take those cards to the office for you while you look for her?
Would you!?
Thanks so much!
Don't worry, I'll take care of it.
You have until one o'clock anyway.
Hinata is so kind...
He's the total opposite of Kiriya.
Now I just need to find Lan!
Where could she be!?

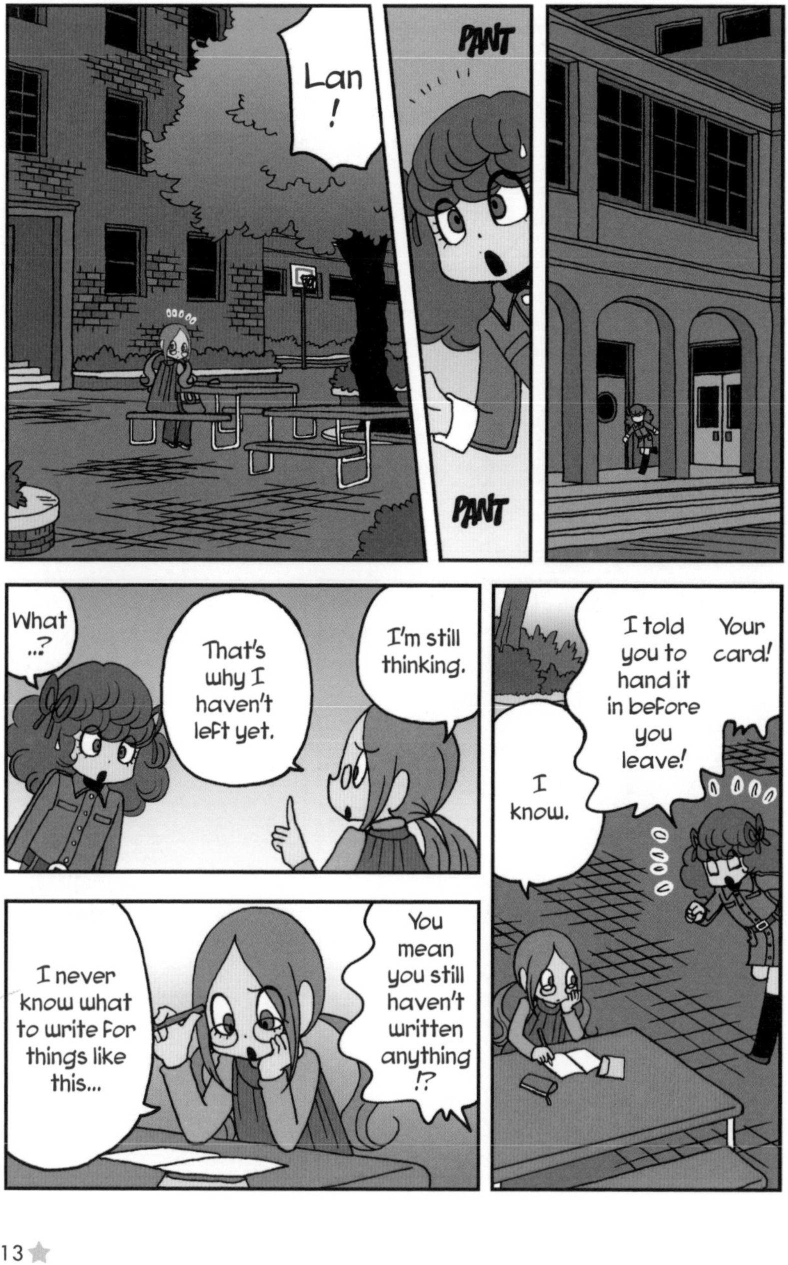
PANT
PANT
Lan !
Your card!
I told you to hand it in before you leave!
I know.
I'm still thinking.
That's why I haven't left yet.
What ...?
You mean you still haven't written anything !?
I never know what to write for things like this...

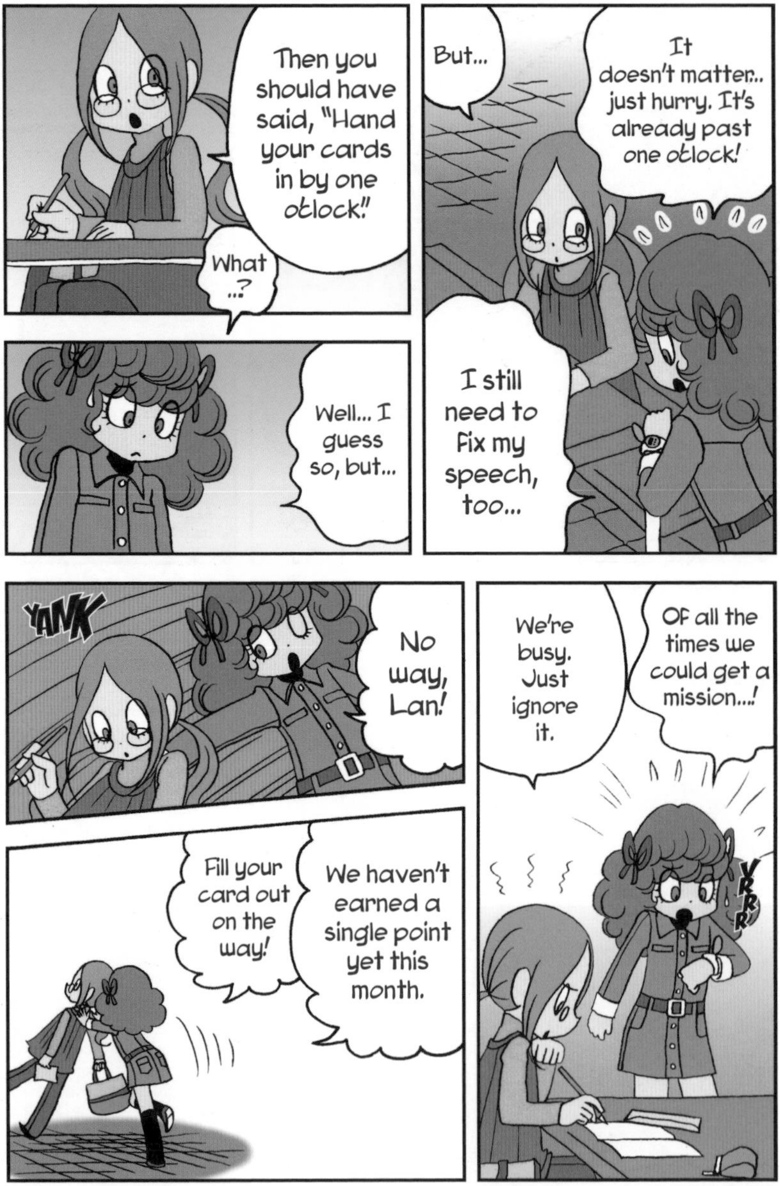
It doesn't matter.. just hurry. It's already past one o'clock!
But...
I still need to fix my speech, too...
Then you should have said, "Hand your cards in by one o'clock."
What ...?
Well... I guess so, but...
Of all the times we could get a mission...!
We're busy. Just ignore it.
VRRR
No way, Lan!
YANK
We haven't earned a single point yet this month.
Fill your card out on the way!

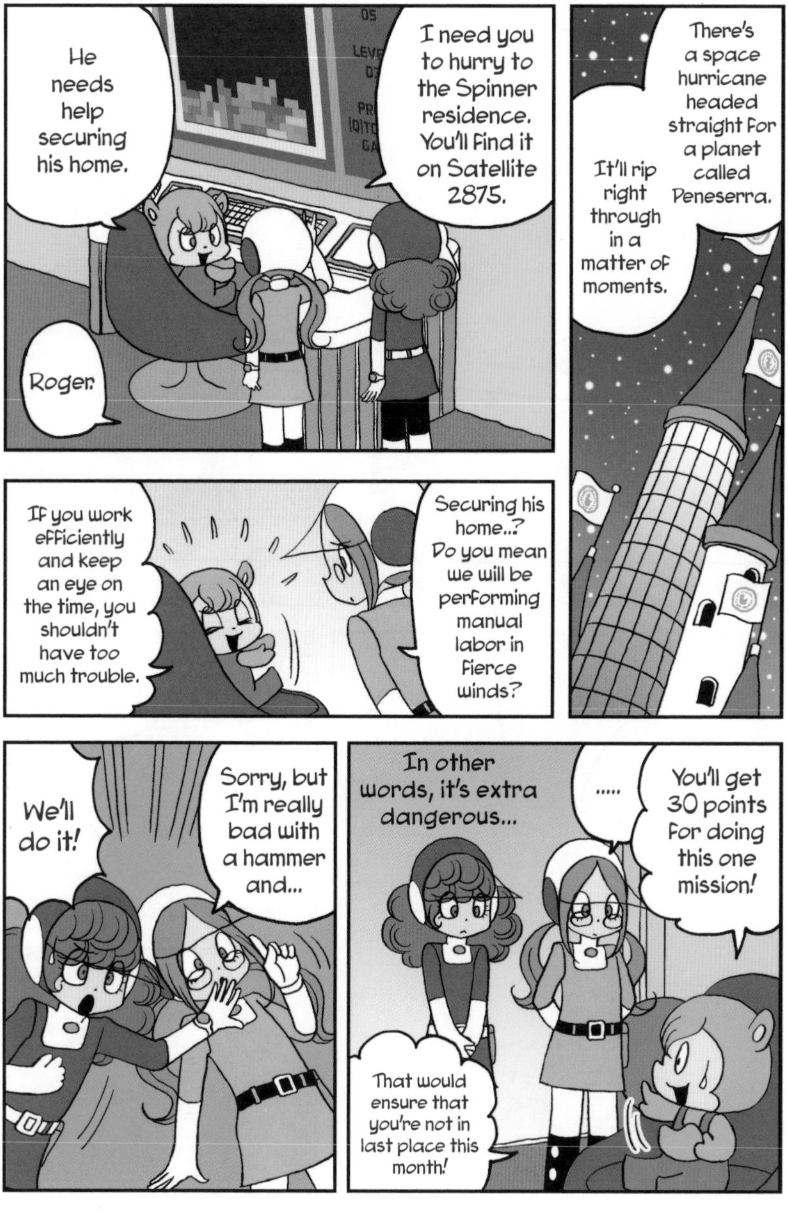
There's a space hurricane headed straight for a planet called Peneserra.
It'll rip right through in a matter of moments.
I need you to hurry to the Spinner residence. You'll find it on Satellite 2875.
He needs help securing his home.
Roger.
Securing his home..? Do you mean we will be performing manual labor in fierce winds?
If you work efficiently and keep an eye on the time, you shouldn't have too much trouble.
You'll get 30 points for doing this one mission!
.....
In other words, it's extra dangerous...
That would ensure that you're not in last place this month!
Sorry, but I'm really bad with a hammer and...
We'll do it!

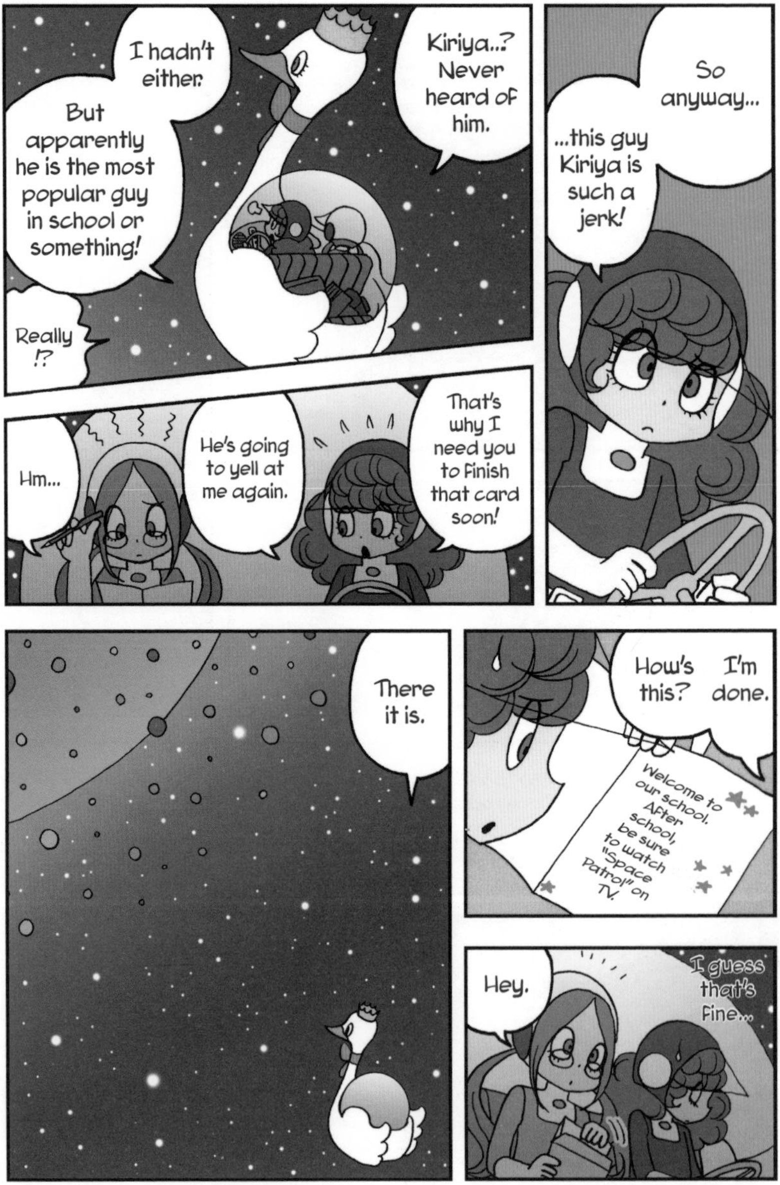
So anyway...
...this guy Kiriya is such a jerk!
Kiriya..? Never heard of him.
I hadn't either.
But apparently he is the most popular guy in school or something!
Really!?
That's why I need you to finish that card soon!
He's going to yell at me again.
Hm...
I'm done.
How's this?
Welcome to our school. After school, be sure to watch "Space Patrol" on TV.
I guess that's fine...
Hey.
There it is.

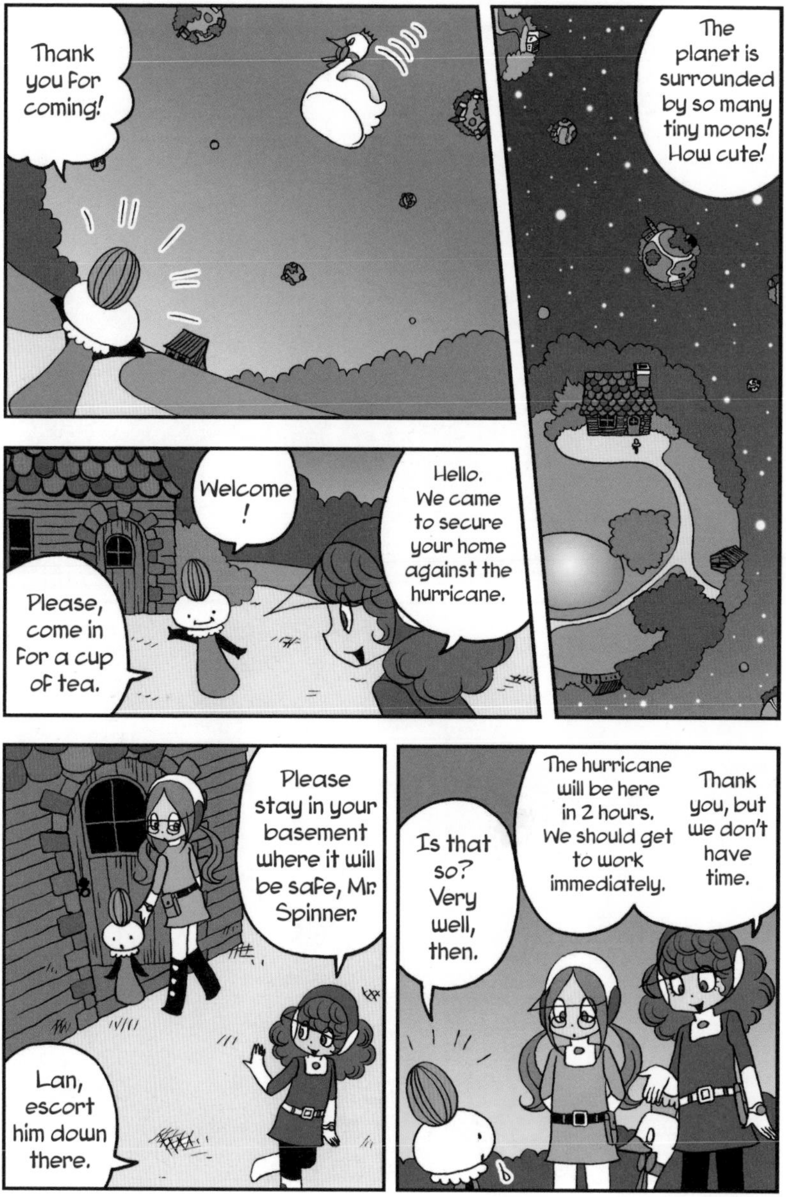
The planet is surrounded by so many tiny moons! How cute!
Thank you for coming!
Hello. We came to secure your home against the hurricane.
Welcome!
Please, come in for a cup of tea.
Thank you, but we don't have time.
The hurricane will be here in 2 hours. We should get to work immediately.
Is that so? Very well, then.
Please stay in your basement where it will be safe, Mr. Spinner.
Lan, escort him down there.

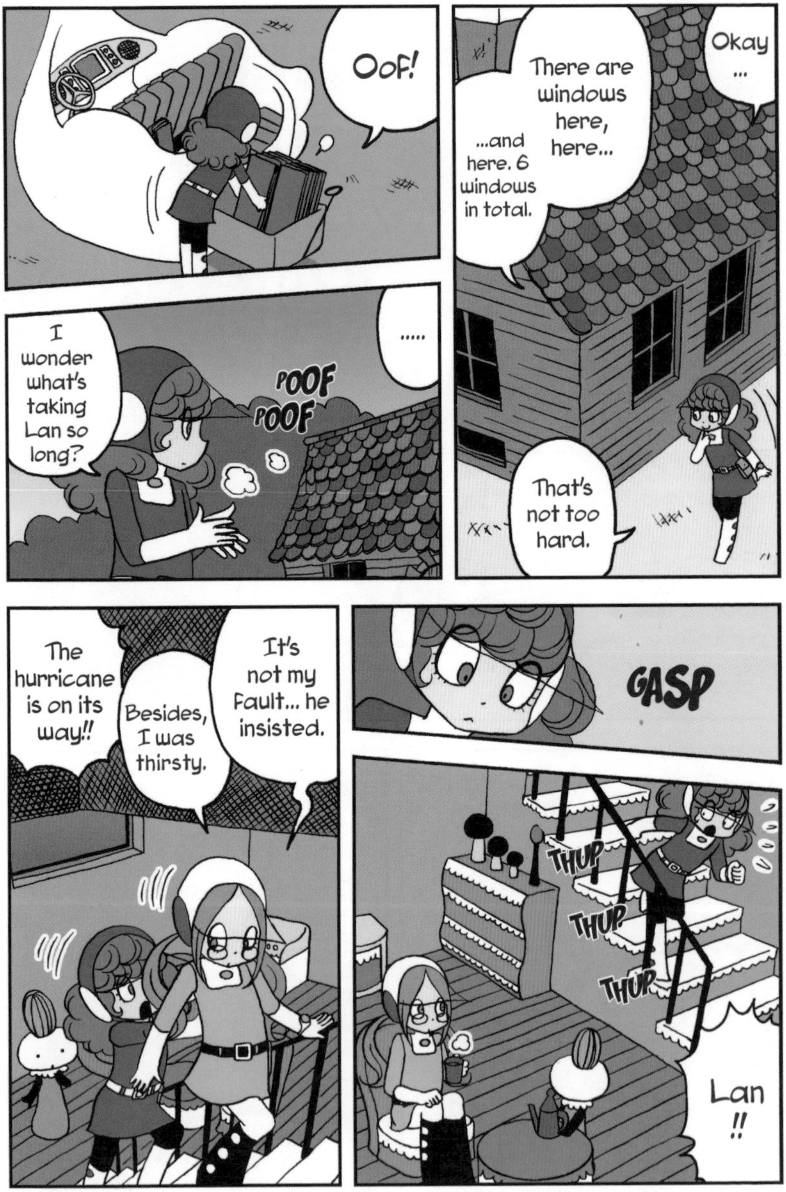
Okay ...
There are windows here, here...
...and here. 6 windows in total.
That's not too hard.
Oof!
.....
POOF POOF
I wonder what's taking Lan so long?
GASP
THUP THUP THUP
Lan !!
It's not my fault... he insisted.
Besides, I was thirsty.
The hurricane is on its way!!

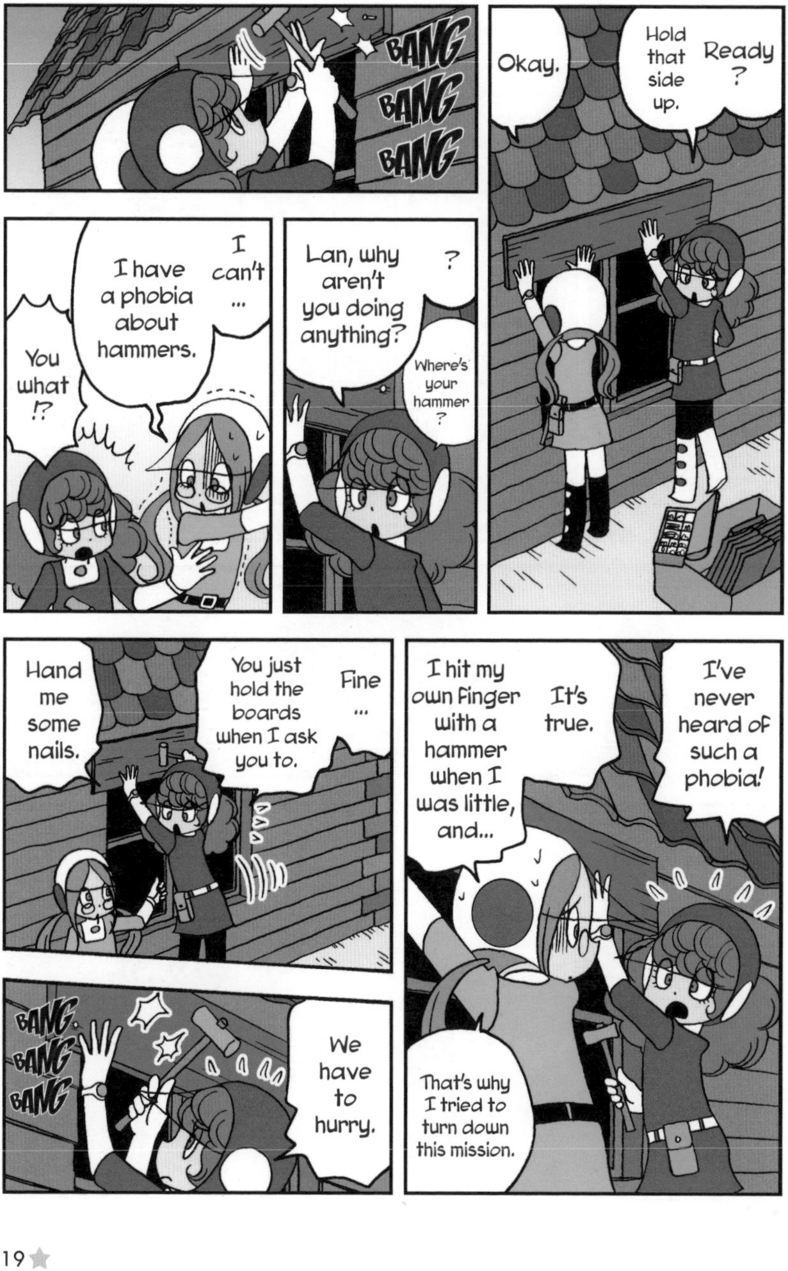

Ready?
Hold that side up.
Okay.
BANG
BANG
BANG
Lan, why aren't you doing anything?
Where's your hammer?
I can't...
I have a phobia about hammers.
You what!?
I've never heard of such a phobia!
It's true.
I hit my own finger with a hammer when I was little, and...
That's why I tried to turn down this mission.
Fine...
You just hold the boards when I ask you to.
Hand me some nails.
We have to hurry.
BANG
BANG
BANG

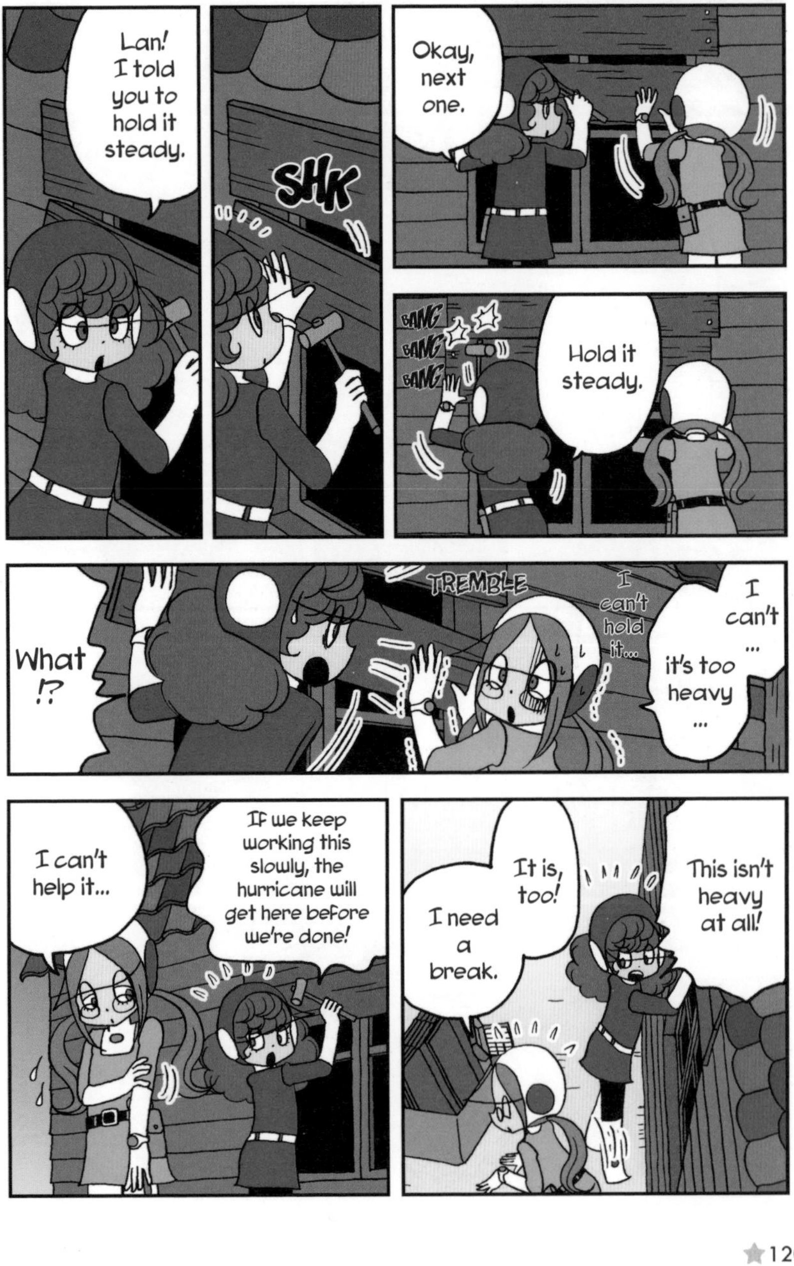
Okay, next one.
BANG
BANG
BANG
Hold it steady.
SHK
Lan! I told you to hold it steady.
I can't ... it's too heavy ...
I can't hold it...
TREMBLE
What!?
This isn't heavy at all!
It is, too!
I need a break.
If we keep working this slowly, the hurricane will get here before we're done!
I can't help it...

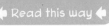

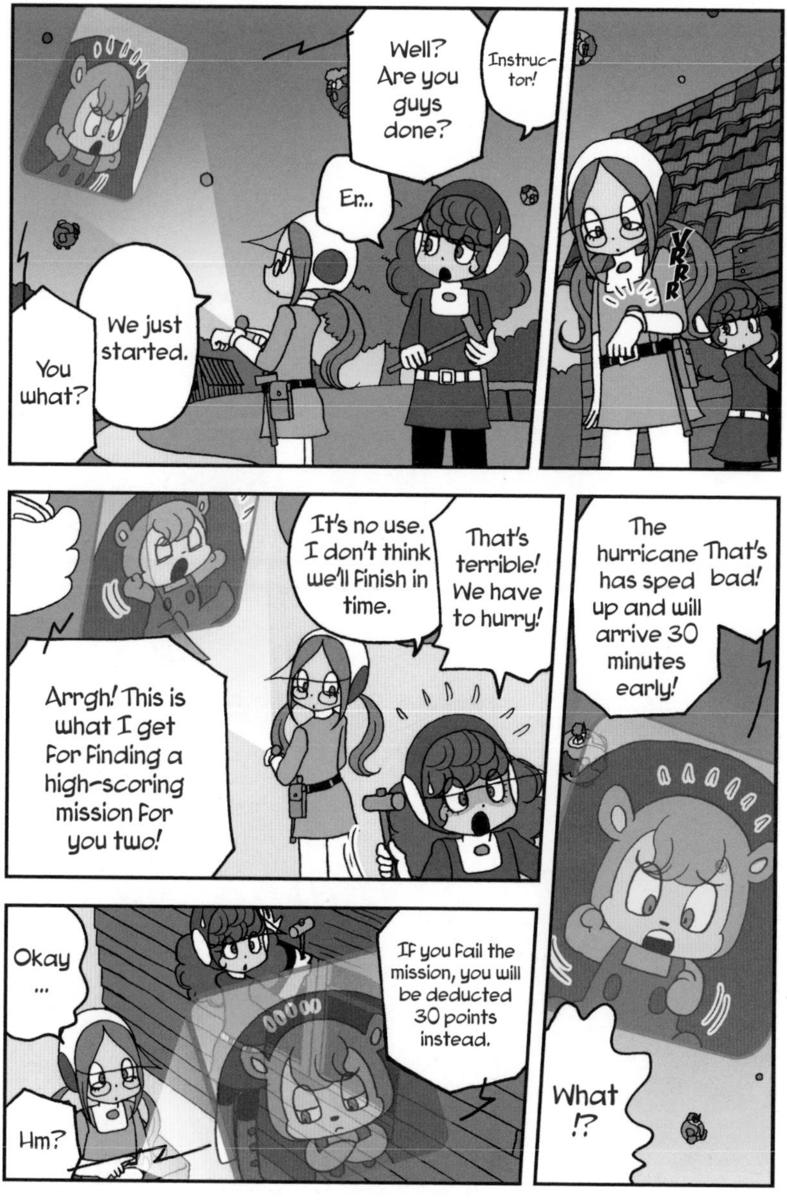
VRRR
Instructor!
Well? Are you guys done?
Er..
We just started.
You what?
That's bad!
The hurricane has sped up and will arrive 30 minutes early!
What!?
That's terrible! We have to hurry!
It's no use. I don't think we'll finish in time.
Arrgh! This is what I get for finding a high-scoring mission for you two!
If you fail the mission, you will be deducted 30 points instead.
Okay ...
Hm?

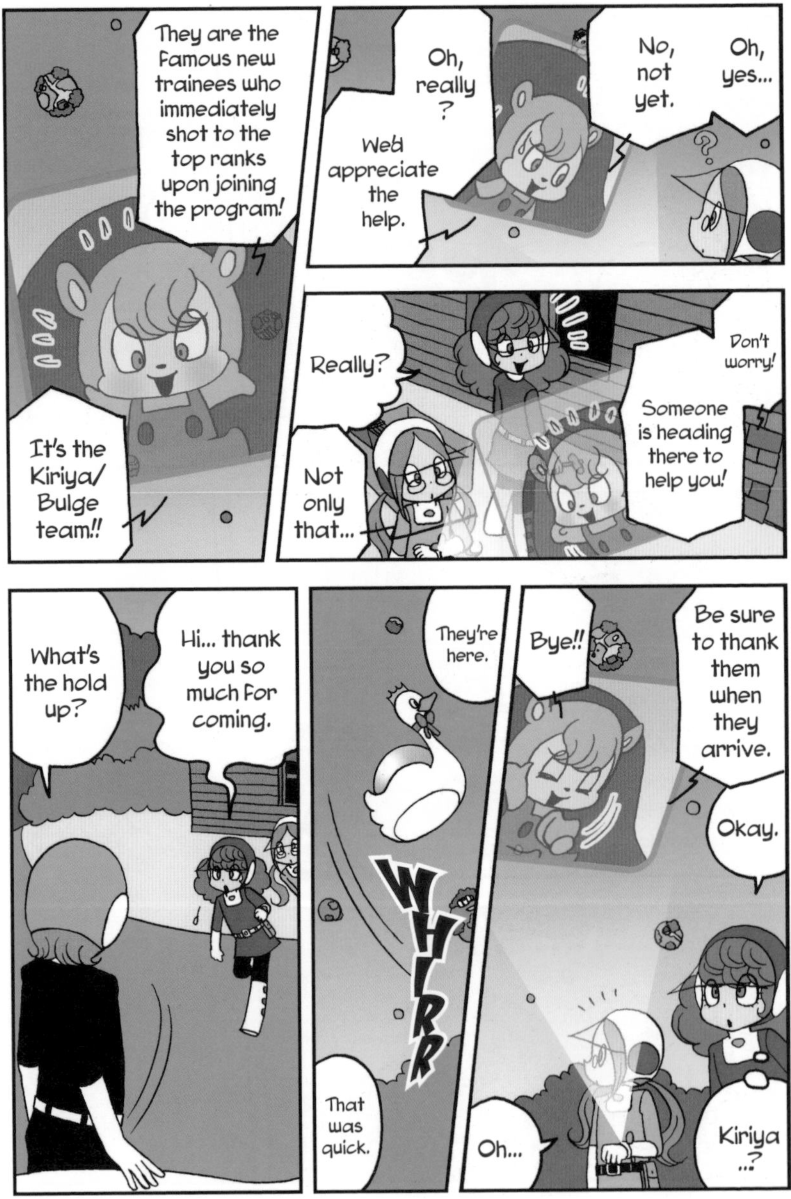
Oh, yes...
No, not yet.
Oh, really?
We'd appreciate the help.
Don't worry!
Someone is heading there to help you!
Really?
Not only that...
They are the famous new trainees who immediately shot to the top ranks upon joining the program!
It's the Kiriya/Bulge team!!
Be sure to thank them when they arrive.
Bye!!
Okay.
Kiriya ..?
Oh...
They're here.
WHIRR
That was quick.
Hi... thank you so much for coming.
What's the hold up?

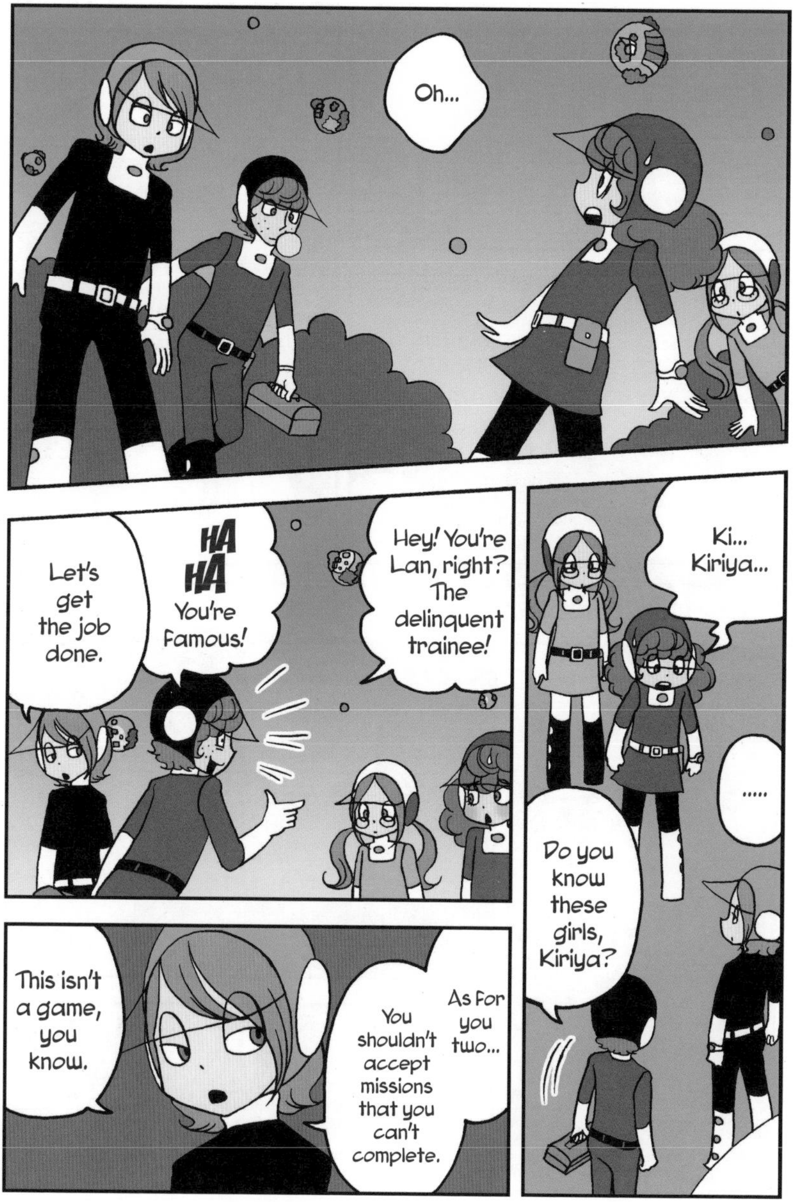
Oh...
Ki... Kiriya...
.....
Do you know these girls, Kiriya?
Hey! You're Lan, right? The delinquent trainee!
HA HA
You're Famous!
Let's get the job done.
As for you two...
You shouldn't accept missions that you can't complete.
This isn't a game, you know.

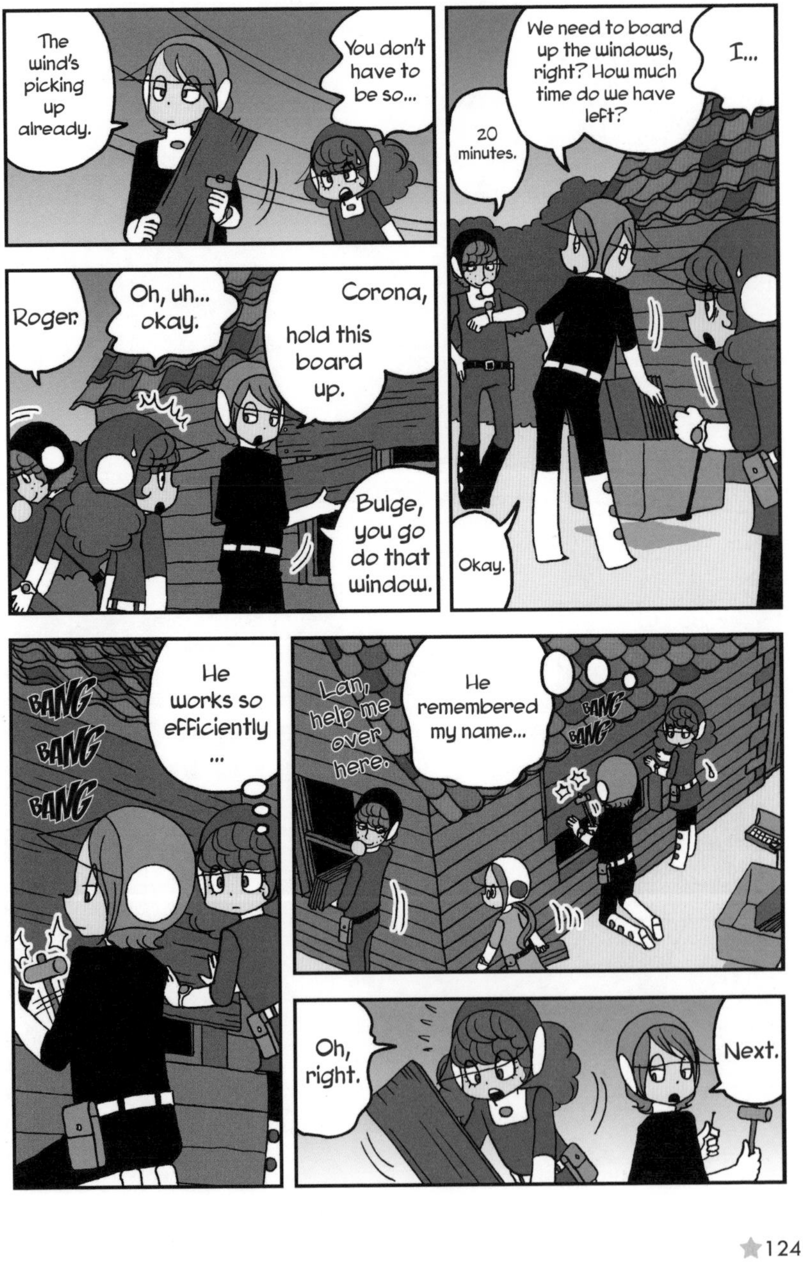
I...
We need to board up the windows, right? How much time do we have left?
20 minutes.
Okay.
You don't have to be so...
The wind's picking up already.
Corona, hold this board up.
Bulge, you go do that window.
Oh, uh... okay.
Roger.
Mu
He remembered my name...
BANG
BANG
Lan, help me over here.
Next.
Oh, right.
He works so efficiently ...
BANG
BANG
BANG

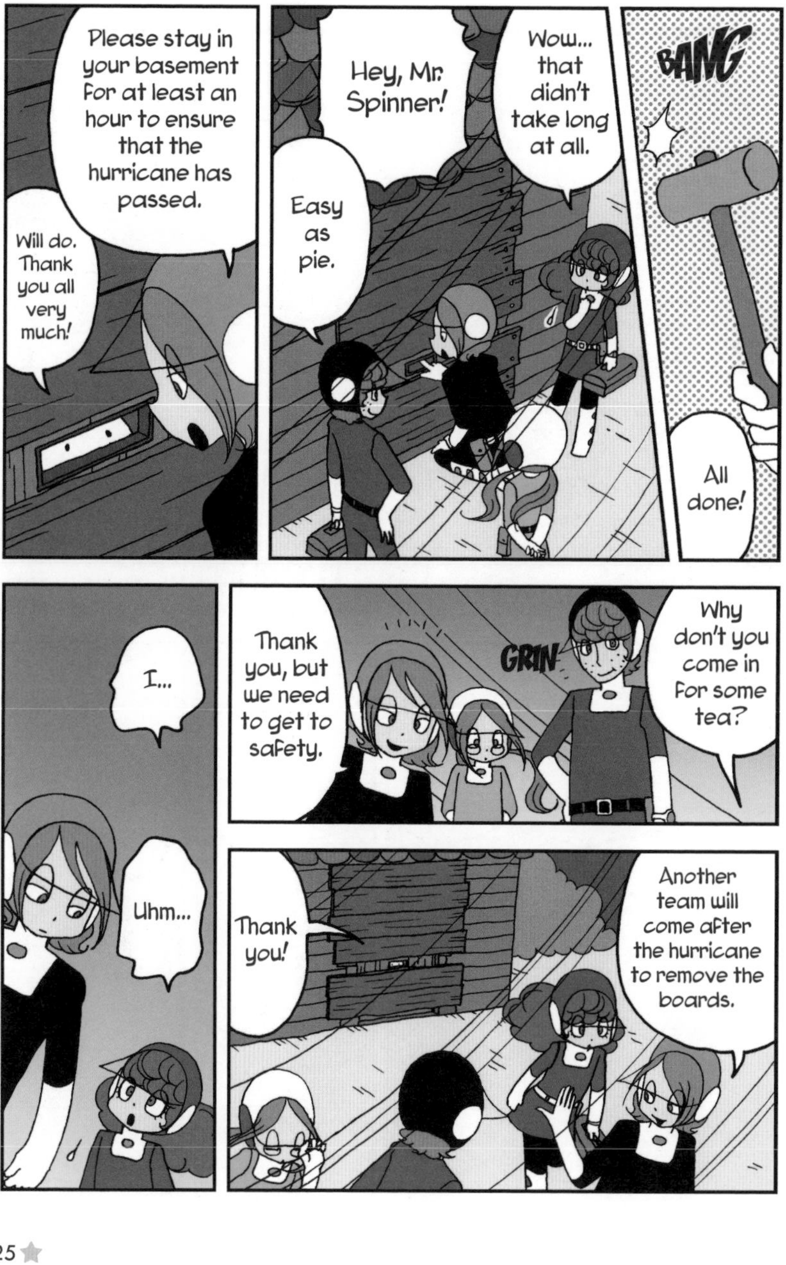
BANG
All done!
Wow... that didn't take long at all.
Hey, Mr. Spinner!
Easy as pie.
Please stay in your basement for at least an hour to ensure that the hurricane has passed.
Will do. Thank you all very much!
Why don't you come in for some tea?
GRIN
Thank you, but we need to get to safety.
Another team will come after the hurricane to remove the boards.
Thank you!
I...
Uhm...

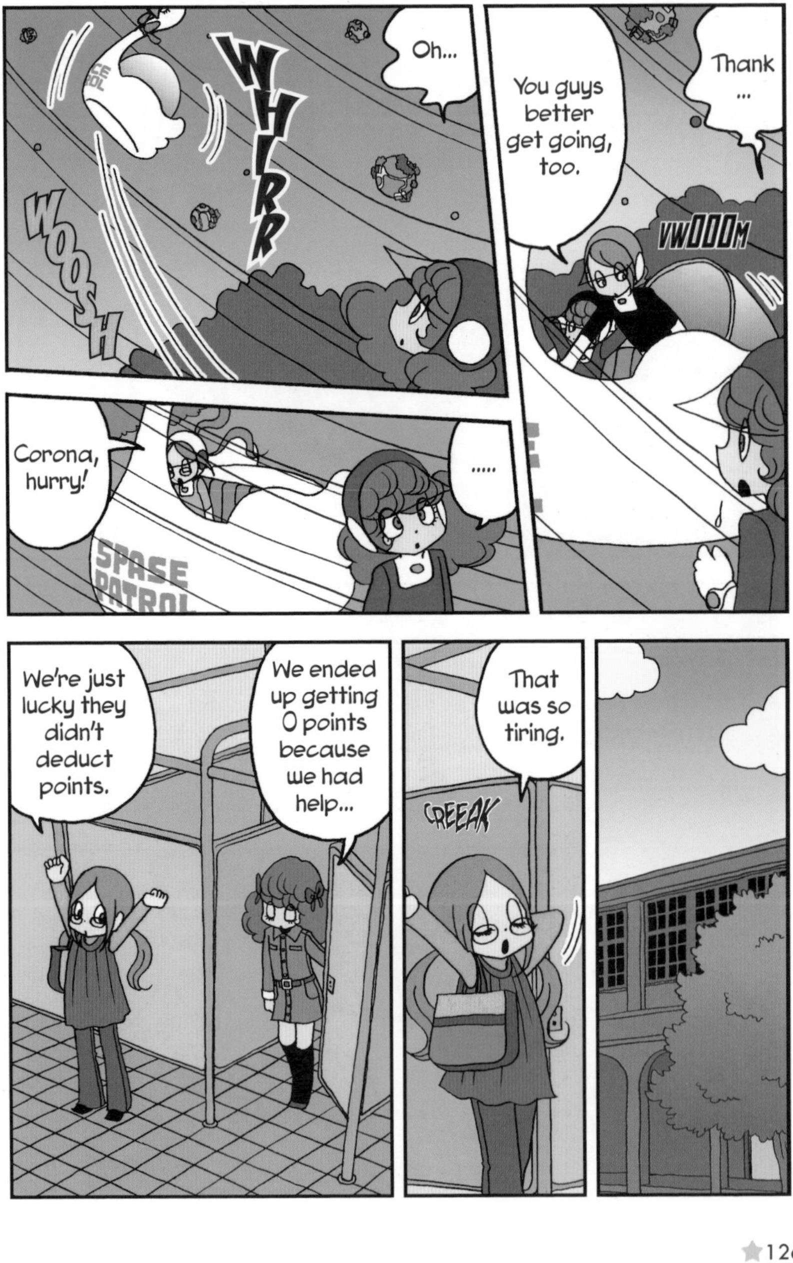
Thank ...
You guys better get going, too.
VWOOOM
Oh...
WHIRR
WOOSH
.....
Corona, hurry!
SPASE PATROL
That was so tiring.
CREEAK
We ended up getting 0 points because we had help...
We're just lucky they didn't deduct points.

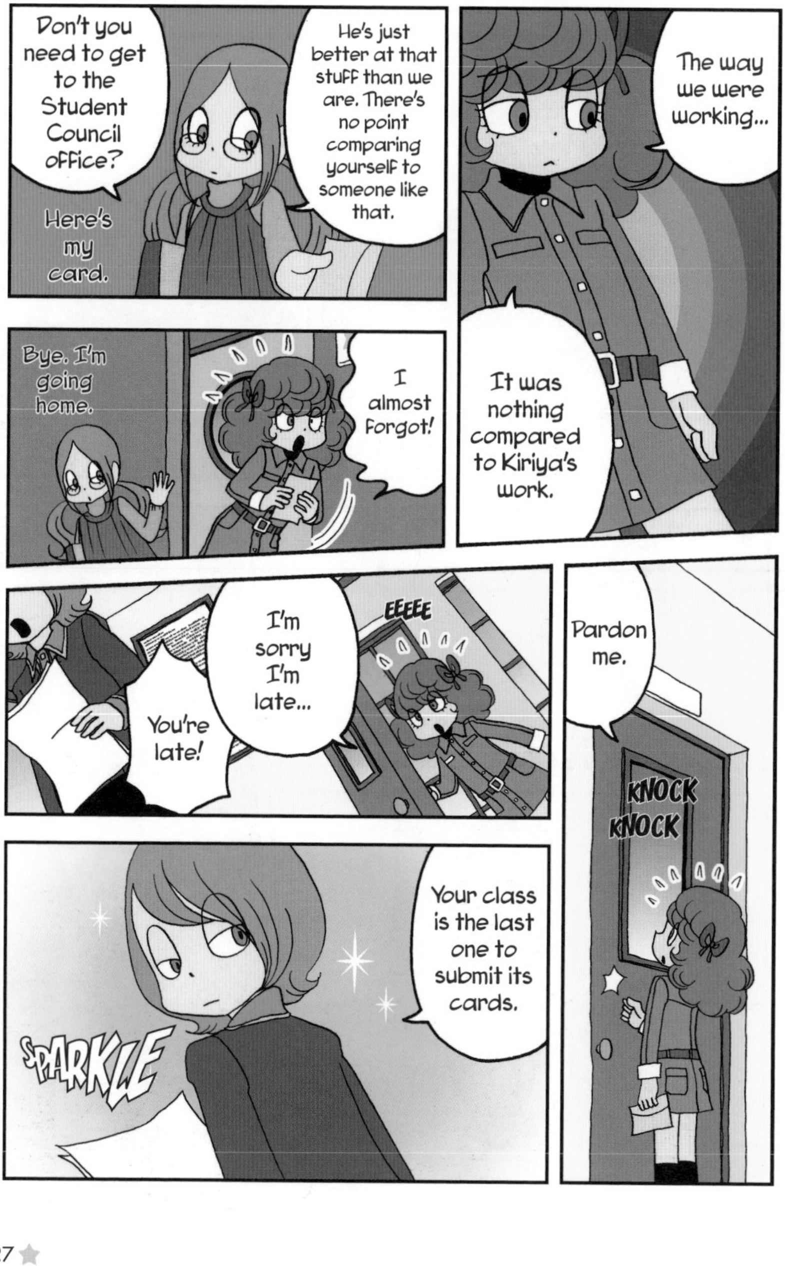
The way we were working...
It was nothing compared to Kiriya's work.
He's just better at that stuff than we are. There's no point comparing yourself to someone like that.
Don't you need to get to the Student Council office?
Here's my card.
I almost forgot!
Bye. I'm going home.
Pardon me.
KNOCK KNOCK
EEEEE
I'm sorry I'm late...
You're late!
Your class is the last one to submit its cards.
SPARKLE

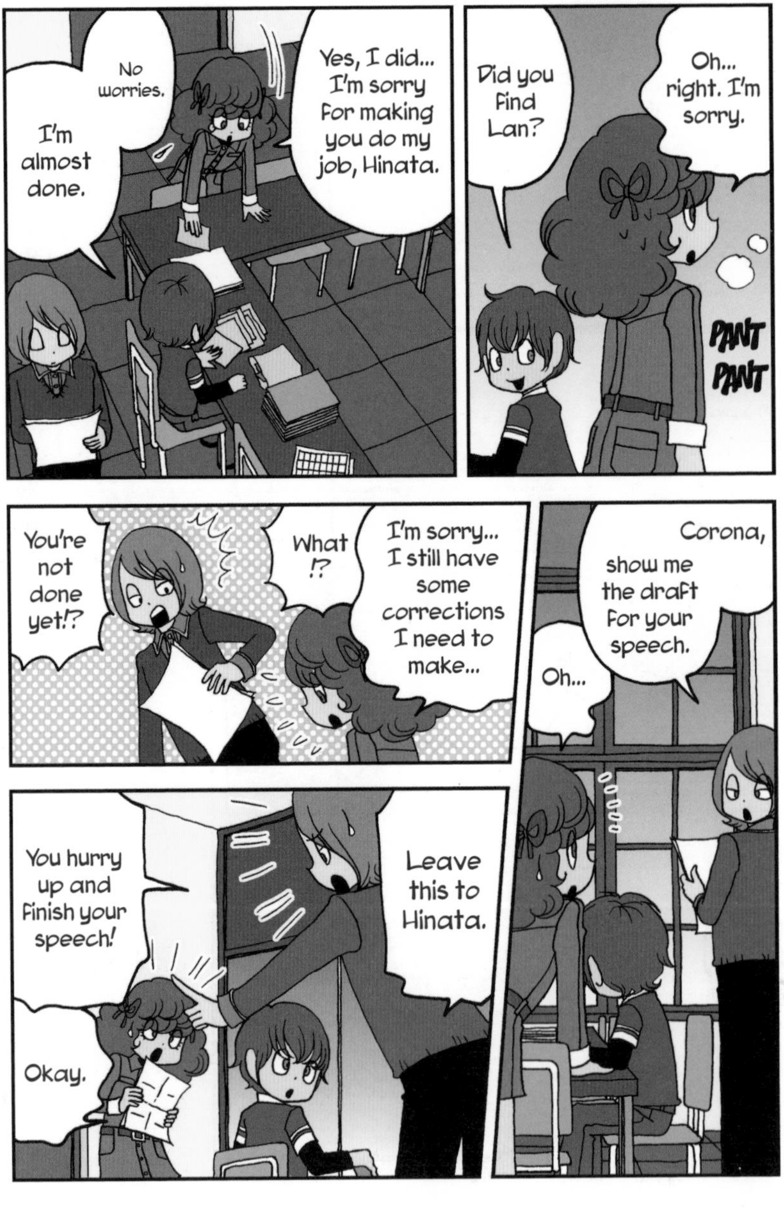
Oh... right. I'm sorry.
Did you find Lan?
PANT PANT
Yes, I did... I'm sorry for making you do my job, Hinata.
No worries.
I'm almost done.
Corona, show me the draft for your speech.
Oh...
I'm sorry... I still have some corrections I need to make...
What!?
You're not done yet!?
Leave this to Hinata.
You hurry up and finish your speech!
Okay.

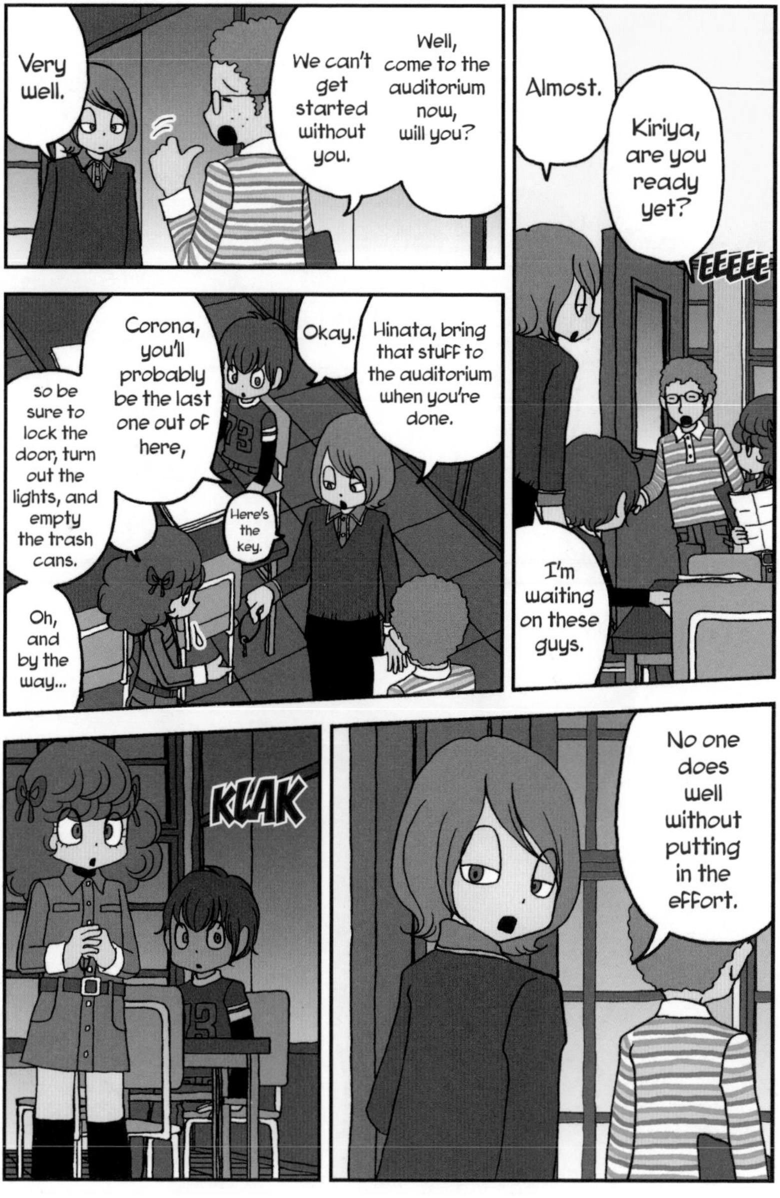
Kiriya, are you ready yet?
Almost.
EEEEE
I'm waiting on these guys.
Well, come to the auditorium now, will you?
We can't get started without you.
Very well.
Hinata, bring that stuff to the auditorium when you're done.
Okay.
Corona, you'll probably be the last one out of here,
so be sure to lock the door, turn out the lights, and empty the trash cans.
Here's the key.
Oh, and by the way...
No one does well without putting in the effort.
KLAK

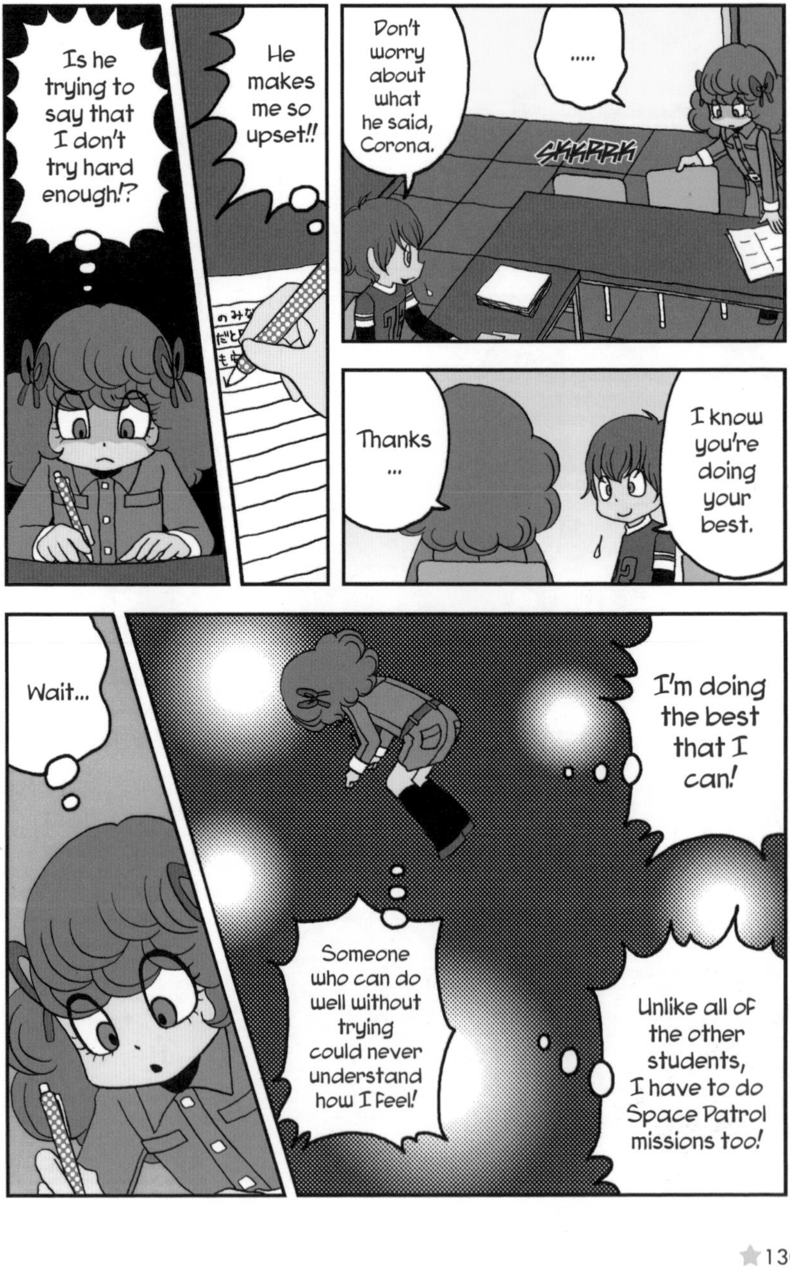
.....
Don't worry about what he said, Corona.
SKKRRK
I know you're doing your best.
Thanks ...
He makes me so upset!!
Is he trying to say that I don't try hard enough!?
I'm doing the best that I can!
Unlike all of the other students, I have to do Space Patrol missions too!
Someone who can do well without trying could never understand how I feel!
Wait...

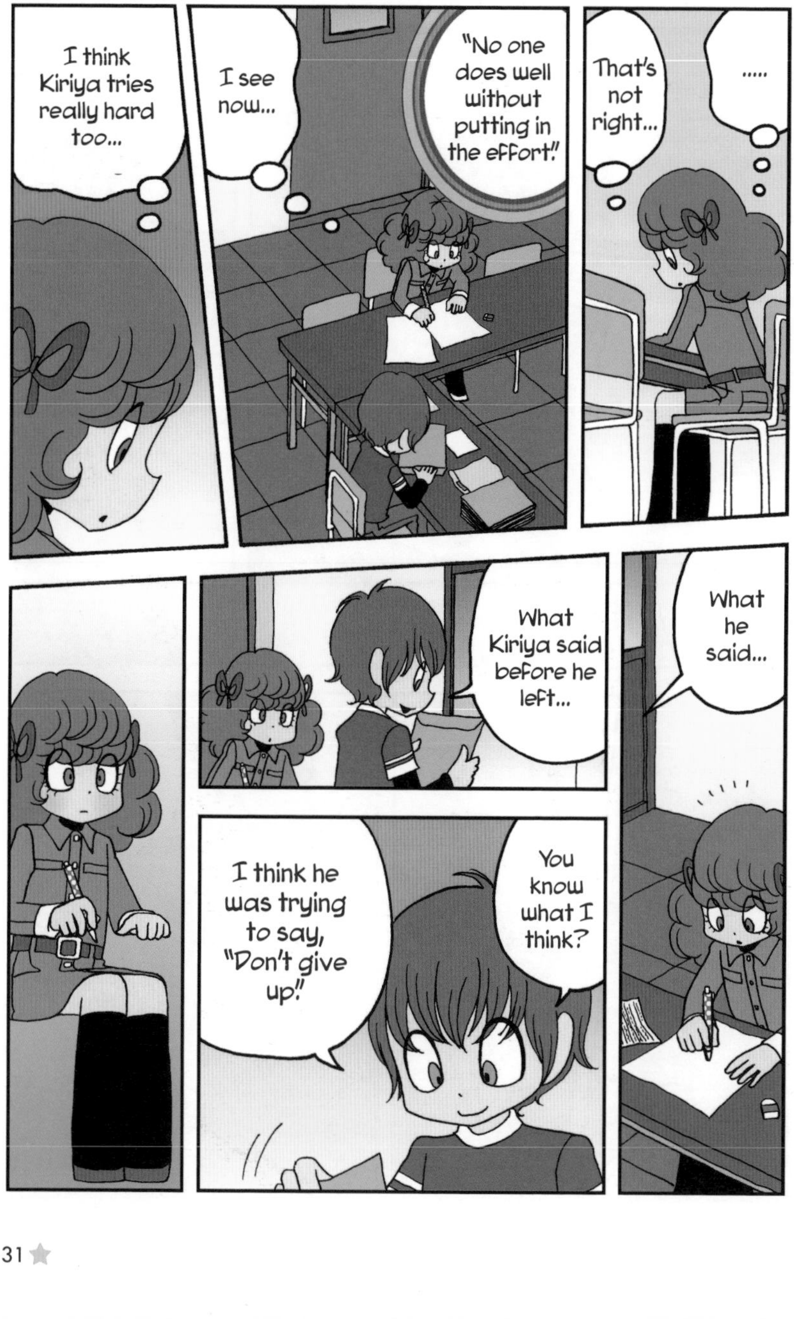
.....
That's not right...
"No one does well without putting in the effort."
I see now...
I think Kiriya tries really hard too...
What he said...
What Kiriya said before he left...
You know what I think?
I think he was trying to say, "Don't give up!"

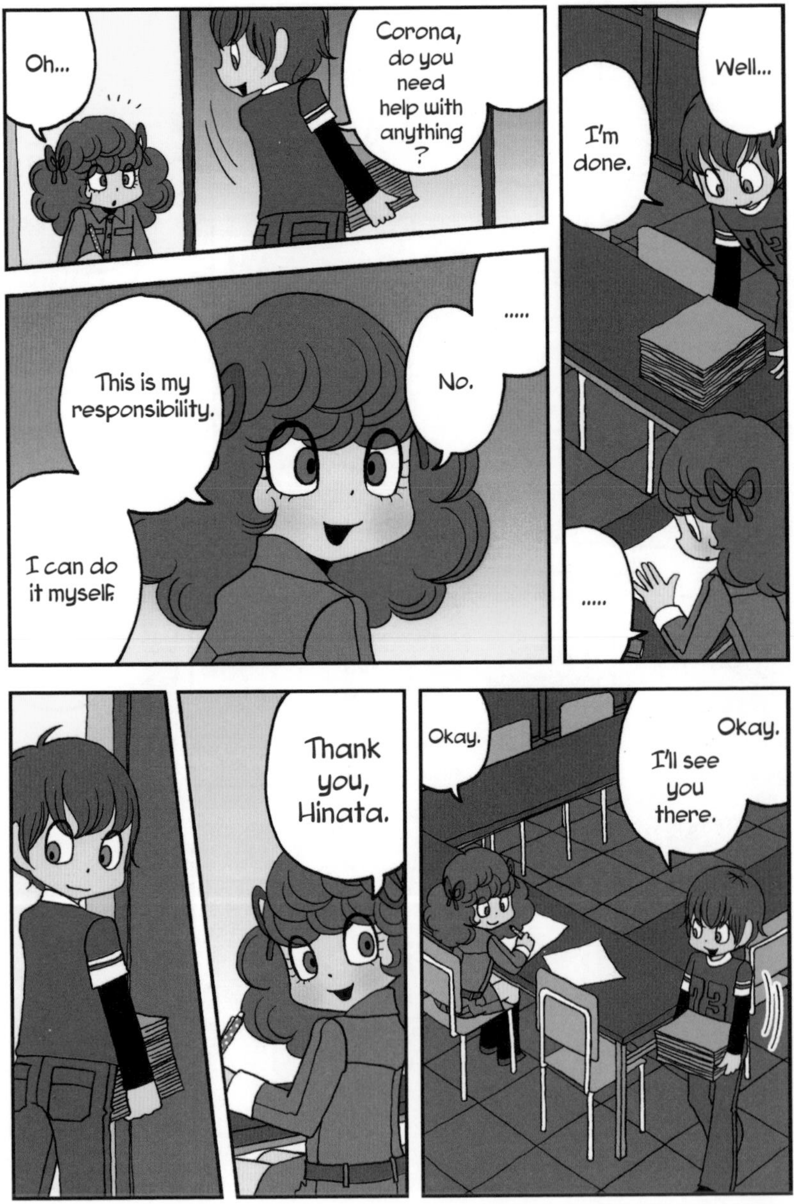
Well...
I'm done.
.....
Corona, do you need help with anything?
Oh...
.....
No.
This is my responsibility.
I can do it myself.
Okay. I'll see you there.
Okay.
Thank you, Hinata.

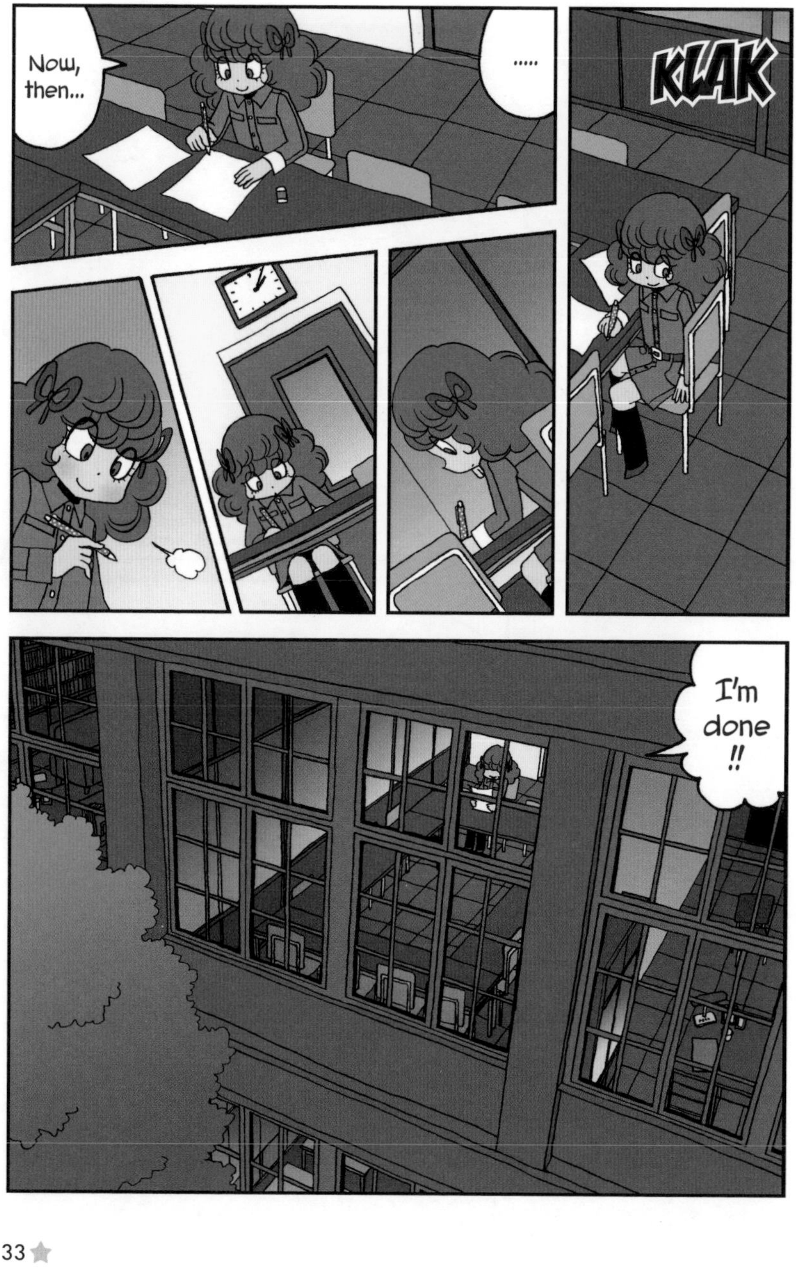
KLAK
.....
Now, then...
I'm done !!

profile
no.01 : Corona Hoshino

Name: Corona Hoshino
Birthday: April 8th
Blood Type: B
Astrological Sign: Aries
Height & Weight: 152 cm - weight is a secret

Favorite Foods:
Shrimp au Gratin
and Mont Blanc

Disliked Foods:
None

Favorite Subjects in School:
Japanese, Gym,
Home Economics

Disliked Subjects in School:
Science

Special Abilities:
Knitting, Getting along
with others

Hobbies:
Making treats,
Watching movies

Treasures:
A necklace she got
from her grandmother

profile
no.02 : Lan Tsukishima

Name: Lan Tsukishima
Birthday: December 25th
Blood Type: AB
Astrological Sign: Capricorn
Height & Weight: 148 cm - 36 kg

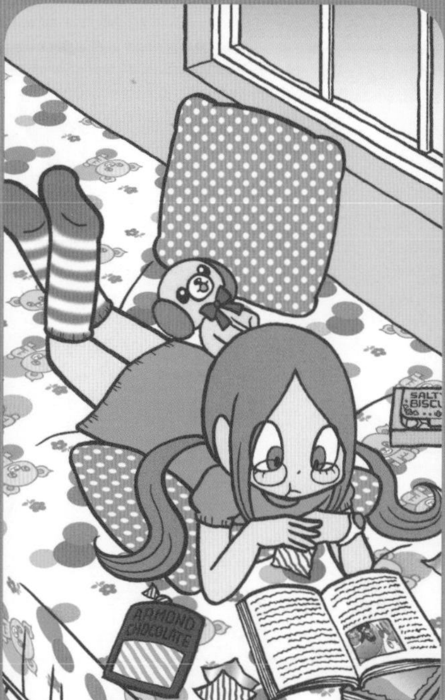
ARMOND
CHOCOLATE

Favorite Foods:
Snacks, Meat

Disliked Foods:
Milk, Pickled food

Favorite Subjects in School:
Arts and Crafts

Disliked Subjects in School:
Gym

Special Abilities:
Can stand on one leg,
Can fall asleep anywhere

Hobbies:
Reading, Researching
about "Space Patrol"

Treasures:
Space Patrol Fan Club
Membership Card

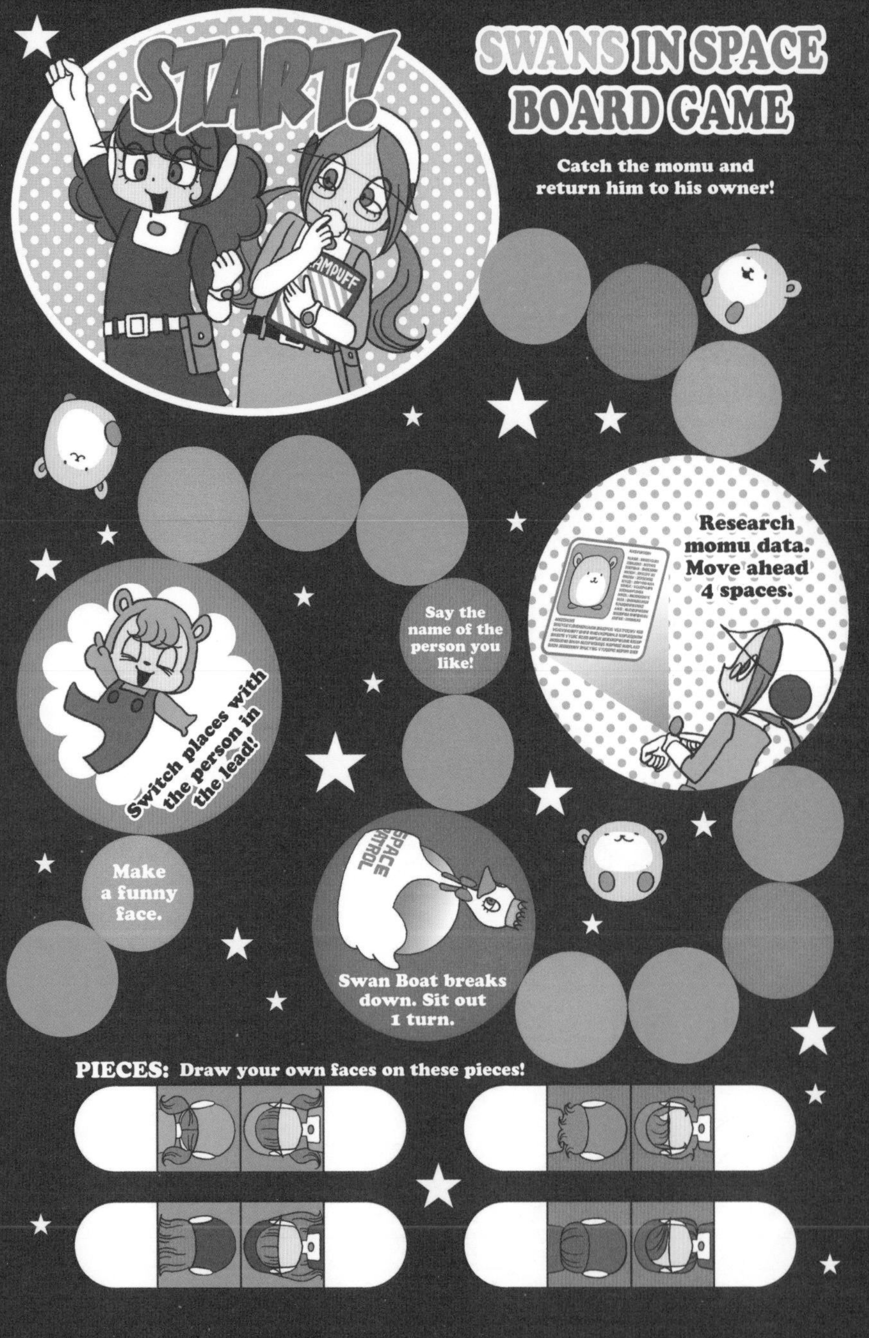
START!
SWANS IN SPACE BOARD GAME
Catch the momu and return him to his owner!
Research momu data. Move ahead 4 spaces.
Say the name of the person you like!
Switch places with the person in the lead!
Make a funny face.
Swan Boat breaks down. Sit out 1 turn.
PIECES: Draw your own faces on these pieces!

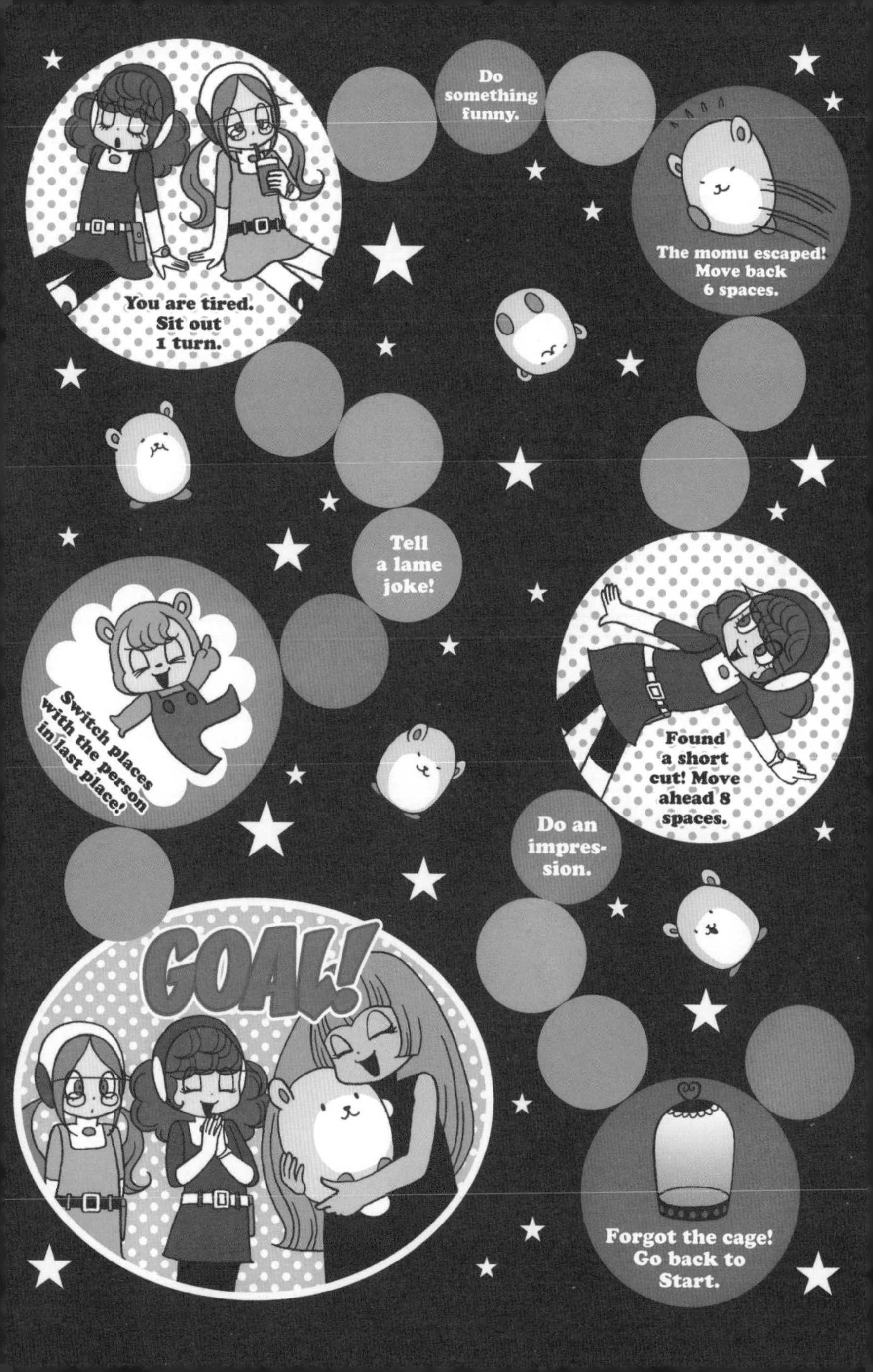
Do something funny.
The momu escaped! Move back 6 spaces.
You are tired. Sit out 1 turn.
Tell a lame joke!
Found a short cut! Move ahead 8 spaces.
Switch places with the person in last place!
Do an impres-sion.
Forgot the cage! Go back to Start.
GOAL!

COMING SOON:

SWANS in SPACE
VOLUME 3

ARRIVING APRIL 2010

SWANS IN SPACE Vol.3
ISBN: 978-1-897376-95-9

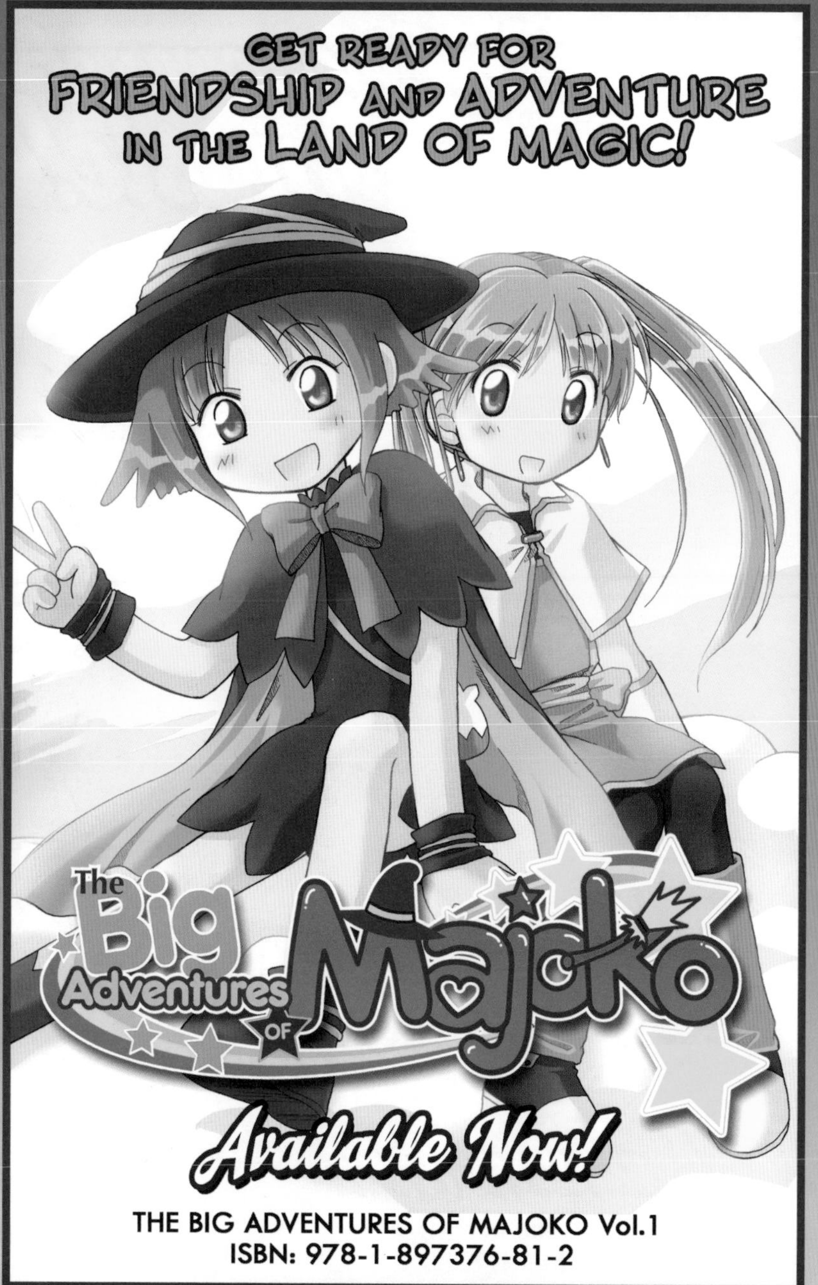
GET READY FOR
FRIENDSHIP AND ADVENTURE
IN THE LAND OF MAGIC!
The Big Adventures of Majoko
Available Now!
THE BIG ADVENTURES OF MAJOKO Vol.1
ISBN: 978-1-897376-81-2

THE BIG ADVENTURES
OF MAJOKO

Vol.1 *(On sale now!)*
ISBN: 978-1-897376-81-2

Vol.2 *(On sale now!)*
ISBN: 978-1-897376-82-9

Vol.3 *(DEC 2009)*
ISBN: 978-1-897376-83-6

NINJA BASEBALL
KYUMA

Vol.1 *(On sale now!)*
ISBN: 978-1-897376-86-7

Vol.2 *(On sale now!)*
ISBN: 978-1-897376-87-4

Vol.3 *(FEB 2010)*
ISBN: 978-1-897376-88-1

FAIRY IDOL KANON

Vol.1 *(On sale now!)*
ISBN: 978-1-897376-89-8

Vol.2 *(On sale now!)*
ISBN: 978-1-897376-90-4

Vol.3 *(JAN 2010)*
ISBN: 978-1-897376-91-1

SWANS IN SPACE

Vol.1 *(On sale now!)*
ISBN: 978-1-897376-93-5

Vol.2 *(On sale now!)*
ISBN: 978-1-897376-94-2

Vol.3 *(APR 2010)*
ISBN: 978-1-897376-95-9